In Search of
Steenie Bergman

Books by Blaine M. Yorgason and/or Brenton C. Yorgason

In Search of Steenie Bergman (Soderberg Series #5)
Decision Point
The Greatest Quest
Seven Days for Ruby (Soderberg Series #4)
Family Knights
The Eleven Dollar Surgery
Becoming
Bfpstk and the Smile Song (out of print)
The Shadow Taker
The Loftier Way: Tales from the Ancient American Frontier
Brother Brigham's Gold (Soderberg Series #3)
Ride the Laughing Wind
The Miracle
The Thanksgiving Promise (paperback — movie version)
Chester, I Love You (Soderberg Series #2)
Double Exposure
Seeker of the Gentle Heart
The Krystal Promise
A Town Called Charity, and Other Stories About Decisions
The Bishop's Horse Race (Soderberg series #1)
The Courage Covenant (out of print)
Massacre at Salt Creek (out of print)
Windwalker
Others
Charlie's Monument
From First Date to Chosen Mate
Tall Timber (out of print)
Miracles and the Latter-day Saint Teenager (out of print)
From Two to One
From This Day Forth (out of print)
Creating a Celestial Marriage (textbook)
Marriage and Family Stewardships (out of print)

In Search of
Steenie Bergman

Blaine M. Yorgason
Brenton G. Yorgason

Deseret Book Company
Salt Lake City, Utah

We express our gratitude to Rudolf Märkle, proprietor of the Hotel Spinne, in Grindelwald, Switzerland, who provided a wonderfully delightful setting for the creation of this book. We also acknowledge the contributions of Jack Schaefer and Will Henry, whose stirring writings launch so many of our own stories and tales.

©1988 Blaine M. and Brenton G. Yorgason

First printing November 1988

Library of Congress Cataloging-in-Publication Data

Yorgason, Blaine M., 1942-
    In search of Steenie Bergman / Blaine and Brenton Yorgason.
        p. cm. — (Soderberg series ; no. 5)
        Bibliography: p.
        ISBN 0-87579-174-3 : $9.95
        1. Utah Expedition, 1857-1858—Fiction. 2. Mormon Church—
History—Fiction. I. Yorgason, Brenton G. II. Title.
III. Series: Soderberg series ; 5.
PS3575.057I5   1988
813'.54—dc19   88-25611
                         CIP

For our great-grandfather, Jons Yorgason,
and Aunt Steenie, his first wife.

Foreword

Blaine and Brenton Yorgason have done it again! As in *Chester, I Love You*, they have worked a special kind of magic, providing a warm and touching story of people (amazingly like you or me or someone else we might know), their fascinating friendships with "lower" animals that possess a "higher" kind of love, and the indomitable spirits of both. The resulting human-animal team provides the framework for another masterpiece that you won't be able to put down until you have lived the experiences of the characters to the last word of the last page.

Add to this the Yorgasons' keen spiritual insight, and you have another classic that should be standard reading for anyone seeking a better understanding of such eternal principles as seeking, hearing, and acting upon the promptings of the Holy Spirit.

My whole family looks forward to each new work by the Yorgasons. Each book provides us with a great family adventure as we read together. More important, each touches our lives deeply and lastingly for good. *In Search of Steenie Bergman* is no exception. I am sure that at the conclusion of the book, you will say, as did my family and I, "We can hardly wait for the next one."

LYNN J. ANDERSON
CONSULTANT TO THE U.S. ARMY SURGEON GENERAL
ON HUMAN-ANIMAL BOND ISSUES AND
PRESIDENT OF DELTA SOCIETY INTERNATIONAL:
INTERACTIONS OF PEOPLE, ANIMALS, AND THE ENVIRONMENT

The king of France with twenty-thousand men,
Marched up a hill—and then marched down again.
                                    —old nursery rhyme

Prologue

The young soldier of Company G of Colonel E. B. Alexander's Tenth Infantry leaned upon his musket on the vast sage plain of South Pass, the windy, level-lying spinal hump of the Rocky Mountains, and watched the slow progress of a train of teamsters. The column of heavy wagons of the firm of Russell, Majors, and Waddell was wending its way westward, carrying the copious supplies of the government's Utah Expedition. Around him more soldiers of the Tenth sprawled in repose, the ten-minute break in the march a welcome moment.

Ahead of him were other companies of the Tenth, and behind him, stretching for miles and miles and even days, were other companies of the Tenth and Fifth Infantries. There were also Phelps's and Reno's Batteries—artillery units with their wheeled cannons that would be used to blast the Mormons into submission.

But the resting soldier now watched the ponderous freight wagons and found himself wondering at them. These wagons were of the style called the J. Murphy Wagon, made in St. Louis especially for transporting goods across the plains. They were big and strongly built, with rear wheels over six feet high and ten inches across at the iron-tire. Their front wheels measured only slightly smaller, and each of these prairie behemoths could carry seven thousand pounds of freight.

The wagon boxes, he noticed, were exceptionally commodious, being about as large as the rooms in an ordinary house—

and were covered with two heavy canvas sheets stretched across high arching wooden bows designed to protect the enclosed merchandise from the weather.

The young soldier had been told that these particular wagons had been sent out from Leavenworth, each loaded with just six thousand pounds of freight so that they could travel faster. The Mormons in Utah were in rebellion, the nation had been informed, and the faster the army and its supplies got to Utah to quash the rebellion, the better off the United States would be. So each wagon was drawn by several yoke of oxen, selected for their endurance and pushed daily to their limits. Speed was truly of the essence if this war was to be fought and won before winter set in.

Each wagon and set of teams, the soldier knew, were in charge of one driver. And most trains, including the one he was watching, consisted of twenty-five wagons, all under the direction of a man known as the wagon-master.

The second in command was the assistant wagon-master; then came the extra hand. Next came the night herder, and, lastly, the cavayard driver, whose duty it was to drive the lame and loose cattle. That made thirty-one men, all told, in each train. The men, as did those in the soldier's company, took turns with their own cooking, being divided into messes of seven. One cooked, one hauled wood, another hauled water, and so on, each having a duty to perform. Besides, all were heavily armed with Colt's pistols and Mississippi yeagers, and every one of them had his weapons at the ready, so they boasted, to "use up" any enemy they might encounter as they pressed toward the valley.

The soldier grinned as he thought of the boastful bullwhackers, but then he saw one of them skillfully use his great long bull-whip, and he thought better of his smirk. The wagon-master was called the bull-wagon boss, and he was usually of the disposition of a teased tarantula. The teamsters were known as bull-whackers, and the whole train was called, by everybody involved, a bull outfit.

Squatting with his yeager or musket still held upright before

2

him, the young trooper considered the train. He had been told that Russell, Majors, and Waddell were operating thirty-five hundred such wagons on the plains to Utah, being transported by forty thousand oxen and being driven by, or supported by, four thousand men. The youth could hardly imagine such numbers, but they didn't stagger him so much as the dollar figure he had also been told. That, the amount being invested to see that the army's goods reached Utah at the same time as the army, was over $2 million. He could not comprehend such a figure, and he felt inclined to doubt the truthfulness of the report, despite the fact that Captain Gove had confirmed it.

"Fall in!" ordered the booming voice of the sergeant of the day, and with a groan the young man forgot the lumbering oxen and wagons. Rising and swinging about, he quickly took up the order of march, a loose order on account of the terrain and sage, but an order that nevertheless covered up to twenty miles a day.

"Say, bunkie," the voice of his tent mate called from beside him, bringing the young man's attention back to the present, "what you reckon is in those wagons?"

"Food, I hope," the first soldier responded with a wry grin. "Either that or new boots. By gadfry, if I haven't worn these about out."

The fellow soldier nodded. "Me too. They say we're in Oregon now. You reckon we'll soon run into Mormons?"

The youth laughed. "Not hardly. According to Captain Gove, we still have a long way to go. The Mormons wouldn't be out this far. Besides, we're the army, and you can bet they'll be afraid to show when we're around."

"I don't know," the second soldier said, shaking his head. "Some of the boys have seen horsemen, way off on the ridges. Clay Purvis told me the captain thinks maybe they are Mormons."

"I wouldn't know," responded the first youth.

"Bunkie, you ever seen a Mormon?"

"Not that I know of. You?"

"No," the second youth replied, "but I've heard plenty, and

3

it gives me the jitters. I heard tell they have horns, little ones you can see in their hair if you look right careful. They say those Mormons can trance you, too, just with one look. That's how they get all those women to be their wives."

"You believe that?"

"About the horns or the women?"

The first soldier laughed. "The horns. Everybody alive knows the part about the women is true, else how could they get so many of them to join up with old Brigham and his boys and go west."

"Yeah, there is that. But tell you what — I'm looking forward to meeting me a bald-headed Mormon after we take the valley. The horns on a fellow like that ought to show up real pretty, that is if there are any."

Again the first soldier laughed. "If you catch one, call me quick. I'd like to take me a look myownself. I'll bet we find horns."

For a time the men marched in silence, the curses of the distant bull-whackers the only sound to break the monotonous tramping of dozens of pairs of number-10 army-issue boots. The ground sloped toward the west, but it was so gradual a slope that it could not be felt, and the men found no joy in marching downhill. Nor did they find joy in the wind, a frigid gale that whistled through the South Pass, carrying foot and hoof-raised dust that seeped through clothing and burned red and raw the soldiers' eyes and exposed necks and hands.

"You all right, men?" an officer asked as he drew his horse close to the tromping soldiers.

"Aye, Captain Gove, we're fine as can be expected."

"Good. Pacific Springs is only a few miles ahead, and we'll camp there for the night. There isn't much shelter, but the water is good, and I've been told that this brush burns hot."

"We'll make out," the first soldier replied. "Captain, how far do we have left to go?"

Captain Gove studied the horizon. "It's about sixty miles to the Green River and Fort Bridger. A man named Yates has a post we'll camp at near there. The Old Woman says we'll wait

4

there for Colonel Albert Sidney Johnston. But I tell you, boys, the old man who leads us now is a doddering old fool! With a bit of a push, we'd be in the valley and feasting on Mormon beef by the time Colonel Johnston got up to us."

The two soldiers grinned, knowing that Gove was referring to Colonel Alexander. The man was indeed old and tediously careful, and he was notorious for not taking stern charge of his men. Instead he kept much to himself, and he preferred gentleness in his dealings with the soldiers. Hence he had been given the sobriquet "the Old Woman."

"Do you think the Mormons will fight?"

"Oh, but I hope so! If they do, boys, then we'll use them all up and winter in the Valley in style. According to some of the boys of the Fifth, they passed some Mormons the other day who were making their escape from Utah. They've been marching five weeks, hiding out much of the time to keep from being murdered by the Mormon scouts that are out searching after them."

"Do you think the Mormons really do that?" the second soldier asked. "I mean, I've heard that they kill all who oppose them, but my Pa met a fellow back on the Mississippi who had lived with the Mormons in Nauvoo for five years, and he says they are the most peaceable people alive. And he sure hadn't been killed when he refused to join their church."

"Well, he was likely a Mormon all along," the first soldier declared, "and just wouldn't admit it."

The second young man shook his head. "I don't think so. Besides that, I can't hardly imagine all the murders I hear tell these people committed. That doesn't make sense for folks to behave that way—no more sense than for them to have horns."

"Sense or not," Captain Gove declared, "I imagine that it is so, for fanaticism produces the worst sort of horrors imaginable. But boys, if the Mormons will only fight, then their days are numbered. We will sweep them from the face of the earth, and Mormonism in Utah will cease. Then our campaign will be at an end, and we can return to our homes and families."

The captain rode away, and the two soldiers walked in silence. A crow cried out from far above them, and then cried again. The wind continued to blow, the dust sifted into their eyes and down their necks, and both men readjusted their neckerchiefs over their mouths.

"You know, Bunkie, Captain Gove can't wait to return to his home and family, which is secure. I wonder how those Mormon folk feel, knowing that we're marching in to destroy *their* homes and families?"

The young soldier looked at his companion but said nothing, and for the rest of the afternoon the two marched in silence, hemmed in by their own thoughts of the impending war.

In spite of the cold wind, the mood around the cooking fires that night was lighthearted. The men sang and danced, and all felt glad that they had crossed the Great Divide and were getting close to the valley of the Mormons. In spite of the rapidly advancing season, there was still hope that with a grand push, they would have no trouble getting through the mountains. Even old Jim Bridger, the mountaineer guide, was hopeful, declaring to one and all that it didn't matter at all that the Mormons had blockaded Echo Canyon. He knew another route, up along the Bear River and down into the northern Utah valleys. It would be fifty miles or more longer, but it would take Brigham and his troops by surprise and would be well worth the little jaunt.

So the men of G and H Companies of the Tenth Infantry were enthusiastic, and as the young soldier stretched out in his bedroll and closed his eyes, he did his best to picture men with horns, glorious battles, and hordes of entranced women anxiously looking forward to the coming of their blue-coated deliverers.

Suddenly he sat bolt upright in bed. He had been asleep, but now his ears rang with the sound of gunfire and a cacophony of other noises, including screaming and the ringing of bells. There was also the thunder of hooves back and forth past his tent, and then the shout, "The mules are free and ours, Port! Let's send them home a'foggin'!"

"Soldiers turn out!" a voice screamed from a tent nearby. "We're attacked!"

The young soldier stared into the inky blackness of the inside of his tent, his heart hammering and his breath absolutely still.

The cry "Soldiers turn out!" rang again and again, and still he sat, terrified. At last, however, his tentmate's own frightened whisper pierced his frozen mind, and he started to snap out of his fear.

"Bunkie, you alive?"

"Yeah, I . . . I reckon."

"You think that was Indians?"

The young soldier shook his head, unmindful of the darkness.

"What? I can't hear you."

"Uh . . . no, I don't. Indians aren't on the warpath right now. It has to be Mormons, I reckon. Besides, I heard them talking English."

"Grief, Bunkie, I didn't think Mormons would fight."

"Well, now you know better. Come on, we've got to turn out."

The two young men scrambled from their tent and into the cold darkness, their pants and boots forgotten as they held their muskets and sought for direction to run or shoot.

"Over this way!" someone shouted, and they turned and stumbled forward, their feet taking great punishment from the rocks and prickly weeds of the high desert country.

"See anything?" the young soldier panted as he ran.

"Not much but dark on dark. Where're we going?"

The young man couldn't answer, so he stopped, then stumbled forward as his tentmate slammed into him from behind.

"Ummph!"

"Sorry, Bunkie."

"No worry. Say!" he then shouted. "Is anybody else out here?"

"Yeah." a quiet voice answered from directly behind them, "us Mormons are out here."

Spinning, the two young soldiers stared at the small group of men who had materialized out of the darkness. "Would you look at that?" one of the Mormons said. "Soldiers without britches."

The others laughed quietly.

"You . . . you going to kill us?" the young soldier stammered.

"Why? You want to die?"

"N . . . no, but . . . but—"

"We *could* kill you," another said, "mighty easy."

"So BANG," another added, and all broke into laughter again.

"All right, young fellers," the first speaker said, drawling his words considerably. "Consider yourselves 'killed.' And remember that us Mormon folks ain't so black as eastern fools would like to paint us. You boys ready to ride?"

"We're ready, Port."

"All right. Let's depart."

The Mormons slapped spurs to horses and were almost instantly swallowed by the night.

The two young men, their weapons forgotten in their hands, stared into the darkness, trying to understand what had just occurred. Then there was a faint halloo from back toward the camp, and finally someone lit a lantern. Using that as a beacon, the two soldiers picked their way through the sage and rocks and back to the tents.

"They got the mules," Captain Gove grumbled. "Those confounded Mormons got the mules."

"Anybody . . . hurt?" the second soldier asked.

Gove looked at him. "Yeah, one man, from Tracy's H Company. He had the heart disease, and it looks like he died of fright. It's a miracle the bloodthirsty devils didn't kill a dozen more of us."

"I like to have died of fright myself," the youth declared honestly. "When I first heard them, I thought the very demons of hell had been turned loose on the camp. For a minute I was too scared even to breathe—I was that slow getting out of my tent."

8

"Well, it wouldn't have done us much good to get out sooner," another man declared. "We couldn't have shot 'em."

"Oh, yeah?" a third man growled. "If I could have found my rifle . . ."

"I found mine," the second man said quietly, "and I got outside. But I couldn't fire."

"Why not?"

"Why? Because those Mormon fellers rode up and down between the rows of tents, close formation, hollering and shooting in the air. I seen them. And there was no way I could have shot at them, not without endangering the boys across the picket from me. It wouldn't have been any different for any of you. Those fellers had us boxed real good, and they knew it. But they weren't trying to use us up, either."

"They could have killed my bunkie and me, too," the second young soldier declared softly, "but they didn't. I . . . I'm with you, I don't think they were interested in killing us."

There was a long silence, and each of the men did his best to digest what he had just been told.

"Probably just afraid to," Captain Gove finally decided. "The murdering cowards. Well, boys, whether they could have killed us or not, now we're in a real pickle. We have no mules, and —"

"Captain," a man suddenly shouted from out in the darkness, "the bell mule is out here! His picket rope got caught in the sagebrush."

Captain Gove sighed with relief. "We're saved. The mules all follow that bell mule, so by morning we should have our animals back. Then we'll truly get after those black-hearted souls."

"Captain," the young soldier said then, "I heard one of the Mormons call another one by the name of Port. That mean anything to you?"

Jesse Gove sucked in his breath. "Yeah. It means that we are by-golly lucky, for that would be Orrin Porter Rockwell, the notorious Mormon outlaw and killer. I've heard that he never

9

takes anyone alive. It is purely amazing that we aren't dead, every last one of us."

"I'm telling you," the second young soldier declared emphatically, "if he'd have wanted us to be dead, we would have been. He and his men had us clean to rights, Captain, and you know it. There was no luck involved. We're alive because the Mormons, including this Rockwell feller, chose to leave us that way."

There was a long silence, and then Jesse Gove spoke again. "You may be right, Soldier. But on the other hand, you might not be. So from now on, we'll be doubling the guard — no, tripling it — so that we have sentinels all around the camp. Anything suspicious, anything at all, and I want to be informed. Sergeant, see that tonight's guard, Cumming, is placed under arrest until we have an inquiry. Now, snap to it!"

He did, and before long the two young tent-mates were lying once again in the darkness.

"You know," the first young soldier finally said, his voice low and quiet, "I think you were right out there. If those Mormons had wanted, we would all be dead men right now."

"I know, Bunkie," the other replied with a sigh. "And I'm starting to wonder about those Mormon folks. Would I be so amazing charitable to soldier boys who were coming to burn me out and string up my leaders? I hope I would, but I don't know. I truly don't know."

And after that comment, the endless wind was all that was heard on the lonely plains of South Pass.

Chapter 1

When I first heard that Steenie had gone, I would not believe. Oh, it made sense, all right, that she would leave. It made all kinds of sense. The trouble was, it didn't *feel* right. There was just too much that had been happening between us for her to simply disappear.

"Ma," I said, looking up from where I sat at our newly constructed table, "Steenie didn't run. I *know* she didn't!"

My mother looked achingly at me, and then she glanced quickly out the window of our small log home. It was early fall, but already the days were getting shorter and the cottonwood grove where we lived was blue with evening shadow.

"Jons," she replied, her tongue struggling to form English words out of her still-Swedish thinking, "Brother Fordham says it iss so, und in spite of vhat ve know of Christena, I yust tink he must be right."

My three sisters looked at me in unison, but at my scowl they dropped their eyes back to their bowls of porridge. Elijah Fordham, our block teacher, had dropped by within the hour, telling us that the Crost family had pulled out during the night before, taking the trail east before Buchanan's Army could get here.

Of course, I had heard of *other* families who had become dissatisfied with our religion, or at least with the almost harsh conditions under which we were forced to live. And those folks had either picked up with a wagon train heading west or had

11

returned to their homes in the east. But this was the first time I had ever known the people who had departed, and I truly struggled to understand.

"Ma," I argued, for once forgetting to be self-consciously proud that I had no such Swedish accent as had my mother and father, "Brother Fordham is wrong this time. He *must* be! I know Steenie too well, and running away is just not something she would do."

"Und how vould you know the girl so vell?" Pa shot back from where he had been silently judging the conversation. "Jons, ve have been only two veeks here in the Valley, und that iss not enough time for a boy to know a girl so vell."

Well, I colored up proper, for I knew that Pa was right. Most young men wouldn't have come to know a girl so well in such a short time. Nor would *I* have known a girl that well, had that girl been any other than Steenie Bergman. But she wasn't any other girl. She was Steenie, and that made Pa wrong.

Ma should have known that, too. She had come to know Steenie almost better than I did. But she remained silent— fearful, I suppose, for what Steenie's disappearance would do to me, her son.

But Steenie Bergman *was* someone special. From the day our dusty wagon had rolled into the area of the Salt Lake Valley known as South Cottonwood, having been released from Mathias Cowley's wagon company, I had known that. And I had known, for almost as long, that for the rest of forever she would be my one true love.

For a moment, I recalled the first time I had seen her—and in spite of myself and what I had just been told about her being gone, I smiled. I had been helping the folks unload what precious little we owned into our newly assigned cabin, when with great clumsiness I had dropped Ma's well-used wooden bread bowl.

Only seconds before, Ma had cautioned me to be careful with it, and teasingly I had told her to mind her own armful, for mine was secure. Instantly, then, the bowl, almost as if it had a life of its own, tumbled out of my arms and into the dirt.

12

Quickly, before Ma could turn and see the mishap, I stooped to pick the bowl up—and that was when I heard from behind me a low, throaty laugh that stopped me cold. Whirling around, I stared at the laugh's wondrous source. And just as instantly I felt my breath cut short—caught up tight in my chest.

Why, she was the loveliest Mormon girl who had ever stared back at a susceptible young convert from Sweden, and I was powerless to do anything but continue to stare.

A little thing less than shoulder high to me, she was creamy tan in complexion, with level blue-gray eyes and a rare dark hair that fired up mahogany-red when the sun shone directly behind it, as it did just then. Her features were regular and fine, and the gentle lines of her figure were scarcely damaged by the ill-fitting cling of her homespun dress and apron.

I continued to hold my breath.

"Look out!" she warned suddenly, and to my mortal shame and consternation, Ma's mixing bowl slipped and tumbled to the earth for the second time in just as many minutes.

Fighting frantically against the red blush that leaped up my neck and across my face, I looked away from her and stooped down, fumbling with my fingers as I again retrieved the wooden bowl. When next I looked, she was no longer standing before me. Instead, she had stepped to the wagon and taken up an armload of supplies.

"Hello," she said, almost in a whisper, as she again reached my side. "Welcome to South Cottonwood."

"Th-Thank you," I replied as I hastily fell into step beside her. "I . . . I am Jons Soderberg. How . . . are you called?"

Again she laughed, and I was becoming more aware by the minute of the musical tinkle that was hers. Glancing at her, I was also aware, and instantly, too, of the profile of her face— a profile more lovely than anything I had ever seen before.

Her forehead dropped almost straight from the soft curl of her hair, the saucy uptilt of her nose met it in the soft arch of dark eyebrow, her full lips had a look of pouting to them that her incredible smile gave the lie to. Her sparkling eyes were shaded by dark, curling lashes and framed by high cheekbones, and her chin, standing firm, dropped subtly and then led gently back and down to the splendor of her neck. From all angles she was beautiful, and I hardly noticed, as we walked, the gentle chiding she gave me for my grammar.

"In America, Jons Soderberg, we say, 'What is your name?' "

For a minute, I couldn't say anything. I had spent hours practicing English while wintering in Keokuk and helping my folks earn the means to cross the plains. Also, during my stay there and while crossing the plains, I had listened carefully to how Americans talked, and I had learned fast. Now most of the time I sounded as though I had been in America for years rather than months. But when I was nervous, I still occasionally allowed my Swedish heritage to seep into my speech.

Nor was I ashamed of my Swedish past. Not at all. But, along with many others, I had endured the hatred and persecution of many of Sweden's most prominent sons when my family and I had converted to Mormonism. And so with my parents, brothers, and sisters, I had put the land of my birth behind me and had set out, with all my heart and soul, to become a free son of America. And I would yet, I vowed daily, achieve that all-consuming goal.

"My name," she continued without a pause, "is Christena Bergman. But my friends call me Steenie."

"And am I your friend?" I asked bravely, still not taking my eyes from her face.

Her reply, given gently and almost in a whisper, thrilled me clear to the toes of the too-small, cast-off boots I was wearing.

"Oh, I hope so," she replied, sounding very sober, and looking once again directly up into my eyes. "I truly hope so."

We walked like that, side by side, up to our small cabin in the cottonwoods, and my mind reeled as I wondered at her words. I don't know how I knew it, I truly don't, for I was too young and inexperienced to discern such things by myself.

But still I knew!

This girl Steenie was saying something to me of loneliness, almost crying it out, and in that instant I added another vow to my one of Americanization. I vowed that I would not rest until

I could hold her close and help to ease the pain that somehow seemed to fill her tender heart.

"Bergman," I said, as I pushed Steenie in the big swing someone had hung south of our home, "that's Swedish, too — isn't it?"

We had been in Cottonwood for two days, and Pa had already been given work in the munitions factory that the Church had opened in the old sugar foundry in Sugarhouse. I had gone there as well, but the bishop who was managing the making of gunpowder for our coming war with the States had decided that he wanted only married men to do such dangerous work. So at the moment I was unemployed, and, frankly, I was enjoying every minute of it.

"It is Swedish," Steenie laughed as I pushed her higher, "though I've never been to Sweden."

"But then how —"

"My parents came to America before I was born and settled in Wisconsin. My mother died during my birth, and my father married again. A year ago, both he and my stepmother died quite suddenly of cholera, and I have been living ever since with my stepmother's brother and his wife and children. Their names are Ben and Maria Crost."

I pushed the swing again, thinking. "And how did you come to be a Latter-day Saint?" I finally asked.

"Two missionaries," she replied as she sailed back and forth on the end of the great ropes. "A good many of our Lutheran congregation accepted their message, were baptized, and emigrated to Zion. We came to the valley last year, and most of us went south past Nephi and into the Sanpete Valley. But my Uncle Ben wished to remain here near Church headquarters, and so here we are."

"Why did he do that?" I asked. "Not that I'm sad about his decision, mind you. Otherwise, I might not have met you."

Steenie smiled sweetly. I gave the swing another push, and again I felt a mighty urge to hold this beautiful girl close and protect her from the evil world we had been born into.

15

"I've thought of that as well," she told me then, "that is, how we might never have met each other if Ben had . . . had . . .

"Oh, Jons, I am *so* afraid of that man!"

"Who?" I asked, catching the swing and pulling it to a stop. For a moment Steenie made no move but sat staring silently at the ground. Then she stood and slowly walked away.

"My Uncle Ben," she then sighed, almost in a whisper. "He . . . he thought it would only be a short time un- til . . . Brother Brigham recognized his leadership abilities and made him a bishop or an . . . an apostle, or *something*. Now, a year later, that call has not been extended. In fact, Uncle Ben still has the calling of block teacher that the bishop gave him thirteen months past, and this rankles him severely. Regularly now he curses and rails upon Brother Brigham and the other Church leaders, and he cannot see that it is within *himself* that the fault lies, not within them.

"I have tried my best to talk with him, Jons — to encourage him to pray to feel the Spirit again that he felt when he was baptized. But he grows meaner by the day. Nor is his dear wife, Maria, any longer able to influence him for good. It is as though his mind has darkened and that he has set his heart against the kingdom of God. In fact, I'm reminded often of the phrases Nephi used to describe his two older brothers — hard-hearted and stiff-necked. There is much yelling and anger and cruelty in Uncle Ben's cabin now, and I can hardly bear being there with him."

With Steenie's words reeling in my mind, I found myself aware once again of the desire that was swelling inside me to rescue her — to get her away from the man that seemed to have such a hold on her life. But I said nothing. Instead we just walked — and before long I had taken her home and was working my way, thoughtfully, back through the willows to my own home.

What could I do? How in the world could a boy like me help a wondrous person like her to be relieved of such great pain? I didn't know, but I knew I had to find a way —

"Oh, Jons, look how beautiful it is!"

I looked, and indeed the Valley was beautiful. It was early the following morning, and Steenie and I stood on a bluff south of Emigration Canyon, but just north of what I learned was Parley's Canyon. The chilly morning wind tugged at the blankets we had brought with us for warmth, and the first rays of the sun cast our shadows sternly before us, sending them tumbling helter-skelter down the rocky and brush-strewn slope. There they were lost, swallowed by the greater night-shadows that yet lingered below.

Off to the west, the Great Salt Lake glistened and sparkled like millions of acres of jewels, and the mountains that rose to the south of the lake, as well as those that formed islands to the north and west, receded in ever-diminishing hues of lavender and blue. Closer in, also to the northwest, the City of the Saints shown as an oasis of green amidst the all-encircling fields of fall-yellow and ochre, the colors of harvest time. It was an eye-catching view, and for long moments Steenie and I both stood spellbound by the sight of it.

Finally a lark trilled in the fields below us, and only then did I speak.

"Do you come here often?"

"Not as often as I would like to, Jons. There is so much work to be done that I have no time. But now that harvest is almost over, perhaps I will begin to enjoy a little more freedom."

"Have you put up much food?" I asked.

Steenie nodded vigorously. "Everything that we could bottle or dry, we have preserved. The Lord has blessed us immeasurably—folks say more than any other year since the Saints' arrival in the Valley ten years ago, and there will be little hunger this winter."

"Was the hunger bad in the past?" I asked.

"Oh, Jons, the sufferings I have seen are simply pitiful. Even last winter it was bad, and many days I spent from daylight till dark grubbing thistle roots from the frozen ground for our supper. For grain we often had nothing more than shorts with bran, and eating twice a day was a luxury that few could afford. Brother Brigham and the other Brethren constantly gave of their own supplies, the bishops distributed the food nearly every day, and still there did not seem ever to be enough."

"I've heard that there were crickets."

Steenie laughed. "Crickets? Jons, they are the most foul, ugly insects I have ever seen. They come in hordes, wave after wave of them, until the sky seems black and the earth is covered. To walk through them, feeling their bloated bodies crunching beneath our feet, is an experience I would rather never have again as long as I live! I fought them last spring, and that is enough for me, forever.

"And they were everywhere! They got into my hair and down my neck, they crawled up my skirts, they flew into my face and even into my mouth, and . . . Oh! I shudder to think about it."

"Sounds pretty bad," I agreed. "But what about the seagulls? Didn't they come and eat them?"

Again Steenie laughed. "Sometimes. They certainly came that first year in the Valley, and they are all that saved the Saints from starvation that year. But since then, well, our bishop says, when he mentions the work of the gulls against the crickets, that in his experience the birds come late and leave early. Most of the work is left to be done by the Saints."

I grinned. "I would say that the seagulls and I were cut from the same cloth. Or at least Ma would say that."

"I like your mother," Steenie smiled, looking off across the Valley. "I don't know your father very well, but I do like your mother. She seems so nice. Jons, please tell me what she is like."

Picking up a small rock, I tossed it over the edge of the bluff. "Ma is wonderful, Steenie, but I don't really know how to tell you what she is like. In Sweden her name was Karna Nilsdotter, but here she is called Caroline. Like you, she is just a bit of a thing, but she is tougher than old boot leather, as they say, and even my Pa, big man that he is, backs down from her once she gets riled.

"She's strong, too, and she can fool you with that. She hardly ever gets sick, and one day, before we left Sweden, when a cow came after one of my little sisters, Ma grabbed it by the horns

18

and twisted its neck until that cow was on its side with her on top of it. I was amazed, but Pa said it didn't suprise him at all.

"The thing I like best about Ma, though, is her love. She loves every person she has ever known, and I truly can't think of an exception. When Elder Lars Nils Larsson was teaching my family and others the gospel back in Sweden, police came and arrested our neighbors, an aged couple name Matsson. They were taken to prison and forced to live sixteen days on bread and water, all because they had been baptized into Christ's church.

"For that entire sixteen days, Ma went to the prision every day and visited not only with our neighbors but with the police as well. She was so filled with love for the police that after the Mattsons were released, the offiers made no more arrests in Vallby province. Later one of the officers united with our faith, and he told my Pa that he had decided to embrace Mormonism because he had been able to feel Ma's love for him.

"Tell you the truth, Steenie, I've even heard Ma praying, the past few weeks, for President Buchanan—and for the officers and men of his army who are on their way this very hour to attack us."

"Praying *for* them?"

"That's right. Pa just shakes his head and, when it's his turn to offer family prayer, prays for the Brethren of the Church. But not Ma. She prays for our enemies, that their minds will be opened to the goodness of the Saints, that their families will be protected while they are away, that they will not be killed or seriously hurt when the Lord begins to assist us in our battles with them, and so forth."

"My goodness. I see what you mean about love. Truthfully though, I don't know if I could ever be that serious."

"Well, Ma isn't all serious, either. She sings all the time, she whistles until Pa calls her his Swedish canary, and she makes up silly rhyme songs about us children that are so awful they are funny. And she hardly ever stops teasing Pa, tickling him and flirting with him in front of the rest of us until he almost goes crazy with it. But we can tell he loves it, every minute of it — and there isn't anything on this earth that he wouldn't do for her.

"Sometimes Ma even takes over Pa's authority to call family prayer, doing if for him because his mind gets so befuddled with worry that he forgets. When I asked her about it once, she told me that it was as much her responsibility as it was his to see that our family got to the celestial kingdom. And she is bound and determined that we are going to get there together.

"She is truly an amazing woman, Steenie, and I am honored to call her my mother."

Steenie looked off across the valley, breathing deeply, trying to control her emotions. Finally, however, she spoke. "I never knew my mother, Jons, but I . . . I think she must have been a great deal like your mother. At least that is the feeling that my father used to give me, before he too passed away."

She paused, and in the silence the lark below us trilled again, a sweet, happy sound that somehow made me think of Steenie.

"Jons," she finally said, "do . . . do you think she . . . your mother, I mean . . . would mind if I tried to be like her? I mean, I have watched many women, but when I become a mother, if I could ever be like any single one of them, I would be most proud to be like *her*. Do . . . you think that she would mind?"

"Not hardly," I said, grinning.

"Then . . . uh . . . do you think she would mind," Steenie asked, her voice filled with apprehension, "if . . . if I were to spend time with her this winter, maybe helping out while I watched and learned?"

Well, I could hardly believe what Steenie was asking. If I had prayed about it, which truthfully I hadn't as yet, the Lord couldn't have answered my prayers more perfectly. Steenie would be getting close to my Ma, and at the same time she would be spending more time being close to me. For a gangly young Swedish convert, life was quickly assuming the glorious and hoped-for aspects of heaven on earth, and I was thrilled beyond words.

"She would truly love it," I declared as I reached out and

20

took Steenie's hand. "But no sense putting off until winter what you can do today. Let us be hurrying back, Christena Bergman, so that you might get about your task at once."

And so, with a giggling and lovely Steenie willingly in tow, I began my rapid descent of the mountain.

Chapter 2

"Could they use your services?" Steenie asked anxiously.

With a sense of great discouragement, I climbed onto the wagon bench beside her. I had already been in the Valley ten days, and other than being able to occasionally help some of our neighbors with the last of their harvests, which services were rewarded with grain and other produce for my family's table, I was still without work.

Of course, I had spent every possible moment of every day with Steenie, and that was pleasurable beyond words. The two of us had grown close in that time — laughing, teasing, walking, and riding about the valley, getting acquainted with it and with each other. And as we explored together, we engaged in long and earnest discussions that at the time seemed so important. And it wasn't all deep and thoughtful probing, either. We always seemed to end up chasing each other here and there among the trees in silly games of tag, or sitting on the creek bank playing jack slaps — generally acting in that tom-fool way that young folks can when they've nothing better to do than to be happy in each other's company.

And Steenie Bergman and I were happy, of that I can testify. In fact, through my entire life I could never remember being so completely consumed with joy.

Steenie had also managed to thoroughly captivate my mother's heart. And that was to prove significant, for in affairs of love, I was to learn, a young man can have no better ally than his own staunch and loyal mother.

Now Steenie and I were at Temple Square, where one of the buildings housing temple construction tools and materials had been converted to the manufacturing of weapons for the coming war with the States. Under Brother Jonathan Browning's able direction, the men were already making Colts' handguns, and equipment for manufacturing rifles had been ordered and was even then en route to Great Salt Lake City.

Elsewhere in the sprawling community, the shops were turning out canister bombs, bullets, and cannonballs, and of course at Pa's factory they were making gunpowder.

Old Buck, as most people called United States President James Buchanan, might be sending an army of Uncle Sam's finest to wipe out us "rebellious" Mormons. But the army wasn't going to get us without a fight, and a good one at that. The Mormons, with what seemed to be the whole world arrayed against them, were cheerfully readying themselves for war. Trouble was, with all that activity, no one anywhere seemed to have permanent use for me.

"They couldn't use me yet," I sighed, looking down into Steenie's captivating, dancing eyes. "Brother Browning told me, though, that in a week or so more men will be called to go into the mountains. He said I should tell my bishop I'm available, and then likely I'll be called to go with them."

Steenie looked at me. "But . . . but you just came from the mountains. Are you sure that you want to go back already?"

I smiled at her. "Steenie, that army is coming to attack our people, and I feel honor-bound to help keep them away. I've even heard the soldiers boast of what they intend to do when they get here, and it's enough to make a man's blood run cold. Many's the night the other fellows and I would sneak to their camps and listen to their ribald deviltry and evil plans."

"You did? *Truly?*"

"It was . . . sort of a game," I said, blushing a little, but at the same time feeling proud of the adoration on Steenie's face. "Our wagon train passed many of the government trains as we came to the valley, and after dark each night a few of us would make dares to see who could get the closest to their fires. Night after night, I've hidden in the grass and listened to soldiers and freighters boast of hanging Brigham Young and the other Mormon leaders; of dishonoring our wives, sisters, and daughters; and of plundering and pillaging our people. They even sang songs about it."

Steenie's expression was one of shock. "They . . . they did? Sing, I mean? I can hardly believe United States soldiers would behave so."

"They surely did, Steenie. One night I learned a verse of one of their songs that went something like this:

> The Mormons knew that Uncle Sam
> Had troops upon the route,
> And Brigham prayed the Holy Lamb
> Would help to keep them out.
> The distance then, one thousand miles,
> Me in the face did stare,
> For Brigham swore no damned gentiles
> Ere should winter there."

Steenie giggled. "You shouldn't use language like that," she said, wagging her finger at me.

"It's only a song," I countered, "and not my song at that. Besides, the army won't get into the Valley. Our people are innocent of the charges against them, and so Brother Brigham's prayers will surely be answered."

"Do . . . the soldiers *all* feel like that, Jons?"

I shook my head. "I don't know. One night I heard some of the troops say that General Harney — he's the leader of Buchanan's army — has fully determined that upon his arrival here, he will capture Brother Brigham and the twelve apostles, execute them, and then winter within the walls of our growing temple."

"Isn't he the one they call 'Squaw-killer' Harney?"

"Why, that's right," I agreed. "I heard one of the soldiers call him that, but I don't know how he got his name."

Steenie nodded. "I do. Aunt Maria says that he got it when

24

he killed all those Sioux men, women, and children under Little Thunder at Ash Hollow a couple of years ago. He was supposedly taking revenge for the Grattan Massacre, but he ended up perpetrating another massacre that was much worse. If Harney is leading the expedition, then the Saints truly have much to fear.

"Have you heard any of the songs our people sing about the army?"

"No," I said, surprised. "Do the Mormons have songs about them?"

Steenie laughed. "The Mormons have songs about most everything. Listen to this one. It's sung to the tune of Yankee Doodle Dandy:

> When Uncle Sam he first set out,
> His army to destroy us
> Says he, "The Mormons we will route,
> They will no more annoy us."
>
> The force he sent was competent
> To try and hang for treason,
> That is, I mean, it would have been,
> But don't you know the reason?
>
> There's great commotion in the east
> About the Mormon question,
> The problem is, to say the least,
> Too much for their digestion.
>
> As they were going up the Platte
> Singing many a lusty ditty
> Saying we'll do this and we'll do that
> When we get to the city,
>
> And sure enough when they got there,
> They made the Mormons stir, Sir.
> That is, I mean they would have done,
> But O they didn't get there."

"That's quite a song."

Steenie smiled. "I hear new verses all the time. I just wish the war wasn't really happening."

Slowly the horses drew the wagon east along Brigham Street, past Brigham Young's large home with the beehive symbol, and on toward the foothills. At Seventh East Street we turned south and followed the dusty road toward Cottonwood, and we had gone almost a mile when Steenie at last broke the silence.

"Jons," she said quietly, "why *is* the war happening? Why on earth has the American government decided to send an army to attack some poor religious colonists and their innocent wives and children?"

Feeling helplessly unable to answer her questions, I shook my head. "Steenie, I've been hearing that question argued and debated from both directions for most of the way across the plains, and at nearly every meal I've eaten or meeting I've attended since I came to the Valley. In that time I must have heard a hundred reasons, if not more. Truthfully, I don't hardly know which of them is correct."

"My Uncle Ben says that the government is right," Steenie then said with an air of sadness. "He says that Brother Brigham has got up a rebellion against Washington, and that he intends to be dictator of his own private empire out here in the mountains."

"That's nonsense," I declared. "My Ma says the coming war has to do with persecution, plain and simple. She says it's a common trial that all true Saints must endure. In her opinion, persecution must exist for the Saints of God no matter what age they live in or under what nation's flag they reside.

"Pa, though, looks at it a little differently, or at least more deeply. Some returning missionaries stayed a night with us out on the plains of Wyoming, and Pa spent nearly until morning talking with two of them. From what they said, Pa has decided that it's persecution, all right—but that it's all got up through Satan's usual method of selfishness and lies and ambition for power."

"What do you mean?"

Gently I urged the horses forward. "Steenie, I'm not hardly

the best one to say, for I wasn't here when all this happened. But Pa tells us, at night, what he learns at the powder factory — and from what he says, the same spirit rages in the hearts of eastern politicians and religionists today that raged when Brother Joseph and Hyrum were murdered. For whatever reasons, folks spread lies and falsehoods, other folks believe them, and innocent people suffer. I think—"

"Say, young folks, how about a ride?"

In surprise, Steenie and I spun around and examined the man who stood beside the road. Neither of us had even seen him approach, we had been so engrossed in our conversation. But now that Steenie looked at him, she gave a little cry of recognition.

"Brother Hanks! Why, we didn't see you. Please climb aboard and ride with us."

"Afternoon, Miss Steenie," the man said as he vaulted up onto the bench, "it's good to see you. And who might be this young buck sitting next to you?"

"Ephraim Hanks," Steenie replied, beaming radiantly, "this is Jons Soderberg, lately from Sweden."

"How do you do?" the man said, holding out his hand. I took it and felt a little shiver at the power I felt there. Brother Hanks was not overly tall. He wore a long, full beard, and he had a pleasant, peaceable look about him that I was later to learn could be quite deceptive. But for then I shook his hand and waited to see what might develop.

"How are your Uncle Ben and Aunt Maria?" Ephraim asked.

"They're . . . fine," Steenie said, dropping her eyes.

Ephraim Hanks looked straight ahead. "Then the Spirit of apostasy is still with Ben?"

Steenie nodded sorrowfully, and Brother Hanks gently patted her hand. "Keep exercising your faith, Christena. If the Lord could part the Red Sea, then he can surely change a man's heart. Say, what were the two of you discussing, that you didn't even see me waving at you?"

"We were talking about the army," Steenie said. "Jons, on

27

his way across the plains, crept to their fires at night and listened in on their plans."

Ephraim looked hard at me. "Is that so?" he asked gently. "What company did you come in with, Brother Soderberg?"

"Mathias Cowley's company, Sir."

"Ah! He told us that some of the young bucks had done a little scouting around, and he seemed right proud of their efforts. Did you scout the soldiers, or the teamsters?"

"Both, but mostly teamsters. They were out ahead of the regular troops."

"And what did you learn?"

This was feeling a bit like an inquisition, but I didn't know how to get out of it, so I went ahead and told him all I had told Steenie.

When I had finished, Ephraim Hanks shook his head. "Evil men—that's what a good many of them are. I find it passing strange that a corrupt government will send out evil, drunken adulterers and thieves to teach a moral, righteous people how to behave themselves. I suppose that's one reason why Brother Brigham has decided to declare martial law. Now we will go forth in the power of Zion's God to defend ourselves against their wicked assault."

"Martial law has been declared?" I asked, surprised.

"It has. I was in a meeting with the Church leaders only an hour ago, and Brother Brigham has signed the proclamation. Even as we speak it is being implemented."

"You . . . you were just with *Brigham Young?*" I asked, feeling awed to be talking to a man who had just spoken with the Prophet of the Lord.

"Certainly was."

"My goodness. I . . . I . . . "

Steenie, sensing what I was feeling, suddenly spoke. "Jons has never seen the Prophet, Brother Hanks. He's not used to being around him as we are."

Ephraim Hanks nodded with understanding. "Puts his trousers on one leg at a time, young man, just like the rest of us. And he has every other mortal problem and trial that the rest

28

of us have, as well. Difference is, God has called *him* to be Prophet. The man Brigham is a great man, but it is the office he holds that I honor and serve."

I nodded, trying my best to understand what this unusual person was telling me.

"Brother Hanks," Steenie then asked, going back to what she and I had been discussing, "why *is* the army attacking us? What have the Mormons done that would get the government so upset?"

Ephraim Hanks grinned. "Do you want the short and simple answer or some rather lengthy explanations of it?"

"We'd like explanations, please."

"Well," he drawled, "since you're giving me a free ride, I'll pay with talk and tell you what I know as best I can. First, for background—as you know, Mormonism embraces all of Christ's gospel, and to most good Christian folk, that doesn't seem practical. Nor does it seem possible to them that, in our own enlightened age, a man would step forth and call himself a prophet. That such happened, and that such self-same prophet declared to folks that all their churches were false, truly grates on the self-righteous nerves of Christiandom. It was those same self-righteous people who saw to it that the Prophet Joseph Smith and his brother Hyrum were murdered, and it's the same ones who, today, have sent the army forth to slay us."

Steenie looked at him, and I wondered at the expression in her eyes. "Brother Hanks," she said, and her voice was full of admiration, "I . . . I've never heard it said quite like that. Now what the bishop and other folks say begins to make sense."

"Well," he said, looking a little uncomfortable because of her praise, "if a man has eyes to see, he sees. I'm just saying what I see.

"Another thing. As far as I've been able to tell, the political appointees chosen by Washington for our people have been pompous, self-serving, immoral, narrow-minded men who neither understand nor uphold the freedoms that America's constitution guarantees her people. Many of them can't see a united people without seeing treason, nor see a people enthusiastically

29

following their prophet without seeing slavery and tyranny. Others decry our doctrine of the plurality of wives while living themselves in the midst of lust, adultery, and sin. And the list goes on.

"In fact, the most recent and wicked of these men, I'm afraid, is a judge who left here a year ago by the name of W. W. Drummond. He, more than anyone else, has brought this current crisis upon us.

"According to what the Brethren have learned, Drummond left a wife and family destitute in Illinois, and appeared here in the valley with a harlot whom he introduced as his wife. With her seated at his side on the judicial bench, that gambler and bully openly declared that he had come here to make money, and that money was his god. He then mocked our laws and institutions and took from the local courts all their powers. Then he struck at the heart of all our most sacred beliefs, rendering judicial decisions that would appall the devil himself.

"When Drummond's unpopularity finally forced him to quit the bench, he addressed his resignation and a letter to the attorney general in Washington, writing many lies and half-truths that were calculated to bring the wrath of the government down upon us. How well he succeeded, especially with that thimble-brained Buchanan, who hadn't the sense to examine the false allegations for himself, is evidenced by the army that even now is pounding on our eastern doors."

"Did Secretary of War Floyd have much to do with this?" Steenie asked.

"I reckon he did," Ephraim Hanks replied. "I don't know how much, but rumor has it that he's been a real force behind mobilizing the troops. Why do you ask?"

"I heard some men talking after meeting a few weeks ago," Steenie explained. "According to them, Secretary Floyd is an avowed secessionist, and the army coming here is part of his scheme to scatter and weaken U.S. forces. It frightens me that such selfish political ambitions are allowed to disrupt so many innocent lives."

"Well," I said, speaking for the first time, "President Buchanan certainly doesn't believe that we're innocent. One of the missionaries that Pa met with on the plains had Buchanan's message to Congress this year. Old Buck is convinced of Brother Brigham's despotism, our all-pervading fanaticism, and even our so-called illegal Indian policy. According to the president, all Mormons are in open rebellion against Washington, and we are all encouraging the Indians to fight the government with us. Why, my goodness, I've never even met an Indian, let alone incited one to war."

Steenie giggled. "Me neither."

"Well, I've met several more than somewhat," Ephraim Hanks declared. "Most of them are good people, too. Or were, that is, before they got corrupted by white men. I've not heard that we were encouraging them to fight, but if we decided to, I don't think it would take much to get them going. Most Americans have treated them shamefully."

"I've heard it said," Steenie then ventured, "that polygamy is the principle cause of this invasion. Colonel Fremont has called polygamy and slavery the 'twin relics of barbarianism,' and I've been told that Senator Stephen A. Douglas has said the same thing on the floor of Congress."

"That's so," Ephraim agreed. "There's no doubt that the doctrine of plurality of wives is the most bitter of all Mormon pills for the sectarian world to swallow.

"Well, young people," Ephraim Hanks concluded, "yonder is where I'm headed. Luck to the both of you, thank you for the ride . . . and Miss Steenie, give my best to Ben and Maria."

Steenie nodded. Ephraim Hanks vaulted from the wagon and strode down a lane that winded away from the road, and in another moment I had the horses moving again.

"He's an unusually good man," Steenie said quietly. "And a dear friend."

"Is he the same Ephraim Hanks who's been back and forth across the plains so many times on the mail routes and helping emigrants and so forth?"

"One and the same. Have you heard of him, Jons?"

"I'll say. Folks sit around the fire of a night and tell tales about him and Porter Rockwell. Some folks don't like them, but my Pa says to pay that no mind. He says that when an elephant walks through town, all the dogs bark."

Steenie giggled. "You do listen to your father, don't you."

I looked ahead, down the rutted road. "Pa's a fine man, Steenie, a deep thinker and a good listener. He and my ma were among the very first, in Sweden, to embrace the gospel. Pa said that from the first time he heard the missionaries, he could see the complete sense of it. The more I hear from him, the more sense he makes, too. So, yes—I try to listen."

Now Steenie looked away. "Jons . . . will your father . . . ever practice polygamy?"

"Pa?" I asked, startled. "Why, I don't hardly know. I don't think I've ever heard him talk about it, at least for himself. But I suppose that if Brother Brigham asked him . . . "

"Would *you* ever enter the principle?"

The question caught me unawares, and I looked hard at the girl by my side. She was still turned away, but I could tell by the smallness of her voice that she was serious, dead serious.

"Well," I said, slowly, carefully, "the young fellows in my wagon train used to talk about it nights, and all of us pretty much decided that, given the chance, we'd each have us a whole harem of pretty little wives."

"Jons—"

"Just trying to live the gospel," I said seriously. "And maybe build up the kingdom a mite, while I'm at it."

"Well, I declare . . . " Steenie sputtered furiously, and I could see that it was time to get out of this mess, and fast.

"Of course," I added, flicking the lines against the backs of the horses, "that was before I met you."

"What?" she asked as she looked quickly at me. "You mean . . . "

"I mean, now that I've met you and discovered what a real woman is like, I can see that a man would be in deep and serious trouble with several such wives hounding and pestering and questioning him from daylight to dark. Yes, ma'am, now that I've become better acquainted with you, I can see that one wife,

32

if she was exactly like you, would be more than enough to keep a fellow hopping along the straight and narrow pathway forever."

" 'A' fellow," she asked coyly, "or one particular fellow?"

"Only one," I replied, "unless you're planning on going into the principle yourself, with a whole harem full of husbands."

"Maybe I should," she mused. "But I'd want to start that harem with just the right sort of man . . . "

"Old, bald, plenty of middle to give him stability?"

"Exactly, Jons. Just the ticket for a good life."

"But not an exciting one?" I asked hopefully.

"Hardly exciting. But then, a woman must always give up something. For stability, most any woman I know would give up excitement, happiness, love . . . "

"Is there some particular man that could make you happy, Steenie?" I asked, feeling still more hopeful. "Say a scrawny sort of fellow who stands about six feet tall and has more than enough dark hair."

"Dark, wavy, beautiful hair," she added.

"Yes, I suppose. But a fellow who has nothing else that could recommend him except the aching deep feelings of his heart."

Embarrassed by my own boldness, I stopped speaking, and Steenie grew silent as well. The horses picked up their gait to a steady trot, and I was riding along beside her with my head in a cloud of happiness when her soft-spoken, husky-throated voice brought me down again, hard and fast.

"Jons?" she said, and again she was very serious and all a trembling.

"Yes ma'am?" I responded, and with her next statement, I felt certain that my whole world had exploded.

"My Uncle Ben wants me to be his second wife," she said tragically, desperately. "Here he doesn't even believe in the Church or the gospel, and he wants a second wife. He's even been to the bishop about it and says he was encouraged. Worse, he's getting mean because I keep fighting the idea, and I don't

33

know what to do anymore to avoid his advances. Help me, Jons! Oh, please help me . . . "

I squatted on my haunches in the corner of our cabin, alone. Ma was off helping a neighbor woman stitch a quilt, my sisters were already enrolled in school, and Pa was up at the munitions plant in Sugarhouse. Before me on the floor, its lid open and back, was a small, musty wooden chest that held the total of my earthly treasures. Now, with a critical eye but with rapidly sinking heart, I examined them.

Inside were what was left of a set of Parker crayolas, two stubs of pencils with a mostly filled pad of sketches, a broken knife that one of Pa's younger brothers had given me before we had sailed from Sweden, assorted hard-fired clay marbles, an almost empty bottle of cinnamon oil, a bedraggled rabbit's foot, a compound-fractured measuring stick that I had found along the overland trail, a slightly burned candle, a single British halfpenney, and my once-treasured and forked-limbed sling-shot.

Picking up the slingshot and sitting back on my haunches, I closed my eyes gloomily. Nothing. Nowhere in this silly horde of leftovers from my childhood was there a single treasure with which I might betroth, as my one and future love and wife, Miss Christena Bergman.

Even then she waited outside, sitting patiently on the wagon bench while I sought desperately within my mind to know what to do. But I didn't know, not how to ask her to marry me nor how to stop her Uncle Ben from pursuing what I frankly felt were his evil designs.

I could always just up and ask her to marry me, of course. But that made little sense, and I knew it. I was young for such a step—just eighteen, the same age as Steenie. But even worse, I had nothing to offer a wife. I had no job and no prospects for one, I had no home, and I had no skills with which I might earn a living. Of course, I had farmed since almost before I could walk, and I felt that I could do passibly well at it, given the chance. But to farm, a man needed land. And of land I had none.

No, I had nothing to offer Steenie that she deserved. Nor did I have any treasure to offer her by way of betrothal. But then, neither could I just stand by and see her forced into wedlock with a man she was already beginning to fear and loathe.

"You could just tell him no," I had said after I had digested the staggering news she had shared.

"But Jons," she had cried, "what if I'm *supposed* to marry him? What if I'm the one to turn his heart back to the Lord? What will I do if the Lord has chosen me for such a task, and I selfishly run from it? Ben tells me that, you know. Every day my step-uncle tells me that I will be his salvation after we are married, that the Lord has called me to be his wife, and . . . and . . . Oh, Jons, I don't know what to do!"

Steenie had wept then, and I had driven helplessly beside her. But at last I had understood the haunted look that came so often to her eyes, the anguish that crept with increasing urgency into her voice.

And so as we neared South Cottonwood, I had begun silently thinking, planning. I would marry her myself! Ben Crost could not be right about the Lord wanting Steenie to marry him — not when it produced such fear and loathing within her. They were no product of the Lord's work!

So, to stop him, I would ask her myself, and we would be married as soon as I could get something established. That would surely put a halt to her Uncle Ben's evil plans.

But now I stared helplessly. Now I could see that there was no reasonable or possible way I could ask Steenie to become my wife —

"Jons?"

Spinning, I gaped in surprise at Steenie, who was standing in the doorway behind me. I had not heard her come in, and the fact that she had been secretly watching startled me.

"Jons, what are you thinking?"

"Uh . . . about being foolish," I told her quietly, resignedly as I rose to my feet.

"What do you mean? I . . . I don't understand."

It was in my mind to say nothing, to just lead her back to the wagon and drive her home. I intended that, and I intended further to simply let circumstances after that day take their course, both for her and for my helpless self. Then we could both see what time brought us.

I intended that, all right. But to my surprise, I heard myself speaking. "I was looking for something," I said quietly, "something precious with which I could . . . troth you."

Steenie's eyes opened wide with surprise. "What?" she whispered. "You could *what?*" And my heart thrilled with the hope I could hear in her straining voice.

"I . . . I . . . wanted to ask you to marry me," I stammered, my boldness suddenly gone. "But I've nothing of value with which to troth you, nothing but this silly slingshot—"

In an instant the worn elm-fork slingshot was lifted from my grasp, and Steenie Bergman was straining against me, her arms lifted and pressed tightly around my neck. "Jons," she whispered, and once again tears were falling from the incredible depths of her blue-gray eyes, "did . . . you really mean that?"

"I . . . did," I replied while I awkwardly fumbled to put my arms about her waist.

"Then with all my heart I accept," she whispered as she buried her face against my pounding chest. "With this precious slingshot I accept thy troth and pledge thee my heart until such future day as we are sealed for eternity by one of God's mortal servants."

"And I'll see to it that you are the most well-taken-care-of woman in the West!" I replied, my eyes suddenly filling with moisture and with gladness.

And then, almost before I knew what was happening, our lips had come together, and I was clinging tightly, desperately, to my one and eternal love.

Chapter 3

I stood alone in the road before Steenie's cabin, gazing at the darkened windows. The log structure was empty, and now I knew that Brother Elijah Fordham had been right. Not only Steenie Bergman but also her Uncle Ben Crost's entire family were gone.

Bending over, I discovered the ruts the wagon had made as it left the yard. Though the only light came from the moon, they stretched plain before me, out into the road. There they turned directly toward the trail up Emigration Canyon. Truly had Ben Crost turned his back upon everything that he and the rest of us had given up so much to embrace.

What threw me, though, was Steenie. Why had she gone *with* him? What about our troth? Did the promises we had made to each other mean so little to her that she would pack up and leave for the wild mountains with winter coming on, just so she could throw herself on the mercy of the army? I couldn't see the reason of it, but neither could I argue with the evidence. Steenie was truly gone.

Numbly I walked to the door, pushed it aside, and stepped in. The cabin, one of the nicer in the area, was empty and clean, and I sensed that I was seeing the work not only of Maria but also of Steenie, both of whom had too much pride to leave the remnants of their living for others to clean up.

Of course, the table was still there, built into the wall, its one cracked leg leaning awkwardly. I looked at that leg, felt the knot that was still receding on the back of my head, and wondered.

Late the afternoon before, with Steenie fervently clutching my silly slingshot, I had brought her home. I had accompanied her inside, still excited but not expecting anything, and before I hardly knew what was happening, Steenie had announced our betrothal to her uncle and his wife.

Maria's face had been a study, so I couldn't tell what she was thinking. But Ben's face had been something else altogether. He had been angry, and he was mean enough to push his anger at me.

"*Betrothed?*" he had stormed as he rose to his feet. "Steenie betrothed to a foreign whelp like you? Over my dead body is she betrothed! Steenie, get to your room. I'll deal with you later. And you, Mister. Get out of here and don't ever let me see your face again!"

I had been stunned! I had never expected anything like that, and I didn't know how to react. I looked at Steenie, saw tears in her eyes, and was just turning back to face her uncle when he had hit me in the jaw, knocking me off my feet.

Astonished, I had gone down hard, my head snapping against the table leg as I fell, cracking the leg. Above me the table had collapsed. I had rolled to get out from under it, and Ben had kicked me hard in the ribs. I heard Steenie and Maria both cry out at that, but I was too stunned to respond. I hardly had enough air left to choke on, let alone to cry out with. But I strained and gasped, got a little wind, and pulled myself to my feet, all the time expecting another blow.

But none had come, and when my eyes had finally cleared enough that I could see, I understood why. Ben had shoved Steenie into her lean-to bedroom, and he was standing at the low doorway, yelling at her and at his wife, Maria.

"Mister . . . Brother Crost . . . " I gasped, "I . . . "

Whirling, the man had come at me like a mad dog, and involuntarily I had stepped backward. Then suddenly I had seen red, and doubling my fists I had prepared for battle. I was taller than he was, but he outweighed me considerably, and he had more experience. But I thought little of that, nor did I care how badly he might beat me. I wanted only to protect and preserve my love.

"Jons, no!" Blinking with loss of concentration, I looked aside at Steenie, wondering what I was doing wrong. I had felt Ben hit me then, felt myself going down the second time, and still my betrothed was all I could see. Her eyes were wide with horror, yet while I watched she stepped from the room and up to her Uncle Ben.

"Jons," she had pleaded with me as she clutched his arm, "don't . . . don't fight. You . . . go home, and we . . . we'll work this out."

Ben had kicked me again. I had staggered to my feet, and the man had shoved me out the door. And as I had reeled off toward the wagon, I had heard Steenie cry out, "I love you, Jons Soderberg! I love you!"

With Steenie's voice still ringing in my memory, haunting me with its agony, I stared down at the broken table. Moving quietly then, almost on tiptoe, I stepped past it and to the lean-to that had been Steenie's bedroom. I had never been inside the small room, and even now I felt nervous as I stepped past the threshold. But I needn't have, for it too was empty, stripped of every item that had been part of Steenie's personal life.

As I looked around the darkened room, lit only by the moonlight coming through the single window, I felt as though I would break apart inside. My stomach ached, my head began pounding, and sudden tears fell freely from my eyes.

What had I done? What could I possibly have done that would have made Steenie want to leave me? Had it been that I had acted the coward? Had she left because I had not fought Ben Crost for her? She had seemed so happy, so excited at the prospect of sharing her life with me. And she had seemed so determined that I would not fight him.

But now she was gone.

As I angrily wiped at my eyes and moved back through the low doorway, I caught a glimpse of something in the chinks between the logs above my head, something that seemed, even in the shadowy darkness, to be out of place. Reaching up, I touched what I had seen, felt its familiar smoothness, and with racing heart pulled from between the logs my old elm-crotch slingshot.

Staring at it, wondering that Steenie had not taken it with her, I wiped at my eyes again and finally became aware of the slip of paper tied around one of the forks. With anxious, fumbling fingers, I worked the string loose, and then I held the paper near the window.

There was writing, I could see that, but between the poor lighting and my difficulty in reading English, I could not make out what it said.

Stuffing the slingshot into my hip pocket, I clutched the paper and ran from the dwelling, intent upon finding someone who had a light, intent upon —

"Jons?"

Spinning to a halt in my headlong flight, I stared at the shadowy form. "Ma?" I asked. "Ma, is that you?"

"Ya," she replied as she walked toward me. "Und who did you tink it vould be?"

"I . . . I don't know," I stammered. "I was hoping it might be Steenie . . . Oh, Ma, what is happening?"

Gently she reached out and drew me down to her, and she held me tightly while I sobbed out my grief and despair. I hadn't needed my mother's arms so badly in years, hadn't supposed that I would ever need them again. But I learned that night that there are times, no matter how old a fellow gets, when the comfort of a mother's love is about all that can pull him through.

"Ma," I said when I had regained my composure, "Steenie left me a note. I found it in her cabin."

"Vhat does it say?"

"I don't know. There wasn't enough light to see."

"Ya," she said as she took my arm, "but there vill be plenty of light at home. Come, my boy, und ve vill see vhat the girl has to say."

Hurrying then, the two of us made our way along the darkened road, and a few moments later we arrived at our cabin.

"Soren," Ma said to Pa as we walked in, "Jons has found a message from young Christena. Perhaps it vill not be as ve have thought."

"So?" Pa said, smiling. "Don't you know from the message?"

Shaking my head, I unrolled the small strip of paper and stared at the writing. Steenie had written in pencil and had apparently been in a hurry, for the writing was light and I could hardly decipher the letters. But I finally did and felt my heart racing as I awkwardly concluded: "Jons, B won't let me stay. He'll hurt the others. Please come. I love you. S!"

Shaking, I read the note aloud to my folks.

"Vell," Ma concluded with finality, "that iss goot to hear."

"Yeah," I agreed, "But now what am I going to do?"

"Do?" Pa said as he turned back to his meal. "You vill do notting, my son. You are but a lad, und the girl iss part of another family. If the man who iss father of that family chooses to go, it iss none of our affair."

"But Pa—"

"Jons, I have spoken."

"Soren, dear?"

Pa looked up at Ma, warned by the sweet but determined tone of her voice.

"Ya?"

But Ma threw him a curve, and my poor father didn't even see it coming. "Brother Cole's young heifer," she said sweetly, "got mired yust before dark, und he vas asking if you might come und halp him."

Jumping to his feet, Pa grabbed his hat. "Voman, vhy didn't you tell me vhen I got here? I yust—"

Smiling sweetly, Ma took Pa's arm. "Soren, you do not need to go. There vill be others, und the calf might already be saved."

"Mother," Pa said as he took her hand from his arm, "I am a Soderberg, und if a neighbor needs a halping hand, day or night, then this Soderberg vill be there halping. Now I must be going."

Again Ma stopped him. "Soren, please listen to me."

"Voman, take your hand from my arm."

41

"There iss no young heifer," Ma stated then, leaning earnestly into Pa's big frame. "Not unless one considers poor little Christena Bergman. Und, my dear, iss she not more important than a cow?"

Pa looked hard at her, and I was having a difficult time not grinning.

"Iss not Jons also a Soderberg?" she continued tenderly. "Vould you want Jons to be less a man than you? Vould you vant that he should turn his back upon a cry for halp from such a sveet und innocent child as Christena Bergman?"

"Vell, no," Pa muttered, collapsing again into his chair. "But he iss too young —"

"Soren, Jons iss as old as your father vas vhen he married your mother und set off on his own. Besides, the lad iss not marrying Christena, yust halping her to come back to her people. The marriage vill come later, the good Lord villing. Now, my dear, vhy don't you halp me get a pack up for the lad. It vill be cold in the mountains, und I tink he could use your varm coat."

Pa grumbled but followed Ma's instructions, and hurriedly I headed out to the shed to get the chores done. My heart was singing again, for I was going after Steenie. And when I found her and brought her back, there would be a wedding. I knew it, for Ma had said so. And to tell the truth, I had never known Ma to be wrong.

Chapter 4

The sky was only just showing gray when I closed the door behind me and strode off toward Emigration Canyon. I truly had no idea of what it would take to find Steenie and bring her back, but ignorance is bliss, and I was feeling blissful as could be.

In my pack I carried Pa's warm coat and blanket, a large bait of food, a small knife, and some other odds and ends that Pa had called "get-along" stuff when he had given them to me. I also had my slingshot and Steenie's penciled note. And, finally, I had my Pa's blessing, pronounced upon my head, that the Lord would go with me and protect me and grant unto me success. With that, I knew I could not fail.

It was a Saturday morning in the latter part of September that I started out, and the day was bright and clear. By the time I topped the foothills the sun was rising, and ahead of me I saw the gathering dust of an incoming company of Saints. Stepping out, I soon reached the road, and there I learned from a returning missionary that the train was Captain William G. Young's company, containing the last of the season's emigrants.

The missionary, A. Milton Musser, was just returning home from a five-year mission to India and England, during which he had circumnavigated the globe, traveling, as he told me, "without purse or scrip." Yet he was anxious to see his family, so I let him go and sought someone else to question.

Unless you've seen an emigrant train on the move, you have

no idea of what it's truly like. In dry weather, first and last there is the dust, billowing clouds of it raised by churning wheels and plodding hooves and feet. It is promiscuous grit, seeping into and around and over everything in the train. Folks are forced to wear neckerchiefs over their noses and mouths just to keep from bogging down in their own mud.

And then there is the noise, a cacophony of sound that at times feels as though it will break the eardrums and render the brain useless. The sounds are made of the creaking and screeching of green wood on hard iron, of ungreased wheels on crooked and worn axle thimbles, the banging of iron-tires against rocky earth, the clatter of hundreds or thousands of hooves against stone, the thunderous bellowing and whinnying and bleating of cattle and horses and sheep, the chattering of many human languages being fused into one, and the shrieking of children's voices that all speak the same universal, and loud, language of childhood.

Next there is the smell, of smoke, dust, animals, and sweaty, unwashed bodies — and over all the pungent odor of crushed sage and cedar. The latter, while pleasant, hardly hides the first. Yet folks adjust, and most live with it for as long as there is need.

And last there are the faces, dozens upon dozens of faces, of men, women, and children. Each is an individual, each reflects through the dust and grime whatever he or she is feeling most strongly at the moment, and each suffers all the weaknesses and frailties that burden the rest of humanity. Yet somehow, over the course of the long trail to the valley, these faces all become fused, and it is almost as if they are a mighty, blood-related family.

That day, as I gazed upon the weary travelers, I saw mostly relief and joy, for the Valley had at last been reached, and the journey was nearly at an end. And even in the faces of those who reflected pain or anger or frustration, I sensed relief. These folks had come from all parts of America and Europe, had been traveling for months and sometimes years, and had each been driven by the urge to gather with the Saints of God in the valleys of the mountains of Zion. Now, at long last, it was accomplished.

"Hello," I called as I moved up the road past the laboring people. "Hello, and welcome to the Valley."

Some folks smiled and nodded in reply, some spoke, and a few ignored me, intent on dragging forward the complaining burdens of their own bodies. At length, however, I saw what I had been looking for, a man apart and alone. As I spied him sitting upon a rock, I thought he might have the time to tell me what I wanted to know.

I got closer and then realized with a start that he was old, real old. He sat still and quiet as a wrinkled lizard, ancient and craglike, weathered and withered to a thin angular shape of bent bones and stringy muscle. His hatchet face under his wide floppy hat brim had been whittled by age to dry leathery skin, and his white straggly whiskers showed thinning that must have reflected the growth on top of his head.

He sat alone, staring off over a herd of grazing cattle, and I wondered if he even saw me coming. Or if he saw anyone else. Or if they saw, or cared, about *him*. He gave the appearance of a decrepit old nuisance, a shiftless relic out of the past, and I nearly turned away before I saw his eyes.

The man, I knew instantly, wasn't as old as he looked, and I kept coming.

"Hello," I said loudly, fearing that he might be deaf.

"Howdy," he drawled in response, and I knew by the quiet tone of his voice that he could hear. I also knew, from the drawled "howdy" that he was a natural-bred American.

I stopped before him, and for a moment we regarded each other soberly. "Jons Soderberg," I finally said, thrusting my hand forward.

Slowly he reached up and took it in a surprisingly firm grip. "Gideon Monson," he replied. "Gideon Peabody Monson. If you figure on talking, call me Gideon."

Grinning, I nodded. "Monson. Are you Svenska?"

"Grandpap was Swedish," he replied. "Most of me, though, is Swiss. From Grindelwald under the Eiger, the Monch and the Jungfrau, up the river from Interlaken. Since Europe, I come by way of Tennessee."

"You a convert?" I asked.

"Who ain't?" the old man replied. "Hand a feller a Book of Mormon, and if he reads it in earnest, he's a convert. You a newspaper correspondent?"

"What?"

"All these tomfool questions can't be just out of general interest. So you're either a correspondent for some eastern paper, or a sheriff with a warrant for my arrest. You look too young to be a sheriff, so I reckon you're a correspondent."

For Gideon Monson that was a long speech, though at the time I didn't know him well enough to realize it. "Neither." I grinned. "I'm just a convert like yourself."

"Then why you heading the wrong way?"

"I'm looking for some folks who I think took the back trail a day ago. Maybe you saw them?"

Gideon stared ahead and did not respond. Above us the sun was sending streamers of pink and gold across the wide land. In a few hours it would be beating more directly down, building layers of late September heat. But right then, the night-cool of the canyon mouth lingered, fresh and sweet, and I took deep gulps of it, savoring the feel. Off to my left, a rock squirrel popped up, stared at us, and then disappeared into the waving grass. Then a high-bowed Conestoga creaked toward us, pulled by three span of oxen, and the noise of the complaining wheels was about all I could hear. Folks called those wagons prairie schooners, and from the way they loomed up like tall ships, it was easy to see why. Once the wagon had moved past, the old man spoke again.

"For six weeks I've been trying to get that idjut to grease his thimbles. Wouldn't do it, and now they're ruint. Serves him right! Why you looking?"

"It's a long story," I sighed. And then I described Ben Crost and his family, Steenie Bergman, Ben's wagon and team, and even the splayed left foot of Ben's riding horse. The last, I think, impressed Gideon Monson.

"For such a young pilgrim, friend, you take note of a good deal."

"I spent a year in Keokuk, farming and hunting meat for a butcher," I told him. "Then Captain Cowley had me on the scout a little, back on the plains. I'm no frontiersman, but I do try to see what I look at."

"Maybeso you do," Gideon grunted. "And I did see your wagon, yesterday about this time. They was beyond Henderson Spring on Little Mountain, going at a good clip. The girl was with 'em."

Gideon's statement was flat, unemotional — and served me instant notice that somehow he knew who I was really after.

"Did you speak with her?" I asked.

"Not hardly. But I looked at her, little wisp of a thing with the fire of a late sunset in her hair and a smile of sweet purity on her lips. She didn't look happy, though, and I wondered if her pa was taking her away from some young buck like yourself."

"He's not her pa. He's her uncle, or second uncle, maybe, and I think he took her against her will. She and I, we . . . well, we had a . . . an understanding of marriage, and I don't hardly think she'd cut and run."

"Never can tell," Gideon commented wisely.

"Maybe not," I groused, "but she left me a note of desperation, pleading for my help, and I won't stop until she's free."

"Luck," Gideon said as he reached down, took up a small stone, and flicked it at a straying crow. And with that, the conversation was over.

Adjusting my pack, I started out again, and as I walked I found myself feeling mighty grumpy about Gideon Monson's lack of confidence in Steenie and me. But the morning was fine, and it wasn't long before I stopped thinking of him and began to notice again the incoming Saints.

Every living soul of them had pain and weariness written on their faces. Many were barefoot, most wore rags and tatters, most were driving wagons or walking along beside them, and a few were in harness, pulling handcarts that contained a small heap of their remaining worldly goods.

Yet I hardly saw a soul who was not happy, and it put me in mind of one of the things Pa quoted from the Prophet Joseph. According to what Pa had been told, Joseph had said that a religion that didn't require the sacrifice of all worldly goods was a religion that didn't have the power to save.

Well, Mormonism, at least for these folks, had surely required the sacrifice of most worldly possessions. So I prayed, as I strode along the dusty trail, that the Lord would please save them, and all the rest of us who had come so far, in his celestial kingdom. And praying for them, I quickly discovered, made me feel better about Gideon Monson and about where I was going and about what I was hoping to accomplish. In fact, I could feel my heart growing wider and wider—

"Hey, you!"

Looking up in surprise, I realized that I had come to the mouth of the canyon. Further, a man with a rifle was standing there, and he had it pointed directly at me.

"Where do you think you're going?" he asked brusquely.

"Up the trail," I replied, feeling a little irritated by the man's rough manner.

"You have a pass?"

"A what?"

"A pass, Son. Don't you know that Brother Brigham declared martial law? It's been ten days now, so you ought to have heard."

Dumbly, I shook my head.

"Well, he did, and no one goes up-trail without he has orders from General Wells or without he tells me flat out that he has quit the Church and is returning to the sin and wickedness of the Gentiles. Which are you?"

"Neither one. I'm just looking for some folks—"

"Say," the man asked, interrupting me, "how old are you?"

"Eighteen."

The man grinned. "Then if you're a Mormon you're conscripted. You've got to report and get sworn in as a member of the Nauvoo Legion. There's a war going on, you know. Or hadn't you heard of that, either?"

The fellow was being a little sarcastic, but I didn't much mind. I should have known about the conscription. What really troubled me, though, was that I wasn't going to be allowed up-trail.

"I know about the soldiers," I said, my mind racing. "We camped near them, crossing the plains.

"You camped? What do you mean?"

"I came in with Captain Cowley's company, a couple of weeks ago, and now I need to go—"

The sound of rapid hoofbeats beat into our consciousness, and within a moment a horseman loomed into sight, pushing past the stragglers of the emigrant company. As we watched, he pulled his lathered mount to a halt near the sentry.

"Wheat," he said, nodding his head in greeting. "Express for Squire Wells."

"Lo, Port," the sentry replied, momentarily forgetting me. It might have been a chance for me to get by him, too. But I couldn't, not with the man on the horse looking down at me.

He was a thin man, roughly dressed, with gray eyes and jet-dark hair and beard that hung in braids far below his shoulders and chest. In spite of the horse's heavy breathing, the man sat easily and seemed calm as a summer day. Still, I could feel something, almost as though the man was seeing through me, and I could hardly move.

Port—Porter Rockwell. So this was the famous guard of the Prophet Joseph, the dangerous man that folks back east were calling Brigham's avenging angel. I tried to see murder in him—tried, but couldn't, for I don't think it was there. Nevertheless, I continued to stare, and after a moment he turned back to the sentry.

"Van Vliet has left Ham's Fork," Port said softly. "He's going east, and he's sounding like ol' Brig ate him up."

The sentry grinned. "Just like we'll eat up the army, happen they try to come into the Valley. What did he say to Squaw-killer Harney?"

"By gum," the man responded, "*that's* what I've been forgetting! Harney's been replaced by a gent name of Albert Sydney Johnston. I hear he's hard as nails, but he's no butcher, either. He's on his way west now and figures to meet the troops by the end of October. Me, I figure it'll take him a little longer."

Port chuckled, and the sentry laughed with him.

"Wheat," the scout continued, "it was wheat with Van Vliet, all the way. He told Colonel E. B. Alexander, the temporary commander that the government blue-bellies are calling the Old Woman, that the Mormons had been lied about more than any other people he knew. He told him that we're innocent and will fight the army to the last of our extremities. And if my name's Port Rockwell, he's dead right."

"They had *better* believe him!" the sentry exclaimed.

"Some do, some don't. The 10th Regiment are young and full of fire, and when Van Vliet tried to stop them with his warning, they swore they would come in and wipe us out anyhow. They made twenty miles instead of ten the next day. One fellow, Captain Gove, figures the 10th alone can sweep our people from the earth and that the days of Mormonism in Utah are numbered."

The sentry shook his head. "The man's a fool. He's never seen Echo Canyon or the determination of our Mormon boys."

The legendary Porter Rockwell grinned and wrapped his leg around the cantle of his saddle, relaxing further. "Well, at least Van Vliet is convinced our boys are serious, and I do believe he's convinced Colonel Alexander that we are, as well. Van Vliet is reading the words of old Brother Jameson wherever he goes, and they're doing much to spread our cause."

"Brother Jameson?"

"Aye, the same elderly gent as was in the Haun's Mill massacre back in Missouri, where seventeen of our men and boys were murdered. Jameson is still carrying a few ounces of lead around with him from that day. He says he wants to pay it back with usury. Says he prays to God daily to send Old Buck's army along, for he wants to have a chance at them when he's armed.

"Then there was the vote in the southern territories, unanimous, that the Saints would torch their homes and lands and fight from the mountain peaks if the army should come in. Mild and peace-loving Brother John Taylor voiced it well when he thanked God, from the pulpit here in Great Salt Lake City, that the Mormons are determined to be free of mobocracy and to have peace, even if they have to fight for it.

"I reckon that Quartermaster Van Vliet was some startled to see the further unanimous showing of hands when Brother Taylor asked for a confirmation of his words. But now Van Vliet is a believer, and he's on his way to Washington to try and cool Old Buck's heels.

"You know," Port continued, combing his whiskers with his fingers, "I joined up with Mormonism as a youngster, with my best friend Joseph Smith, on the very day it was organized. Yes sir, the Prophet baptized me on the 6th of April in the year '30. But I tell you, even though Brother Joseph told me it would be rough goin' even after our people got to the Rocky Mountains, I didn't figure on all of this."

"Say," he drawled, still seeming to be unaware of my presence, "is Squire Wells yet in the Valley?"

The sentry nodded. "He hasn't passed here, so I reckon he is."

"Then I'm off," Porter Rockwell announced, and with another cry of "Wheat!" he had spurred the horse past the two of us and was pounding past the emigrants down-trail toward the city.

My mind whirling, I watched the man disappear. Then I turned back to the sentry. "Was that *the* Port Rockwell?" I exclaimed.

"One and the same," the sentry replied, still looking at the departing horse and rider. "The purified article. He'd do to ride the river with, too, I'll guarantee. Why, one time —"

"Brother," I interrupted, feeling an increasing urgency to get about my errand, "I must get up that trail."

For a moment I thought the sentry wavered, but then his face set up and he shook his head. "Not unless you have a pass, young feller. I'd suggest that you get down to headquarters, down on Brigham Street, and get signed up. Maybe then you can be assigned to Echo. Otherwise, I reckon you'd better be giving it up."

There are times when a fellow can see that a man can be bluffed, but there are also times when it is just as obvious he can't. This was one of the latter. And so, sorrowing and truly baffled about how I was going to get to Steenie and help her away from her wicked uncle, I turned around and headed back into the dust of the still-descending emigrant company.

I would definitely go down and sign on with the Legion, but I had my reservations about that, too. I had no weapon but my slingshot, no horse, nor no real supplies, and I knew that my chances of getting assigned to the Eastern Expedition were terribly slim. Yet somehow I had to find my way to Steenie.

"Mighty fast trip, wasn't it?"

Startled, I looked up and was surprised to see Gideon Monson, still seated on his rock. Neither had his horse moved, nor the grazing cattle. He was obviously not in any big hurry to reach the valley.

"Sentry won't let me past unless I'm a member of the Legion," I told him. "Brother Brigham has declared martial law, and folks going up-trail have to be apostates or have a pass. Besides, I'm of age and haven't yet signed up for service."

Gideon's hat brim bobbed slightly. "I reckon. But what about that flame-haired gal?"

"I'm going to try and get assigned to Echo. Maybe from there I can find her."

"You don't sound awful hopeful."

"I'm not," I replied, kicking at a rock. "I have no horse, no gun, no supplies. So I have little hope of going. But maybe some other Saint will see her need and help her."

"I thought you loved her."

The challenge was short, terse, and I snapped my head up. "I do, but—"

"Then hang it all, young feller, why you letting that sentry buffalo you? Man loves a woman, he does what it takes to see that she's cared for and protected. He surely doesn't leave it to other folks."

52

"But the sentry, the conscription . . . "

Gideon slowly unlimbered himself from the rock, setting his floppy, wide-brimmed hat more firmly in place as he did so. "Friend Soderberg," he growled as he creaked to his feet and staggered toward the hanging reins of his horse, "never let it be said that you was overly struck with the brights. You suppose that dusty trail yonder is the onliest way on this green earth over them mountains?"

"No, but—"

"Don't 'but' me, young feller. You want that little gal so bad, go after her!"

"But I have no pass or gun—"

"Hang it all, there's that 'but' again. Young feller, for two cents I'd blaze you a trail back over these mountains myownself. But I don't hardly know if you could foller me."

For a moment I stood still, staring up the oak-clogged slopes that stretched away to the east. My mind was whirling, and I was getting a whole new sense of direction. Finally, I looked back at the old man, who was now seated precariously in his saddle.

"I don't have two cents, Gideon Monson, but I do have this old elm-crotch slingshot and a note from Steenie Bergman."

"You asking me to go with you?" Gideon said slowly, quietly.

"I . . . I . . . "

"Well, are you, or not?"

"I . . . can't ask you to leave your family."

"Kettle-belly here is the onliest family I have, and he goes with me."

"Well, if you don't have anywhere else to go . . . "

Gideon stared off into the valley. "I don't," he said slowly. "I've got no family left alive at all—nothing holding me here but these fool cows. 'Sides, likely the brethren out on the plains could use an experienced hand. So if you wouldn't mind my company . . . "

"I wouldn't. I mean, I'd surely appreciate your help."

Turning his horse, Gideon kneed it forward, and I ran to keep up. Moments later he reigned in near one of the last of the lumbering wagons. Quickly the driver whacked the lumbering oxen to a halt, and then he looked up at the mounted Gideon Monson. "I'm going on a scout," Gideon declared. "Zeph, you and the missus have been good to me, mighty good. I appreciate it, and one day I'll see that you're repaid."

"Gideon, there's no need of that."

The old man reached down into the wagon and pulled out a small pack and long-barreled rifle. "The pendulum always swings," he said as he creaked back upright with his possibles. Then he turned to me.

"Friend Jons, you'll start right now in learning. You see what I just did?"

"Took your pack and rifle out of the wagon?"

"That's correct. But I did it wrong, just so's you'd notice. Did you?"

Mystified, I shook my head.

"Then you'd better open your eyes. Pulling a loaded rifle, barrel first, out of a wagon, is like riding a mule's tail. Both can get you gut-shot. Now, what say that you, me, and Henrietta be on our way?"

"Henrietta?"

Gideon patted the polished, burled stock of the rifle. "Henrietta. She's true as can be, and other than old Kettle-belly here, the dearest thing I have left on this earth—that is, since my Abby-girl and the children was taken . . .

"Tell the missus so long, Zeph," he said, tearing his thoughts away from his past. "I'll look you and the cows up once we all get settled.

"Now leave us be on our way, friend Jons. We have us a splayed-hoofed horse to be catching."

And with that, Gideon Monson urged his horse on its long-gaited way to the north and to the next narrow draw that sliced eastward into the mountains.

And I, with my pack as firmly in place as my determination, set out on shanks pony to do my best to follow him.

Chapter 5

It was cold where Gideon and I hunkered over our small fire, and we were hungry. But the fire helped, and so did the weather, which continued to remain dry. Of course, even as I held my hands over the fire, I knew that the warmth was no substitute for food. But, as Gideon had laconically pointed out, being warm and hungry beat out being cold and hungry six ways from Sunday.

And it was cold up on that mountain. We had been moving for three days, mostly with me hanging onto the tail of Gideon's horse, and we were making tolerable good time, what with having to blaze a whole new trail. But now we were high up, and cold.

That first day, Gideon had led me up what I later learned was Red Butte Canyon, and from the head of Red Butte we had worked our way southeast below Lookout Peak to the top of Killyon Canyon and Little Mountain. Below us a mort of Mormon soldiers had been camped, heading east — so we had stayed shy of them, camping alone. The next day, we had continued east past Fort Big Mountain; had skirted Little Emigration Canyon, Mormon Flat, and Camp Clayton; and had camped above the spring at Kurzy Hollow, just below the mouth of East Canyon. And all the way we had had to take care, for the trail was thick with men and animals heading out to meet the armies of Uncle Sam.

Now we were camped in a little swale high upslope of Spring

Creek, about four miles southwest of the Weber River, and we were hungry. The difference between Gideon and me was that Gideon said little about it, and I could hardly stop complaining.

"Gideon, do you think those fellers down below would spare us a bait of grub?" I asked.

My companion made no reply, so I sat and stared longingly at the fire that winked up at me through the brush and trees below. We were too far upslope to hear what was being said, but there was a large crowd of men down there, and I could occasionally hear voices. Even worse, though, was that at least twice I had distinctly smelled the aroma of frying bacon.

"You think we could go down there and ask to join them for supper?" I asked hopefully.

Almost imperceptibly Gideon shook his head. "Not hardly. Them pilgrims would likely send us back under guard faster than lizards scoot off hot rocks. Besides, one of them might think that thieves had ought to be treated like treasure—buried with care and affection."

"Then could we maybe—just *borrow* . . . some food?"

"You mean thieving."

"Not exactly," I argued. "Gideon, if we're all on the same side, then maybe a little requisitioning between troops would be smiled upon with divine favor."

"Divine favor," Gideon grunted as he pulled himself up from his kneeling position over the fire. Then slowly he hobbled to where his horse cropped sparse bunches of dry grass. At his approach, the horse lifted its head, and with a soft nicker it rubbed its muzzle against the old man's gaunt chest.

Reaching out, Gideon scratched behind the animal's ears. "What d'ya think, Kettle?" he asked the round-bellied animal softly. "Am I hungry enough to become an ordinary thief?"

The horse nickered again and shook its head, and Gideon stared out into the darkness. "Horses is funny animals, friend Jons," he said quietly. "And that goes especially for these scrubby little wild critters that folks call mustangs. Every one I ever saw is smallish, thin and bony, from living off next to nothing at all, and having to travel hundreds of miles to find even that.

"Look at him—grass-bellied, cat-hipped, hammer-headed. Hardly anything at all worth noticing. But there's something there, all right," Gideon grunted, seeming to get more worked up by the minute. "Thing is, it just doesn't show. The spirit is there, and the hardihood, as well as the stubborn clutch on freedom. This little gelding was bred by adversity to survive in a land where only those fitted to it can survive. Kettle here and his kind have been honed by summer drought and winter storm and the fangs of the wolf pack and the claws of the mountain lion to the knife-edge of endurance. Motion is the very meaning of their existence, and in motion they endure. Lookee here, Son. In Kettle's chest are the mightiest lungs on earth, the strongest heart. In his legs are steel springs, his hooves are rock-hard, and buried deep in his lean flanks is the strength to gallop clear to the far edge of eternity and all the way back again."

Once again the little horse muzzled the old man, and again he scratched behind its ears.

"Son," he continued, still not looking at me, "Kettle and I are two of a kind. Neither of us shows much, but as he has been bred to run, I have been bred to become like God. Deep down, I've always known that. Now I've finally found me a religion that teaches I am right. Christ's gospel shows me how to keep the commandments so I can become who I was eternally bred to be—and I am not about to throw it all over for a bellyful of food. No, nor a wagonload of gold, nor anything else of mortal value."

Now Gideon turned back toward the fire and grinned gently. "So if you're hungry enough to steal, Son, you're hungry enough to travel on alone."

He grew still then, and I sat stunned. First, he had said more in that few minutes than he had said in three entire days. But more importantly, he had said things I had never before considered. But he was also right, and I knew it. Like the old man, I had been created to be with God, and to be like God. So was I willing to throw all that away for some foolish, temporary

57

mortal convenience? Not hardly! Not when I thought of it like Gideon put it.

Poking a stick into the fire, I stood up. "Brother Gideon, you are a wonder. What's more, you are right. I am not exercising much faith. My pa gave me a blessing that I would be successful on this little scout, and I suppose that includes filling my belly. I just need to wait until the Lord brings that promise to pass."

Slowly Gideon creaked back to the fire, walking stiff-legged on account of his arthritis. "I call that waiting," he grinned wryly, "living the 'law of the last minute.' For a fact, though, the real name of that law is 'the law of the *true* last minute.' "

"What do you mean?"

"I mean, you and I don't decide when the last minute is supposed to come along. The Lord does. That's why it's called the *true* last minute. Why, I recollect one time . . . "

Gideon suddenly grew still, and he lifted his head slowly until I could see that he was listening, trying to hear something that I couldn't make out.

"What is it?" I whispered.

For a moment he didn't answer, but then slowly he lowered his chin. "Don't know," he replied quietly. "Thought for sure I heard something crying."

It came again then, a faint whimpering that sounded part animal, part human. And that time even I heard it.

"You get a bead on it?" he asked.

"I think," I whispered, "it's off that way, behind you."

Gideon nodded and lifted his rifle. "Me, too. Think I'll have me a looksee."

Well, I don't know why I did what I did then. It made no sense at all, and when I think about it now, it still doesn't. Not unless it was a prompting by the Holy Spirit. Of course, I didn't recognize it as such, but I'm learning that such promptings are most always little more than feelings, small impressions that come into a person's mind like a stray idea. And that is what happened then. A feeling came over me that Gideon and his rifle were not needed out there in the darkness. What was needed was *me*, and I had better be up and getting out there.

"Gideon," I grunted as I rose to my feet and stepped around the fire, "you stay and take care of that arthritis. I'll call out if I need help."

"You ain't armed, Son."

That was true. I wasn't. On the other hand, the same feeling that I was needed out there was making me feel like I didn't need a gun either. Call it crazy, or call it anything else — I don't think I could have possibly stayed by our fire right then. I had to get out in that darkness, and I had to get there in a hurry.

"I'll be all right," I murmured. And without giving my elderly friend a chance for further argument, I slipped into the darkened brush.

As I made my way forward, I was thankful that I hadn't been staring into the flames. A man stares into the flames, he blinds himself for several seconds, and that can be the difference between life and death. On the trail west I had learned to look past a fire, not into it, and fortunately the habit was still with me.

Moving carefully forward, I hadn't gone more than fifty feet when I was abruptly made to halt. The growl that did it was low, animal, and unfriendly. It came from directly before me, and without hesitation I turned to run.

But the brute in the darkness had apparently gotten my scent, and the warning growl became instantly a whine of entreaty. As well, the plea was accompanied by the thumping of a plumed tail upon hard earth.

"A *dog*?" I breathed, instantly forgetting my hunger. "Alone in this wilderness?"

The animal's reply was another whine, another series of hopeful tail thumps.

Searching, I found a sulfur match deep in one of my pockets. Striking and cupping it, I gave close scrutiny to the animal I had found.

Lying there in a dark patch of its own blood was an emaciated creature that looked starved coyote, but that was acting more dog than any dog I had ever seen. I saw that, and I saw

59

also, before the match sputtered out, that this particular coyote-dog had need of human friend far beyond ordinary measure.

"Just so, boy," I said quietly as I reached down and gently scratched him behind the ears. "You need help, feller, and I'm willing to give it if I can. But I've got to get you back to the fire. You willing to be carried?"

The wounded creature responded with further, though noticeably weaker, thumpings of his tail. So, shaking my head, I reached under the animal and eased it into my arms. Rising, then, with my absolutely silent and motionless burden, I made my way back to Gideon and the fire.

"Lawsy," Gideon grinned as I walked in, "you've gone and found some supper."

"Not hardly I ain't," I responded, using some of the old man's own language on him. "This poor brute is hurt, and I'm going to do what I can to help it."

"Son," Gideon said, shaking his head, "that there is a wild prairie wolf. It regains consciousness, you'll likely lose a good chunk of your anatomy, and get the hydrophoby, to boot."

With my foot I scraped a place, near the fire, bare of stones and twigs. "He's conscious right now, but barely. Besides, he may look coyote, but he acts dog."

"That so?" Gideon asked, sounding more interested. "Then likely he's a cross and has been man-trained. What ails him?"

Setting the animal down on the area I had cleared, I bent to examine it and without much trouble found a wickedly broken leg.

It was a cruel wound. Some hours old, it had apparently been caused by a rifle or pistol ball. The radius, or long front bone of the left foreleg, was badly broken near its juncture with the humerus, or upper leg bone. The dog had been licking the wound, so little infection had developed. But to reduce the fracture, and to splint it in such a way as to prevent crippling or gangrene, was going to require the help of far more than my severely limited medical education.

"What you aiming to do, Son?"

"Right now . . . well, to tell the truth, I'm praying."

"Praying?"

" 'Inasmuch as ye have done it unto one of the least of these,' I think the Bible says. Gideon, would you hand me my bedroll there?"

Unrolling the proffered bundle, I sorted quickly through the get-along stuff that Pa had sent with me. For injuries, there was a homemade swab, a wound compress, and a small bottle of carbolic. Knowing that such tools would have to do, and feeling thankful that I had watched Ma do more than a little midwifing, I took out my knife and cut off two short, stout oak limbs from a tree behind me. Then I tore two long strips from the tail of my shirt.

Finally ready, I eased back down beside the shallow-breathing dog. "Are you with me in spirit, good friend?"

The dog whined, licked my hand, lay back upon the earth, and then was still. "Trust in the Lord, you told me," I said with a wry grin to the intently watching Gideon Monson. And then I took up the crude swab and bottle of carbolic and went to work.

An hour later, finally finished, I sank back against a tree and closed my eyes. "Whew! I hope that takes care of him."

"It'll do the trick," Gideon responded, and I was surprised at the tenderness in his voice. "Son, you have a real way with critters. In all my days, I never saw the like."

I opened my eyes and looked at the old man. "Pa has it more than me, and he says he got it from his pa. Maybe it runs in the family. But he can gentle-talk a mad bull into wearing pinafores in five minutes."

Gideon chuckled.

"Likewise," I continued, "back in Keokuk they never brought him a horse he couldn't ride, if he could talk to it a mite before climbing aboard. Come to think of it, I haven't been thrown in some time myself."

"Been on some wild ones?" Gideon asked hopefully, his eyes brightening as he sensed a new friendship forming.

"No," I said, "haven't hardly been on a horse at all, ever in my life. That's why I haven't been thrown."

Gideon grinned and tossed a pebble at me. I ducked, and suddenly I felt good. Gideon had been impressed with something I had done, the dog was probably going to be fine, and I was going to find Steenie and take her back home with me. In short, the world was shaping up as a wonderful place to be.

Sensing my mood, the wounded animal thumped its tail a few times, the small fire crackled warmly, and I stretched back further against the tree. In another two or maybe three days, I would come up with Steenie, and then she and I —

"Hello the camp," a voice called softly from the darkness.

Jerking my eyes open, I was surprised to find myself alone in the small clearing, alone except for the crippled and low-growling dog. Gideon was gone, and —

"Hoist your hands up where I can see them," the quiet voice ordered. "Now!"

Obediently I raised my hands, but still I kept my eyes focused on the rim of darkness where the man's voice seemed to be coming from.

"You alone?"

"Except for this almost dead dog," I replied honestly.

"Other men?"

"Do you see any?"

There was a soft chuckle, and a bearded man materialized on the edge of the firelight. I started then, for I knew him. Or at least I knew that I had seen him before. The trouble was, I couldn't remember where. Nor could I remember his name.

He looked at me, and the single eye of his rifle glared in my direction as well. "Two bedrolls," he said softly, and once again I felt a little shiver of recognition. "You and the dog travel in style, don't you."

"We do."

"But no grub, nor pot for coffee. Friend, I don't understand this a'tall."

"Well," I said, careful not to move my hands, "put down that rifle, take up a rock, and I'll tell you my woeful tale."

"I'll sit, but you've some tall talkin' to do afore I lower this rifle. There's a war on hereabouts, some wild Indians are out taking slaves and lifting hair, and a man can't be too careful. Now, how come you and the dog be rusticating in my own private mountain camp?"

"*Your* camp?" I echoed in surprise. "But there were no signs of previous fires when we —"

"We?"

"We. The dog and me."

"It have a name?"

"Lazarus," I responded, thinking quickly. "If he lives through being shot and my doctoring, he'll have been literally raised from the grave. So, why wasn't there sign of fire?"

"Because I always clean my camps. Now, Son, normally I'm right friendly — but when a man holds a gun on me, especially from ambush, I get sociable as an ulcerated back tooth. You tell that feller behind the rock yonder to come out with his rifle lowered, and maybe we can all make a little medicine."

Turning, I stared as old Gideon slowly rose to his feet, his rifle trained on the man across from me.

"I'll come," Gideon said easily, "but if we're lowering weapons, we had *all* ought to do it. I'd hate like thunder to break your arm."

"Not kill me?"

"Not hardly. I don't hold with killing. Besides, breaking your arm would be a whole lot more beneficial. Give you time to ponder the evil ways of man, and maybe do a little repenting. Now, what's it to be?"

The man, whom I still could not place, chuckled again. "It appears we have here what Dan Jones's friend Kit Carson from down to Taos calls a Mexican standoff. Either hand opens the ball, both hands dance to the tune. I think I'll lower my rifle."

Slowly he did so, and with a sigh of relief I lowered my hands. Carefully then Gideon limped forward until he too was in the light, and then we all glared at each other.

"So, are you Mormon, or otherwise?" the man asked.

"Which are you?" Gideon responded instantly.

The man nodded. "Very well, I'll go first. I'm Mormon."

He watched our reactions for a long-held breath, and then,

apparently satisfied, he plunged ahead. "Name's Ephraim Hanks. I'm on a little scout for the Prophet."

"Ephraim Hanks!" I exclaimed, my memory of my wagon-ride with him and Steenie flooding back, "I met you—"

"Friend Jons," Gideon warned, cutting me off, "it's hard to put a foot in a shut mouth. You forget mighty fast that martial law has been declared back yonder, don't you?"

I gulped, knowing Gideon was right. But still, this man had been very friendly to Steenie, and I felt certain that, given the chance, he would be the same to us.

"We've met?" Ephraim Hanks asked then, exactly as I had hoped he would.

"Yes, sir. The other day. You rode a piece with Steenie Bergman and me. We spoke of the war."

Hanks beamed. "Of course we did. And you're Jons . . . "

"Soderberg."

"That's right, Soderberg. How do you happen to be up here, Son? The way Christena was looking at you and hanging onto your arm, I'm surprised she let you get this far out of the valley."

"Steenie's gone, Brother Hanks. Ben Crost and the whole family pulled stakes and lit out, four days ago. Thing is, I think he forced Steenie to go with him against her will. She asked me by note to come after her, and I'm doing my best to do just that."

"Is this your father?"

Gideon snorted. "Grandpappy, more likely," he growled.

"Is that so?"

"No, sir. I met Gideon Monson on the trail, and he—"

Ephraim Hanks stood up in surprise. "Gideon Monson. *The* Gideon Peabody Monson?"

Gideon's eyes crinkled down at the corners, but he said nothing. Nor did he have to. Ephraim Hanks was saying it all.

"Captain Monson," he said as he stepped forward and held out his hand. "Old-timer, I'm right proud to make your acquaintance. My first wife's father fought under you at the Battle of New Orleans, and I have heard the tale a hundred times of how you took a handful of men and whipped back a regiment of the British, saving his life and the lives of—"

"An old-timer is somebody who's had a lot of interesting experiences," Gideon declared soberly, "some of them true."

"Well, my wife's father swears what he saw you do in that battle was true."

Gideon shook his head. "It weren't no regiment. They was hardly more numerous than we were. Besides, the War of 1812 is a long time past, and everybody was saving everybody's life in that battle. In a war, there ain't never any real heroes."

"Likely," Ephraim grinned. "But I'm still more than a little happy to make your acquaintance. Have you . . . joined the Church?"

"Two years past."

"Why, that's wonderful. Won't my wife be pleased to hear this." Then Brother Hanks turned back to me. "And Ben Crost finally tucked his tail, did he? Well, he didn't act like he had much staying power. And you say that you're after Christena?"

I nodded.

"You sure she wants to be found?"

"The note she left me says she does."

Hanks smiled. "Luck to you, Son. I wish I could help, but I'm under orders and can't do it. I hope you find her, though. With Captain Monson along, I'm sure you will. Now tell me why the two of you are up here on the slope instead of down with the rest of the brethren."

After a nod from Gideon, I told the rest of it, including how Gideon and I had come up Red Butte Canyon, giving the sentry the slip.

Ephraim nodded occasionally, but he was quiet until I was finished. Then he chuckled. "So that's what's been bothering the two of you. No passes, and you've neither of you signed up for the Legion. Well, it'll sure have to be done."

"You mean to stand there, all bold-faced and hairy-fronted, and tell me that a stove-up old fool like me's supposed to sign up for this war?" Gideon exclaimed.

Ephraim looked stunned. "Why, Captain, I . . . I thought you'd *want* to join up."

Gideon snorted. "Not hardly. I'm too old for conscription, too, and you know it! No, sir, I've had me enough of fighting in this life. If Old Buck's army boys want to use me up, why, I'll do like them Lamanite fellers did in the Book of Mormon. I'll lay myself down and make it easy for them. Yes, sir, I am a converted man of peace, ever since I promised the Lord I'd never join nothing else after I joined his onliest true church."

Ephraim grinned. "Then why the rifle?"

"Him," Gideon grunted, nodding at me. "I'm only up here because I want to see the boy find his woman child. Normally I'd say that a feller ought to never marry a woman with the kind of looks he'd like to see on another man's wife. But from the brief looksee I had of Christena Bergman, all bets and uncommonly good advice from an old soldier like me are off. I would say that little sister is a prize worth chasing."

"She is, at that. So, neither of you is interested in stopping the government forces from wintering in the Valley?"

Gideon shot me a warning look, but he needn't have. I wasn't interested in anything but finding Steenie, and Ephraim Hanks could see it in my eyes.

"Because," he continued slyly, "if you'd be interested in helping us out, why, I might be able to work it into our orders so that I could help *you*. Interested now?"

Gideon and I looked at each other, and I imagine he too could see the beam of hope in my eye. With a muttered grumble he swatted his leg with his bedraggled hat, and then he sank down on his saddle to stare into the fire. "Be thankful for fools," he growled to himself. "Without them, none of the rest of us would look like much. You call it, Boy. I'll ride along, whatever it is."

"Then you have a deal," I said to Ephraim Hanks. "So long as it gets me closer to Steenie Bergman."

Grinning, Ephraim nodded. "Brother Al," he called then, "why don't you come on in now."

Gideon started up, and I simply stared as a man rose from

behind the very rock where Gideon had hidden earlier. Then he lowered his rifle, and with a brief nod he stepped into the glow of the fire.

"Gentleman," Ephraim Hanks declared soberly, "may I present Brother Al Bagley. Al, meet Captain Gideon Monson and Jons Soderberg, the two newest *non*-members of the Nauvoo Legion."

And Al Bagley smiled and said hello.

Chapter 6

"Well, boys," Al Bagley declared after we had stuffed ourselves with the best fatback and frybread I had ever eaten, "ol' Eph here has done it again."

"Which is?" Gideon questioned.

"Prophesied. Yes, sir, sometimes Eph out-Brighams Brother Brigham himself. This morning as we were saddling up, Eph told me we'd run onto some reinforcements for our little two-man army, and he thought that we'd about double it in size. Well, here you are, and again he was right."

"This . . . this prophesying happens often?" I asked.

"No, not oftener than every day or so."

I looked with wonder at the bearded man who sat silently across the small fire, picking his teeth with a wood sliver. Ma and Pa were often close to the Spirit, but the process had so far eluded me, and I truly wondered what it would be like. I also wondered how a man could get to be close to the Lord, but I had never seriously considered that it might happen to somebody like me. Mostly, that was because I was too comfortable having faith in the faith of others. I just didn't want to pay the price to develop my own.

"How do you do it?" I finally asked, thinking I might learn some shortcut to out and out becoming righteous.

Eph looked up. "I don't. The Lord does all the work. I just listen and say what I think the Spirit is impressing me to say. Usually it comes out about right."

"Only if your heart is right," Al qualified.

Eph grinned. "Wouldn't know about that."

"Likely," Al grinned back. Then he turned to me. "Son, the kicker to hearing the Spirit is in being worthy. Brother Brigham reminded us yesterday morning, while we were eating breakfast together, of the Lord's warning concerning the Spirit. The Lord told Brother Joseph, in Doctrine and Covenants 63:16, that if a man can be pure hearted, not harboring any lustful or unclean thoughts, then he can *have* the Spirit. On the other hand, if he lets his mind grovel around in the mud of lust and unrighteousness, then he won't have it. The Lord made Joseph that promise."

"There's more," Eph enjoined quietly. "If a feller throws up his hands, so to speak, and gives up to wickedness and lust, he not only loses the Spirit, but the next thing you know, he starts denying the faith. Once that happens, he's apostatized, and the Lord says that from then on he'll be filled with fear."

"Meaning?"

"Meaning," Gideon stated, speaking for the first time, "that a man gets jumpy as a fly-bit bull once he loses the Spirit. He's offended at the least little thing, and he's certain-sure that others are out to get either him or what he thinks is rightfully his. Left alone, the poor soul will be led by the devil all the way down the darkened road until murder is the only option he sees left."

"The Captain's right, Jons, and it's obvious that he's seen this in others."

"Durn tootin' I have. Not only seen it, but heard about it and read about it, too."

"Read about it?"

"In the Book of Mormon. Friend Jons, you need to start reading that book. Every time any righteous man, Nephite or otherwise, lost the Spirit of the Lord and apostatized, he got filled with a spirit of murder and was heaps more wicked than the regular wicked folks he hung around with. Wicked Nephites were always worse than wicked Lamanites, and were always chosen to be their leaders because they were so bloodthirsty.

Way I hear it, wicked Mormons were the ones who led out in the murders of Joseph and Hyrum Smith, so things ain't hardly changed at all, then until now."

Gideon stopped talking, and in my mind I could see Ben Crost, Steenie's uncle. He had acted jumpy as could be the minute I came along, and all of a sudden I began to wonder about that man's thoughts and morals. No, that isn't so. I already *knew* about his thoughts and morals, for he had been trying to force himself upon Steenie for some time. And it wasn't any righteous plural marriage he was advocating. No sir, he didn't believe in that, or the Church, or the prophets. He believed only in himself and was advocating out-and-out lust. And now it became clear as day what had happened to the man. As the Lord had prophesied, he had committed mental adultery, had lost the Spirit, had denied the faith, and was now so filled with fear that he had fled east, thinking that his life was in danger. And so it was—his *spiritual* life. His soul was dying of slow strangulation, and he didn't hardly know it at all.

"Ben Crost's a good example of all this," Ephraim Hanks said, confirming my thoughts. "He's made a lot of boasts about what he accomplished in his past, but a self-made man usually comes to the point where he worships his own creator. Ben has lost the Spirit, and now he worships only himself."

"Anyway," Al Bagley concluded as he nudged a small stick into the fire with his boot, "worshiping the one true God is the trick ol' Eph here has learned. His heart is pure as the driven snow. The Lord knows it, and that's why he blesses Eph with the spirit of prophecy."

For a time then no one spoke, and I looked at the men who surrounded me. I had never before met such men, and each of them was giving my think-box, as Gideon would have said, whole wagonloads of new fodder to chew through.

Finally Eph got up and rolled out his bedroll. "Yes, sir," he breathed as he stretched out, "it was a mortal pleasure taking breakfast from Brother Brigham. He's full of confidence that the Lord will keep the army out of the valley this winter, and so am I. Fact is, I feel better with just the four of us and the

Lord than if I had a whole legion of men behind me. Boys, before our little scout is over, it will be determined whether a legalized government mob can force themselves on us against our will or not. But I say we go in the strength of Israel's God, and the army will not prevail."

"Jesse Earl came in from the plains yesterday," Al Bagley stated, "and he reported that Uncle's boys are marching on very unconcerned and deliberate. He says they are not dreaming of trouble but instead are anticipating fine times in the Valley this winter, walking over our people, hanging our rulers, and ravaging our women."

Eph grunted. "They'll be some surprised where they do winter. In fact, I feel to add my prophecy to Brother Brigham's. If we go out meekly, shedding no blood, that army will never get to the Valley this season. Instead, they will winter in the cold and blizzards of the mountains, where their love for rapine and murder will be somewhat cooled."

"That's a sure prophecy," Al grunted, "because Brother Brigham said it already. That's the kind I could make."

Eph laughed easily. "There, Jons—you see? Prophesying's not much harder than listening to the Lord's anointed servants and then repeating what they say. It's still the Lord who has to do all the work."

Things got very quiet then, and we all sat silently in the mountain swale, thinking. Overhead, the tiny lanterns of the stars glittered in the frosty sky. The black bulwarks of the trees stretched upward as if in sentinel circle, mostly sheltering us from the frigid winds that dropped down from the mountains to the east. Occasionally a log popped in the fire, but other than the sighing of the wind and the occasional distant murmur of voices from down below, there was no sound on the mountain at all.

I looked down at Lazarus, and the animal, sensing my gaze, weakly thumped his tail. I grinned and rubbed between his ears, but I still worried. The dog was not well, and I had no idea how he would live once we departed in the morning. I just hoped that—

71

"So you doctored the dog?"

I looked up at Eph and nodded.

"Son, you did a fine job, and you've won a true friend. That dog will live, and one day he'll return the favor—with interest."

"Sir?" I questioned, not understanding.

"You've saved his life, Jons. The Spirit whispers that he'll save yours, maybe more than once."

Now I really looked at the man. But he just smiled, laid back on his saddle, and closed his eyes.

"So you're after a girl?" Al Bagley asked then.

"Yes, sir. She left me a note on . . . on something I had given her, asking for help, and I plan on aiding her back to the Valley."

"You give her a ring, or something?"

"No," I said, feeling unaccountably embarrassed. "It was . . . my old slingshot."

I expected laughter, but Al only looked at me. And then Eph spoke from his bedroll. "Funny thing what sorts of foofaraw a woman sets store by. My wives are the same. Little trinkets hooked to memories mean more to them than all the world's wealth. A smile of real happiness from one of my wives is worth more to me than a whole mule-train of pure gold. So, more and more I'm working to give them reason to smile."

"You a polygamist?" Gideon asked.

"That's right. I'm married to Harriet Decker Little and Jane Capener. They're both fine women. Besides that, last winter I met a young woman out on the plains name of Thisbe Read. She was part of the Martin handcart company. If my impressions are correct, one day she will become my third wife."

"Well," Gideon said, shaking his head, "I've heard tell that 'For better or for worse' usually means for good, but Mormons take the cake both for numbers and marital longevity."

"How much?" Al Bagley asked, sounding confused.

"Sticking together for eternity," Gideon explained. "I used to say that you can never trust women, or tenderfeet—but the wife I had was so all-fired wondrous and trustworthy and loving that I'd quit mortality right now if'n I thought she and I wouldn't be together for eternity. Nor would I ever want to try it again with another."

"That's sort of how I feel about Steenie," I said softly. Gideon and Eph looked at each other and smiled, but I didn't mind. I was falling deeper in love by the day, and I didn't see how it could possibly end up any other way than for Steenie and me to get sealed up to each other for eternity.

"Is your little gal truly worth this chase?" Al Bagley asked me.

"Moreso," I said. "Besides being pretty as a picture, which she surely is, Christena is warm, tender, loving, gentle — truthfully, I can't think of an angelic quality that she doesn't have."

"Yep," Al said, "he's sure smitten."

"Learning fast," Gideon agreed. "Given enough time, Jons'll come to find out that a year of traipsing around the mountain don't hardly equal a day of sweetheart'n. But he ain't old enough to know that yet. Way I see it, a man doesn't have sensible thoughts about a woman until he's thirty-five. A'fore that, all he has is feelings, and they run four hundred to the ounce and are mostly blind."

"Is she a smart one?" Al Bagley asked next, when the others had stopped chuckling.

"Questionable," Gideon teased, "seeing who's she's fallen in love with."

"She's smart," Eph declared, finally standing up for me. "I know her, and she's real bright."

"Well," Gideon said, "that's good, Son. Marry a woman with brains enough for two, and you had ought to come out about even."

Everybody but me laughed at that — and I would have, except that I didn't want to encourage too much more of their persecution. But I should have laughed, for it continued anyway.

"If she's all you brethren say she is," Al Bagley declared, "then maybe I'll give young Soderberg a little competition when we come up to her."

"Won't work," Gideon declared. "I've seen it a'fore, and

I'll see it again. She loves Jons, so he'll get hisself hugged for sneakin' a kiss from her, and you'd just get yourself slapped."

"You said she was beautiful?" Al asked.

"Pretty as can be," I told him.

Al grinned widely. "Then I don't reckon she's hardly worth my trouble."

"What? But—"

"Young feller, most women are as pretty as they *can* be. Thing is, that's not usually saying much."

Well, I threw a stick at Al Bagley, he ducked and tossed another back, there was a little more general teasing and poking fun at me, and then Ephraim Hanks grew serious.

"If you catch Ben Crost, Jons, what do you aim to do with him?"

"Beat him to a bloody pulp!" I growled.

"Ahh, the laying on of hands method of teaching the gospel."

I grinned sourly at Eph's humor. "Well, he laid his meat-hooks on me the other night. I would say he has it coming."

"And then?"

The question made me uncomfortable, not because it was asked maliciously, but because I really didn't know. I'd tried to think it out, but as far as I could get was seeing Ben Crost's nose smashed flat. After that, things didn't show up clear at all.

"The man might get real mean," Al put in. "Are you prepared for that possibility?"

Again I squirmed, for truly I wasn't. Pa had always taught us to be peaceable and quick to forgive, leaving vengeance for the Lord. But Steenie was important to me, terribly important, and it seemed reasonable that I needed to put my hand in this pie and pluck out the only plum there. But if it came to violence beyond a good fist fight, I didn't hardly know what I would do.

Gideon, I think, sensed what I was feeling, for it was then that he spoke up. His voice wasn't loud, and it had the squeak of age in it. But nevertheless we all listened intently to his tale.

"I come from the high-ups of the Cumberland Plateau back to Tennessee," he said, talking only to the night. "Me and my folks ran a side-hill farm that was long on rocks and short on crops, just out of Jamestown. Still, we mostly had a good life.

"Then we were set on by a few fellers who were determined to make theirs what we had already made ours. In that fight my older sister died under their hands. But Pa was a peaceable man with a love of God in his heart, so we buried my sister and moved on, leaving what we had to them.

"Trouble is, those same fellers came again, some two or three years later, at our new farm. You see, they had got a place from us once, it had been easy, and they wanted more.

"That time Pa and me stood against them, and one man of theirs went down. But they didn't learn from that, and a week later they came a third time. They shot Pa up real bad, burned the cabin, and thought they had us treed. But I got into the woods with Pa's Henrietta here, and when the last of the smoke had cleared, three more of their men were on the ground dead, including the big old he-bull who had been running their rawhide outfit. After that they pretty much left us alone."

"You did right," Al Bagley declared. "Even the scriptures tell us to defend our families."

Gideon nodded. "I know. Trouble is, dead men make mighty poor bedfellows. I don't think there has been a day in my life that I ain't seen those fellers lying on the ground. They may have had it coming, but I surely paid the price."

"Unless under very particular conditions," Eph then declared, "bloodshed is never a good idea. The Saints are facing the same thing today. We can have bloodshed, or we can follow the Prophet and avoid it. If we use up that army, then Brigham says we will have blood to our heart's content, and a good measure of it will be ours.

"You see, boys, a man's blood is a sacred thing to the Lord. I don't know how it works, or even why, but blood is terrible important to him. That's why the scriptures say that Christ's blood purifies, sanctifies, and cleanses us from sin. And any murdered man's blood, including Joseph's and Hyrum's, will cry unto the Lord for vengeance until vengeance is taken by the heavens.

"So you see, blood is important to the Lord, or maybe a better word is sacred. If it is spilled unrighteously, then the Lord is bound to see that justice exacts a penalty upon those who spilled it. And we will yet see that penalty exacted upon this nation, for they have spilled the blood of innocent men, women, and children, ever since this Church was founded.

"After the mobbings in Missouri, Joseph prophesied that America would have blood and mobbing to their heart's content, and they will. But to me, it would be a pity if the Saints, in the heat of anger, spilled the blood of those poor soldiers and had to be punished, themselves."

"What about the soldiers who want to spill ours?" I asked.

"Some of 'em might truly want that, Jons. From them the Lord will protect us, if we do as Brigham said. Most of the soldiers, though, are just following orders, and are as innocent as you or me. Trouble is, over the sights of a rifle, innocence is hard to detect. That's why I, for one, will not fire a shot in this campaign."

"But we're making guns and powder . . . "

Eph grinned. "We sure are, and those things will come in handy for hunting, and such, in the years to come. But to use them on people? We won't have to do it if the Saints will do as they've been counseled."

"But the speeches, the factories . . . Why do the Brethren talk about fighting like they do, if they don't really want us to fight?"

"Good question. I'll answer it, and then let's pack it in. Jons, folks have to feel involved to become united, and the speeches and the gun factories are to get the Saints involved. Once we're all united and willing to do what needs to be done to protect our wives and children, to sacrifice whatever needs to be sacrificed, then the Lord will step forward and fight our battles for us.

"We'll slow the soldiers down and make life as miserable for them as we possibly can, and if the Saints will continue to work and prepare in unity to the best of their abilities, then I promise you that there will never be a war. The Lord will fight it and win it for us, and not a shot will ever be fired."

"Is that another prophecy?" Gideon asked.

"Yeah," Al Bagley responded, "that is another one. He said the same thing to Brother Brigham yesterday, and the Prophet blessed him and told him that the Lord had revealed that idea to him. So now we'll watch and see it come to pass."

"You're saying, then, that I won't need a gun on my quest to find Steenie?"

"You don't have a gun?" Al Bagley asked, surprised.

Silently I shook my head.

"Boy, you're crazy. Not to mention the army out there, what if that Crost feller decides to shoot you? He might not take too kindly to your taking the girl back, you know. How you planning on defending yourself?"

"I . . . I don't know . . . "

Al Bagley laughed, but Ephraim Hanks stopped him with a raised hand. "Do what you're supposed to do, Son," Eph then said quietly, "and for the rest of your life you'll never need a gun to point at another man. In fact, the Spirit whispers that if you are worthy, you will one day be a bishop in this Church. And good bishops must be free of the blood and sins of their generation. You keep the commandments and seek the Spirit, Jons, and for the rest of your life, the Lord will fight your battles for you, and you will be free of that blood and those sins.

"Now," Ephraim Hanks continued, "if you boys are ready to turn in, I'll lead us in a word of prayer." He did, and for a long time after that I lay in the dark, thinking. Not about me maybe becoming a bishop. That was too staggering, and I had to let it alone. But I did think a lot about the other. Eph was right about me not shedding blood, and I knew it. I just didn't know if I could hold to that, happen Ben Crost had done something awful to my Steenie. And it was while I was worrying my teeth on that bone that I finally fell asleep.

Chapter 7

"You don't have a horse?"

Feeling even sillier than I had felt about not having a gun, I shook my head in response to Ephraim Hanks's question. "But I'm a good walker," I declared.

"What about your dog? That wound looks mighty serious, Jons. In my experience, breaks like that can take weeks, even months, to heal."

I looked down at Lazarus, who lay on the ground looking up at me. "I guess I'll carry him," I replied. "For as long as it takes."

Eph shook his head. "I don't know, Son. We need to move fast, and I don't think you can do it carrying a worn out coyote-dog. But if you're that all-fired serious, then maybe I can carry it for you, at least until we can find somebody to care for it."

Walking over, he reached down to lift Lazarus but stopped short at the low and threatening growl from the animal's throat.

"Is it just me," Eph asked as he straightened back up, "or is this critter so overly fond of everybody?"

"I don't know," I told him. "Gideon, maybe you can carry him on your horse."

My elderly friend reigned over, and I lifted Lazarus toward him. But again the growl issued forth, and Gideon pulled back his hand just in time to avoid losing a couple of fingers in Lazarus's snapping jaws.

Al Bagley grinned. "Boy, Eph was right. You've got you a

one-man dog, and he'll be your friend for life. I've seen it in others, a time or two. But he's no good to the rest of us, so if you want him along, you'll have to carry him yourself."

"Then I will."

"Jons," Eph asked as he looked down at the dog and me, "did you pray before you worked on that critter?"

"He sure enough did," Gideon responded for me.

Eph grinned. "That explains it, then."

"Explains what?"

"My impression. I feel to tell you that the Lord will work a miracle on that animal. You will yet see it brought to pass. It will heal quickly."

"Truly?"

"Absolutely. Now we'll ride ahead," Eph concluded, "and do what we can to scare you up a horse. You have any preferences?"

I grinned. "Not hardly. Folks say I have a way with animals, so I imagine about anything will do. If it has a saddle on it, I'll be able to ride it."

"You ride a lot?" Eph asked, sounding surprised.

"He ain't rid a'tall," Gideon told him. "But he does have a way with critters."

"Well, like I always say," Al Bagley interjected, "never tamper with the natural ignorance of a greenhorn. Let's go find the boy a horse."

After giving me directions on where to follow, the three rode away, and I was left alone with my new and crippled companion, a mangy but grateful coyote-dog.

"Well, Lazarus," I said as I adjusted his weight in my arms, "it's a fine day for a tramp through the woods. Let us be on our way, as well."

And so we were. It was a beautiful morning for walking, too. The air was fresh and clear as spring water, birds sang in the trees, several times deer bounded away up the slopes before us, and it felt good to Lazarus and me just being alive and in the mountains. I didn't even feel bad that the others had gone on ahead. I knew they were rounding up a spare mount for me, and so in patience I strode along after them.

I thought too about Steenie, wondering where she was and what she was doing. Probably traveling, all right. But a wagon couldn't make as good time as I could, and I knew it would only be a matter of days until I caught up with her.

And wouldn't she be excited then! In my mind I could already picture our reunion, with each of us in the other's arms. What a grand time we would have then. Of course, first I would need to take care of Ben Crost. But I would, by cracky—not maiming him or killing him, I had finally decided—but by teaching him a sound lesson, nonetheless. Yes, sir, what a glorious day that was going to be!

And with that thought in mind, I began to consider the strange turn of events in my life since I had left the Valley. I had met up with the most unusual and most righteous men I had ever known—other than my folks, of course. And they had taught me, too. The thing that was interesting to me was how much better I now felt, knowing that my resolve to live a higher law had been directly related to the company I had been keeping. Sort of made sense, too. Pa always said that the winds of others' words either set a person's ship on course or pushed it out to sea. And right then and there I made up my mind that I was going to be on course. I would get my Steenie, we would marry and settle down, and our children would be taught as these fine brethren had taught me.

With such high and lofty thoughts racing through my mind, I made my way off Hogback Summit, past Jack Beard Springs, through Parker Hollow, and finally into Main Canyon. There I followed the whispering, gurgling creek out into the valley of the Weber River. From that point I turned right, and after what seemed no time at all, I was approaching Echo Camp, at the mouth of Echo Canyon.

"Jons Soderberg! Yo, friend Jons!"

Looking up, I saw Gideon Monson waving at me from the top of a pole corral, maybe a hundred yards away. I grinned, waved back, hitched Lazarus up in my weary arms, and shifted directions. Then I set out to make my way to the corral.

I found the mouth of Echo Canyon to be like one great village. Men were camped everywhere — in tents, willow huts, mud huts, cottonwood bark huts, and even out in the open. Cooking fires were also everywhere, but it was late in the morning, almost eight o'clock, by the time I got there. And by that time most of the fires had burned out. The men were now at work, here and there, building up the defenses of the canyon, getting ready, should it become necessary, to repel Ol' Buck's army of boys in blue.

"Hello, Gideon," I said as I finally hove up at the rough corral and placed Lazarus on the ground. "Been waiting long?"

"Not overly. Put the mutt down, climb up here, and take a look-see."

I did as directed and saw Al Bagley and Eph Hanks standing in the pole enclosure with as scraggly a little gray horse as I had ever before laid eyes on.

"That one for me?" I asked sorrowfully.

Gideon nodded soberly. "It is if you want it."

"Gray?"

"Son, a good horse is never a bad color. Gray, black, dun, I've found the best color for a horse is *fat*, and that one is."

"But . . . but it's so small."

Gideon sighed. "Admire a big horse, Jons, but saddle a small one. You'll ride easier and farther, and that's a purified fact."

"I don't know, Gideon. That horse looks half dead."

Gideon now shook his head. "Boy, for some folks, assets are brains. For you, all they are is baby donkeys. Now you listen to me. When a man gets too old to set a bad example, he hands out good advice, and now I'm handing it to you. That little horse is a good one, and you'd do well to stop your jaw-jacking and accept her."

"All right," I said, doing my best to sound happy, "against my better judgment I'll take your word for it."

"You ain't got no confounded judgment at all," Gideon

muttered. "But you had best be careful anyway. Those boys have a hooraw going—"

"*Her?*" I asked, interrupting my friend. "It's a *mare?*"

"And a fine one, too," Gideon grunted, closing his mouth against me with finality. "Hey, Eph, the kid finally says he's interested."

"Well, Son," Ephraim Hanks said, grinning at me, "that's fine. Come down here and let's see if you can outride her."

I jumped down into the corral, and as innocent as a baby robin I waltzed up to that little gray horse. But I should have been suspicious. Busy as the men in that camp were, I should have realized that there were way too many of them hanging around that corral. For there were, dozens of them, doing this and that and the other—seeming to pay no mind to me or Eph or Al Bagley or the little gray mare.

And I paid them no mind, either. In a moment I was beside my companions, ready to claim my horse. Al had the little gray by an ear, twisting it back and down, and the animal was standing still and motionless before me.

"What do you think?" Eph asked innocently.

"She looks good enough for me."

"Glad to hear it. She may buck a little, but most horses do that. Just hang on, and that will wear her down."

"You don't need to tell him that," Al grunted. "The kid is good with animals. He said so himself."

I looked at the man, surprised a little by his tone of voice. But he grinned at me and winked, and my mind was once again at peace.

"Mount up," Eph Hanks ordered.

And so with great excitement I scrambled onto the back of the little mare. The stirrups didn't fit exactly, but I bent my knees and pulled up the hackamore reins until it felt about right.

"Don't take too short a hold," Gideon hollered, "or she'll jerk it right away from you the minute she bogs her head."

I nodded, starting to feel a little nervous.

"All set?" Al asked.

Again I nodded, and Al turned the mare loose.

One jump, I think, was all she made, but it was all so quick that I couldn't hardly tell. For the next thing I knew, I was on the ground with both hands and one mouth full of dirt. Still, it hadn't hurt me any, and as soon as Al Bagley "eared" the little gray down again, I made another try. It was just as short and sweet as the first ride, but this time it dazed me some, and so I wasn't near so quick getting up off the ground. But Al Bagley eared her down again, and again I climbed back on.

"Never mind the hackamore this time," Gideon shouted. "Just get hold of that old horn and screw down on it!"

I nodded, then looked down at the grinning Al, blinking a couple of times trying to see if it was really him. Then he turned her loose a third time.

And on that ride I did real well, or at least I thought I was doing well. I pulled every scrap of leather off the wooden saddle-horn and managed to ride that little mare through four jumps, and I was starting to think that I might stick. But then the little mare switched ends on me, my foot came loose of the stirrup, and the stirrup flew up and caught me over the right eye, knocking me loose again. Next jump my shirt caught on the saddle-horn, and when I went sailing the shirt stayed behind.

I must have sat on the ground for some time after that, trying to remember where or who I was. For when I finally became aware of the laughter, it had almost died out. Looking up, I saw the top pole of the corral lined with grinning and laughing men, and I knew I had been hoorawed for sure.

Slowly getting back up, I could hardly keep my balance. I took one step, then another—and Gideon was there on one side, while Eph had hold of me on the other.

"He's some wobbly on his pins," Gideon declared.

Al Bagley had the gray by the ear again, and he was grinning, as Gideon later said, like a jackass eating cactus. "You ready for another try?" he hooted, and there were chuckles all around me.

"You bet," I mumbled, and staggered forward.

"Whoa, boy," Eph said softly, "you proved your point, and we all got our chuckle. Now we'll go find you a decent horse . . . "

I broke loose of the two men and limped toward Al Bagley. I think he was some nervous at the expression on my face, but I didn't intend doing anything to him. Not then, at least. Instead, I wanted information.

"Who's is the horse?" I mumbled when I had reached it.

Al released the animal's ear and stepped back. "I . . . I don't hardly know. It's part of a string the Church sent up."

"So if I want it I can use it?"

"Hold on," Eph called. "Jons, we'll be in need of making time, not fighting bad horses. Now let's find you another mount and be moving on."

But I wasn't about to be dissuaded. "Gideon," I asked, "didn't you say this was a fine animal?"

"I did, Son. But —"

"Then this is the horse I want. You fellows need to hurry along, go after it. I'll be up with you by nightfall."

All three of my companions looked at me as if I was crazy. And maybe I was, I don't know. Thing is, I had been shamed but good — and keeping that little mare was the only way I could see of regaining some sort of face — an item of mighty importance to a boy my age.

"You sure?" Gideon asked.

"I am, Gideon, if you are."

"I'm certain," Gideon declared. "She's mustang, and they're good little horses, when they're trained right."

"I'll train her," I stated flatly.

"Then I say let him keep the horse," a man on top of the corral called out.

"I second it," joined in another.

"All in favor?" was the next cry, and that was followed by a wild and cheerful chorus of ayes. The men then applauded and cheered as Al Bagley untied the snubbed-short rope and handed it to me. Five minutes later I was alone with the unsaddled mare, trying to gentle her down.

She had been ridden before, I could see that, for she still

bore saddle scars from some hard use. She had also been ridden earlier that morning, for she had sweat some, and it had mostly dried. That meant, at least, that she had been broke to ride. Good. Then all I had to do was gentle her down a mite, and we would be fine.

Carefully I looked her over, talking softly the while — and the more I looked, the better I felt. I didn't know much about horses, but I was surely getting a good feeling for the gray.

"Her name is Perdition," a man said as he brought me a used saddle and blanket the quartermaster had assigned. "And she's a real son of a . . . Well, that is, she's a real daughter of perdition. Funny thing. I never thought there would be such things as daughters of perdition, but that was before I met this little mare. You be careful, Son. She's mean clear to the bone."

"Perdition," I mused as I looked her over. "Well, first thing to be changed is the name. Instead, little gal, I'll just call you Perdy, because of a truth, I think you are — real perdy."

The horse looked at me and rolled her eyes, so I reached out to pat her neck a little and try to gentle her down. She snapped at me, however, a vicious snap that would have ripped my arm open had she connected.

But she didn't connect, and she was lashing out to give it another try when there was a sort of low snarl from behind me. The next thing I knew, old crippled Lazarus had somehow hobbled into the corral, jumped into the air beside me, and clamped his teeth into the mare's soft nose.

Well, I never heard such a squealing and a ruckus in all my life as I heard then. That poor horse thought she was going to die, and *I* thought the dog was. But it turned out Lazarus knew what he was doing, and in the next few seconds, both me *and* the mare were going to learn that.

I don't think Lazarus had hold of that horse's nose for more than ten seconds, and for five of them she was too surprised to react. Then she squealed and rose up to snuff the life out of the crippled creature hanging from her snout with teeth and pawing hooves.

Only the dog was no longer there. Instead, old Lazarus had

85

let go of the nose and had launched himself at the mare's exposed belly, taking another nip there.

Well, down she came with another snort to stamp the life out of the pesky dog with those same rock-hard hooves, and again that dog was gone. Crippled as he was, I never did figure out how Lazarus moved so swift and careful. But he did, and the next attack was on the hock of Perdy's near hind leg.

She kicked at that, got only air, and was just spinning to fight when from nowhere, it seemed, old Lazarus was on her nose again.

Well, there was more squealing and more stomping, and that tawny-brown, splint-legged coyote-dog was here and there and everywhere, nipping and snarling and drawing flecks of blood. But in all of that, Lazarus never barked. I learned later that only dogs bark, but that coyotes and wolves snarl and growl and howl. I didn't know that then, but I did know that whatever noises the critter made or didn't make didn't make one bit of difference. Old Lazarus had that little gray mare kowtowed to a faretheewell within a short two or three minutes.

And suddenly it was over. The mare was standing with flared and bloody nostrils, her chest heaving, her head down, and her eyes rolled back, facing the panting dog. And Lazarus, his tongue out and his sides heaving, stood wide-legged, facing the horse.

They stood like that, facing each other, and then the dog did the confoundedest thing I ever saw. Instead of snarling, he whined a little in a low sort of way, and then stiff-legged he moved slowly toward the mare.

She snorted and stepped back, Lazarus stopped and growled, the mare stopped, Lazarus whined and moved forward again, and that little scene was repeated two or three more times. But then the mare didn't move at Lazarus's advance, and the next thing I knew, that dog was up to her and licking the blood from her wounded nose.

Oh, it startled her some, all right, and she jerked back at the first wet lick. But Lazarus growled deep, and in another minute or two he was licking all the blood away, with the mare letting him do it. From there Lazarus moved to her belly and her hocks, and for the rest of the time he was cleaning her up, that little mare quivered all over but never moved hoof again.

It was almost like he was saying, "Friend horse, I beat you, and I'm sorry it had to hurt. So why don't you let me clean up this little bit of a mess I made, and maybe it won't pain you so much any more."

I don't hardly think the dog thought that way. I don't even know for sure if coyote-dogs think. But I did, and I was absolutely astounded. So, apparently, were others, for only then, when I heard a murmuring of voices around me, did I become aware that the crowd had regathered around that pole corral. I looked at them, felt surprised that I hadn't seen anyone, and then one of the men started to clap. Soon all of the brethren joined in, and I clapped with them. We had seen a real show that morning, and I don't think I have ever seen another like it since.

"Friend Jons?"

Turning, I was surprised to see Gideon in the crowd. And next to him were Al Bagley and Ephraim Hanks. So they too had heard the ruckus and had come back to see the fun.

"Son," Gideon called, "that wolf critter's gentled the horse down for you. Now saddle up and get aboard quick, while the mare is still kowtowed. Besides, it's time we were heading up-trail."

Nodding, I took the saddle and walked slowly to the quivering mare. She started to move, Lazarus growled, and from that instant she was still. I put the blanket on, threw the saddle over her, and pulled the cinch-strap under her belly. I then threaded it through the ring, and even when I put my knee against her and snugged it tight, Perdy didn't budge. Of course, Lazarus was right in front of her nose, watching, and I think he was some incentive.

Finally, with wildly beating heart, I stepped into the stirrup and hoisted myself aboard. I felt the mare's muscles bunch, set myself for another awful bite of corral dust, and then slowly let my breath out as I felt her relax.

Then, like I had seen Pa do it, I climbed up and down, in and out of that saddle, several times, just getting her used to me and my weight. I then stepped in front of the mare and led her around the corral a couple of times, with Lazarus hopping painfully along beside us, getting her used to seeing me and following me around.

That accomplished, I climbed aboard again and nudged the mare forward. And to my joy and intense pride, she obediently stepped out. There followed more applause from the pole-top bleachers, with a few offers to buy Lazarus, to which I replied that he wasn't mine but was just traveling with me. Finally someone let down the poles, and we rode out to where I had stacked my gear.

Perdy flinched a little when I dismounted and hoisted my pack, but what surprised me most was when I lifted Lazarus to the saddle and then climbed aboard behind him. That little Perdy mare couldn't hardly stand it, not being able to see the dog. She turned and turned, trying to get her nose close to his, and probably she would have become jittery again had not Lazarus started in to whine and lick her neck. Instantly she gentled down, and from that day forward I almost never saw those two creatures separated.

Lazarus would sleep, and Perdy would stand over him, dozing too. Lazarus would go off on some business of his own, and Perdy could hardly stand it, waiting for him to return. And when she was free, she followed him constantly. Those two critters became the talk of the Legion, and I didn't lose any notoriety from it myself.

So I had the respect and admiration of the men of the Nauvoo Legion, Al Bagley and Ephraim Hanks foremost among them. But the best of all was that I also had a horse and a dog, both of whom mended quickly and gentled down to good service with no trouble whatsoever.

And both animals were destined to play major roles in my life from then on, though of course I had no knowledge of that at the time. I just knew that I was on course to find my Steenie, and that I was more saddled up with good companions than I had ever before known.

Chapter 8

Steadily the wagon moved down the wide draw, pulled by the two straining span of horses. On the wagon bench rode Maria Crost, the lines to the teams in her hands. In the wagon amongst their things, or up on the bench beside her, rode the three children, too small to walk without causing more problems than their walking might solve. Beside the wagon, high on his splayed-hoofed horse, rode Ben Crost, his eyes missing nothing and his determination keeping the wagon rolling steadily forward. And ahead of him, near the heads of the lead team, walked the silent but hopeful Christena Bergman.

She knew that Ben Crost was behind her, and she knew as well that he insisted on following her for two reasons. The first was so that he could be sure that she didn't try to escape. But the second reason, which revolted her mightily, and which poor Maria had no idea of, was so that he could watch Christena walking. And he did watch, of that she was sure. Constantly she felt his hot eyes burning into her back, and it took all the will power she possessed to ignore it and keep moving forward.

But with an inner strength born of righteousness she did move forward, and in spite of her anger and disgust she kept walking, dry-eyed and steadily—and that was one small but significant part of her plan. And to Christena Bergman's credit, she did have a plan.

Wearily she raised her head, staring off across the brush-covered table lands of western Wyoming. Ben had pushed them all, and there had been times in the past four days when she had been certain that she could not take another step. Besides the constant walking, for she had not been allowed to burden the teams by riding, there had been meals to fix, horses to be cared for, and children to feed and clean. Maria had worked as hard as Christena, of course, but Ben had changed and now did no work at all. Instead, he was constantly on guard, watching for the posse he was certain would be following.

And there *was* a follower, Christena was equally certain of that. Not a posse, exactly, but one who followed, nevertheless. Somewhere back there, one day or maybe two, but coming steadily on, was Jons Soderberg, the wonderful young man whose love she carried firmly in her heart. He would have found the slingshot by now, with her note attached, and he would be coming after her, of that she was certain.

In her mind she could see him, standing before her, walking beside her, sitting facing her, and she couldn't help but smile with joy as she thought of him. He was tall with dark, wavy hair. He was quite thin, and he had the bluest eyes she had ever seen. When she looked up into his eyes, which she had done only a pitifully few times, she saw sky and heaven and the wide reaches of eternity—and the depths of his eyes thrilled her to the bottom of her soul.

He also blushed easily, and Christena had taken great delight in teasing him once she had discovered that characteristic. Nor did it seem to matter what she said or did. Almost anything embarrassed him, and like fire the color would sweep up his neck and face, leaving him stammering and silly, and so pathetically vulnerable and wonderful that it took great stamina for her just to keep from hugging him every time he blushed.

But now he was behind her, coming on, and soon he would arrive and take her away—

Her blistered and bleeding feet made her look down, and in dismay she chanced to glance at her hands. Once they had been so soft and white, with perfect nails. But now they were brown, with calluses, and the nails were stubby and cracked.

Would Jons mind that, she wondered? If he didn't, then she didn't care. But if he did —

Lifting her gaze, Christena strode forward. Jons wouldn't notice such things as her hands and feet, and she knew it. Nor would he look with disdain upon her dirty, stringy hair. He loved *her*, not how she looked, and Christena knew that she had to keep that knowledge uppermost in her mind.

"Wilbur," she said quietly to the big horse who plodded along beside her, "Jons is coming, you wait and see."

The horse snorted and shook its head, and a large jackrabbit broke from the brush ahead and sped away, traveling at an amazing speed.

"See that rabbit?" she said to the horse "Jons will be coming just about that fast, and when he gets here, you can bet I'll be leaving that fast with him."

The horse said nothing, and so Christena stopped talking too. But still she dreamed, and still she did her best to plan out a way to stop Ben Crost so that Jons could catch up with them more easily.

Long ago Ephraim Hanks had told her something, and lately it had come forcefully back to her mind. "The secret of victory," he had said, "is to attack — always attack. If an army has ten thousand men, attack. If it is only yourself, attack. If you do that, a way will always open up for you to become victorious."

So, was there a way for her to attack Ben Crost? Was there something that she could do? One thing she knew — she wasn't going to sit by, waiting to be destroyed, either body or spirit, by her step-uncle. But what could *she*, an unarmed woman with no horse, do? What weapons did she have?

Well, she had the love of Jons Soderberg, and she had the truth. Yet she was not so naive as to believe that truth alone would prevail, without any effort on her part. Still, it was a weapon, and if wisely used, it might divert Ben Crost from her. And Jons's love would give her hope until such time as she could determine how to use the truth against her uncle. So she would choose her time, and then she would move. But what time? When? How?

She was not afraid, but she knew what fear was, for she had felt it the night Ben had beaten Jons to the floor and thrown him out of the cabin. That night she had felt fear. And it had grown worse, only an hour later, when Ben had pushed her into her room with the command to pack her things and get them into the wagon. Until the idea to put a note on Jons's slingshot and leave it for him had occurred, she had been terrified. But since then she had been at peace, for she knew that Jons would find it, being led by the Spirit, and would come after her—

"Still dreaming of that stupid, gangly Swede?"

Spinning, Christena looked up into the leering face of Ben Crost, and suddenly she knew that she could hold herself back no longer. She would speak her mind to the man now and worry about the consequences of her words later on.

"You're mighty deep into some silly dream," he continued. "Was it of him?"

"He'll be coming," she answered quietly, firmly.

Ben Crost laughed. "He'd better not, else he'll return again almighty sore and bloody. You saw what happened the last time he came at me."

Christena looked away, but her voice had a ring to it that the man couldn't miss. "You're a coward, Ben Crost, and that's the truth. He didn't come at you, and you know it."

"Why, you impertinent little—"

"Further evidence," Christena said, smiling smugly as she looked back up at him. "Only cowards curse or strike at women."

With an oath Ben regained control of himself, but Christena wasn't through with him, not at all.

"Ben Crost," she declared, speaking softly enough that Maria couldn't hear her, but loud enough for the mounted man beside her to hear clearly, "you have been sorely deceived."

"Have I now?" the man asked sarcastically. "And I suppose you intend to testify to me of the truthfulness of the Church so I can be set straight?"

"Oh, no, dear uncle. Christ said not to cast our pearls before swine, and so I will not even mention those eternal truths that you once considered so important, but which Lucifer has wrested from your understanding. No, Ben Crost, I will speak to you of another truth, and of life, and show you how, by the laws of the one, you have lost the right to have happiness in the other."

"My, my," he sneered, "so you have become the little philosopher, have you?"

Christena lifted her chin. "If I have, you would do well to listen. Ben Crost, coming west to gather with the Saints is a way for all of us to start over. By coming to the Valley, we wipe clean the slate of our past, so to speak. Whatever any of us is to be need have nothing to do with what we were before, but it begins the day we enter the valley.

"That holds for you, too. If you had had courage, done your work and Church callings well, and had been a man of your word, people either would have been thrilled, or would not have cared at all, about what you had done in the past. If it had been bad, you would have been forgiven. If it had been good, you would have received high praise and would have done even better.

"All sorts of people have joined the Church, Ben Crost, great ones as well as those with problems. Some have had trouble with the law, some have been too far into debt, and some just didn't fit into any mold. Others, as successful as you had been, and even more so, have also joined. If you had proven yourself a responsible person, as many of them have done and are doing, then you would have been the equal of anybody in the Church and would have been chosen as leader over many."

"I don't know what you're talking about," Ben Crost growled.

"You don't?" Christena pressed forward fearlessly. "Oh, I think you do. You had a good past, but you made a mistake when you got to the Valley. You assumed that people would see the same importance in you that you had come to see in yourself. But they didn't see it, simply because it is no longer there. You have not put forth any effort to earn it or to continue it, and so the past you brought with you is of no value.

"But now, Ben Crost, and this is what you do not understand, you have a new past; new and terribly evident. You have shown yourself to be lazy, conceited, arrogant, and cowardly, and you're a bully, as well. And there isn't a soul I know who can't see it."

Ben Crost cursed again, but Christena ignored him and concluded her thought.

"People are tolerant, but only up to a point, and the Lord is the same. Because you have chosen to walk in your own light rather than in that of the Savior, you have forced your family to give up Christ's true religion and to leave the Valley. But worse, you have beaten up an innocent young man, and you have forced me to leave my home and loved one against my will. Those things, Ben Crost, push tolerance of good people beyond its limit and force the Spirit of the Lord to withdraw. I fear that the result, for you, will be very abrupt and very, very final."

Ben Crost laughed. "We'll see, my little Christena, we'll see. But was I you, I'd forget the Lord. If he's there, he obviously doesn't care what's going on down here. And I'd not put much store in that scrawny young Swede being a factor in my 'final result,' either. He ever does catch me, he won't last much beyond that."

"You're *pathetic!*"

"Maybe. But I'm also here, and don't you forget that. One of these days you'll change your thinking of me. I'll be coming to you, and you'd better be ready."

Ben Crost pulled his splayed-hoofed horse back by the squeaking wagon, and Christena Bergman strode forward alone. She was furious, but helplessly so, and with all her heart she wanted to cry. Only crying wouldn't help Jons to win her freedom — not yet it wouldn't.

But when they got a little closer to the Green River and the trader Yates's post, then she would get very, very sick. And her pain, tears, and complaining to any who would listen, a complaining not yet seen on this entire journey, would force Ben

94

Crost to stop at the post so that she could rest and be cared for.

That, she thought grimly and with great determination, was the rest of her plan. And if love and faith counted for anything at all, it would be enough. In the time that diversion gave him, Jons Soderberg would catch up with them and take her away.

Chapter 9

Echo Canyon, at least for the first four or five miles up from the mouth, was a real beehive. Legioneers from all over the territory had been called up and were hard at work at a place called Echo Station, making the canyon as defensible as possible. We met and visited briefly with the leaders of these men — Majors Pugmire and Sharp of Great Salt Lake City, Major D. P. Curtis of Davis County, and Major Munroe of Ogden — commanding among them some 411 men. We also passed a Major Taylor and fifty men from Ogden, and I learned that the horse company who had given me the little gray had been under the command of a Captain Bannion. And there were others, but Eph was in somewhat of a hurry, so we didn't speak with them all.

"Hear the echo?" Eph asked as we rode along. "William Clayton was the first to tell me of it, and of course that's how it got its name. He described it to me as very singular, the rattling of wagons resembling carpenters hammering at boards inside the highest rocks. The report of a rifle resembles a sharp crack of thunder, and it will echo for some time. The lowing of cattle and braying of mules seems to be answered from beyond the mountains, and music, especially brass instruments, have a very pleasing effect, with every note being imitated. Too bad we don't have a bugler with us now, so we could test it out."

As we rode up the canyon, we passed crews damming the stream and flooding the bottom so the government wagons would bog down. Others were digging new channels for the creek so that the water could be used to greatest advantage in future flooding. On the steep slopes, men were hard at work digging rifle trenches and pits, and on top of the honeycombed cliffs that hung several hundred feet above us, others were building stone ramparts, from behind which they could fire down upon the advancing army.

And the army *was* advancing. Expresses passed us twice that day, each with word that the army was within thirty miles of Bridger, and coming on. We also had word that General Daniel H. Wells and his staff were behind us and coming, their destination Fort Bridger, up on the plains of Wyoming. So there was a real hive of activity going on.

Word had also gone ahead about Lazarus and the gray mare, and we drew a lot of attention as we passed by. But lest I get the idea that I had been the recipient of some sort of out-and-out miracle, Gideon went to some pains to tell me that he had seen wolves and coyotes pull the same stunt in the wild, wearing down animals so they could eat them. Of course, that hadn't been Lazarus's objective, as Al Bagley quickly pointed out. And Eph felt certain that the hand of the Lord had been in it, miracle or not. Anyway, it made for a lively discussion and gave me further opportunity to reflect upon the blessings that had so recently come to me.

Another thing—every time we stopped, I found men who had seen Ben Crost's wagon. It was less than a day ahead of us but was moving fast. And more and more Ben was telling folks that he was in a hurry because there were those after him who had orders from Brigham Young to "use him up," meaning, I suppose, to take his life.

Well, that was utter nonsense, for I was the only one after him, and I certainly wasn't under orders from Brigham Young. Nor did I intend to kill him—come within an inch or two of it, maybe, but not kill him. But more and more it put me in mind of what we had talked about the night before, of how a man loses the Spirit, then denies the faith, and ends up being filled with fear. Ben Crost was certainly fitting the mold.

Most everybody also remembered Steenie, and that was starting to trouble me. From what folks said, she did not seem overly anxious to get away from her uncle. Oh, I know I had my note from her, but I couldn't help thinking that if she had wanted to badly enough, she could have escaped. Or said something to the men along the trail so that they would stop Ben from taking her with him. Or anyway talked to one or two of them about *something*. But in all that day, I never met a man who had heard her say a word or give any indication at all that she was not perfectly happy and in agreement with the company she was with and the direction she was going.

And *that* was starting to bother me.

"Friend Jons," Gideon told me after I had worried aloud to him, "women seem passing strange to most men, but that is because they don't understand them."

"Do you?" I asked.

"Mercy, no. But I lived with a good one for nigh onto fifty years, and I did come to understand one thing—womenfolk think different than men do. They run long to feelings and ain't bothered so much by the sense of an issue. To a woman, it's how she feels about something that counts, no matter what color it actually shapes up to be. Why, I've seen a perfectly good woman back up the meanest, lowest-down skunk alive, just because she loved him and believed in him. I've also seen beautiful, lovely sisters turn their backs on the best men the Lord ever made, for the same loco reason. They didn't have any feelings for 'em, no matter the logic of it.

"On the other hand, a good woman will laugh in the face of temptation that would bog a snipe, it is so all-fired bad. And if such a woman sets her sights on the straight and narrow path to celestial glory, then heaven help the poor sorry man who tries to lead her astray. Unlike most men, no matter what is offered, such a sister cannot be bought.

"All's I'm saying, Son, is never expect a woman to do something just because it's what you would do. You'll likely end up disappointed." Then Gideon grinned. "On the other hand, never be surprised if a woman does *exactly* what you would do.

That often happens. But if you press her as to the why of what she did, you'll sure enough end up confused again. Oh, she'll know why, all right, but it won't even be close to the same trail you would have taken to get there. Like I said, womenfolk think different than men do."

"That means," I said, doing my best to understand, "that I shouldn't try to understand why Steenie is still with Ben Crost?"

Gideon grinned. "That's right, Son. You forget the whys of a woman, and just concentrate on the whos. If she's a good woman, then be satisfied with that. You do that all your life, and you'll live and die a happy man."

"I'll try, Gideon, but I'm still worried—"

"Dad-blast it, you young whippersnapper, listen to me! Worrying's like sitting on a rocking horse. No matter how hard you work it, the fool thing ain't never going to get you anywhere. You want to find and help that little gal of yours, stop all the fretting, trust her, and keep your eyes and ears open. Then, when it's time, you'll be worth something to her!"

Well, that ended that particular conversation, and I was still going over it, trying to make heads or tails of what I had been told, when a shot rang out ahead of us, the sound echoing back and forth. With no hesitation, Ephraim Hanks sank spurs to his horse, the rest of us followed suit, and a few minutes later we pulled rein near a clustered group of men.

"I didn't mean it," a large man was pleading. "I just didn't think it would go so far."

Two men held him by the arms, while the others stood around him, glaring. But the big man had no strength to fight them, and he didn't even try. He just wept and told us over and over that it had been an accident.

"Boys," Eph Hanks said as he dismounted, "I'm Major Hanks. Why doesn't someone tell me what happened?"

The big man started crying again, but Eph held his hand up, silencing him. "Well?" he said to the others.

Finally one of the crowd cleared his throat and spoke. "Brother Hanks, Neilsen here just shot William Simmons through the head with his Yeager, killing him on the spot."

"You see it happen?"

"No, sir, but these men did."

Eph turned to the others. "Who of you saw it?"

"I did."

"Me, too."

"So did I."

"And was it like the man said?" Eph asked the three.

"Well, yes and no."

"What do you mean?"

The man took a deep breath. "Sir, Frederic Neilsen here is best friends with William Simmons. He killed him, but he didn't mean to do it."

"That's right," another agreed.

"It can't be," the first man argued. "Man, you saw it. Neilsen pointed the Yeager directly at him and shot. How could he have *not* meant to do it?"

At that a young man about my age spoke up. "It was an experiment, Sir. That was all. We'd been digging those trenches to dam the creek, and Neilsen and Simmons and the rest of us got to arguing about whether or not a person as far away as the tops of those cliffs, where we'll be hiding, could hit a man all the way down here in the bottom.

"Well, Simmons had the idea to climb up there to the top and then have someone fire at him so he could see just how far the ball might fall short. He chose the Dane here, Frederic Neilsen, because he is a former soldier and knows how to handle the Yeager, and because they were such good friends.

"Major Hanks, none of us had the slightest notion that the ball might ever fly so far or so true."

"For some folks," Gideon muttered, shaking his head, "it was too late to get wise the day they was born. I never heard of such tom-foolishness."

Ignoring the old man, Eph looked around at the others. "That the way you saw it?" he asked a lean man in a real funny hat.

"Aye," the man replied, "the kid told it right."

"And you?" Eph asked of the third man who had claimed to be an eyewitness.

"It be like hisself has said," the man replied in an Irish brogue, nodding at the youth. "We've tried to tell these gents that it were an accident, but the blathering fools've not been believing of us."

The man grew still, there were dark looks all around, and a moment later four men came down off the slope with the body of the dead Simmons between them. They laid the man at our feet, and I was very much affected at the sight of him. Except for being so white, he looked as though he would awaken at any second, get up, and get back to work.

Nor was there much blood or sign of damage upon him. The ball, it was quickly determined, had entered in his left temple, leaving a small, bluish hole, and had come out of his right ear, which was also where the only blood showed.

And poor Frederic Neilsen. At the sight of his friend's lifeless body, the Danish convert crumpled to the earth sobbing, and no amount of effort seemed able to console him.

"What do we do, Major?" the man who had spoken first finally asked.

Eph, his hands buried deeply in his pockets, stared upward as if waiting for some sign from heaven. Whether he was or not, I do not know, but after a moment he gave quiet, precise, and simple directions.

"The man's body must be taken to his home for burial. Detail two men to do that, two who were not witnesses to the shooting.

"Because this is wartime and we are under martial law, Neilsen here must be placed under arrest and given a speedy trial. General Wells is right behind us and is on his way to Bridger. He will conduct the trial. All of you who are witnesses must stand ready to testify in behalf of what you saw and know. Do not leave the area, or I swear that you, too, will be hunted down and arrested. Until General Wells arrives, all of you get back to your work. And unless orders are given, there will be no more shooting. Am I clear?"

The men nodded. One then put a blanket over Simmons's lifeless body, and then slowly the men returned to their trench digging.

"Tragic," Eph said as he swung back on his horse. "That is so sad. A man's life gone, and it should never have happened. If we would only learn to use good common sense . . .

"Well, enough of that," he said, shaking his head as if to clear his mind. "Al, I have the feeling that we need to hurry to Cache Cave."

Al Bagley nodded with a wry grin. "Now, that is passing strange. I've been sitting here feeling the same urge myself." Then he turned to us. "Brethren, there are another ten miles to go, and we'll be pushing. Are you up to a hard ride?"

Gideon nodded silently, and I patted a panting Lazarus and told Al that I thought we could stand it too.

So slapping spurs to the horses, we quickened our paces eastward.

Chapter 10

There were three of them, three men who rode up from the south, across the high country, and down into the foothills that made up the north slope of the Uintah Mountains — three stone-faced, weather-stained men who rode slack and easy on their ponies like all men bred to horseback, but whose eyes were narrow-tense and hard and crinkled at the outer corners from a habit of long watchfulness. All were alike in these ways, though in another they differed widely. Two were Ute Indians, renegades who had been expelled from their people and who had then joined with the third man. From him they had picked up many of the ways of the whites — ways of greed and distrust. For the third man, the undisputed leader of the three was white — and not a shining example of that race, either.

He was a mountaineer and fur trapper and trader, one of the remnants of that hardy breed who had tracked out and explored the vastness of western America, risking life and limb to fill their pockets with eastern and European gold.

But by 1857 the great market for beaver and other furs was largely a memory, and so a man with a taste for the wild, free life of the wilderness did what he could to pad his purse and hold body and soul together. Nor was he likely to be particular about how he did it. If the reward was there, so was the willingness to participate. And of late, these same three had found great profit in the running of slaves, Shoshone and Snake Indian women and children, who were much in demand in the Mexican colonies of Santa Fe, Taos, and Abiquiu.

It was a good business, this slave trade, though not as good as it had been when Ute Chief Walker, or Wakara, had been alive. The prominent chief had been one of the greatest traders of human flesh in the mountains, and though Brigham Young and the Mormons had dissuaded him from the practice some years before, others had willingly kept the trade going.

Now Arapeen, Walker's brother, was continuing it, as were other tribal leaders to the south, including Hunkootoop of the Pahvants — and the price was holding steady at $50 to $75 American dollars for children and $100 to $150 for young women. Of course, the Mormons were formidable foes who arrested all who were captured with slaves or who were suspected of selling them. But still the slave-hungry Mexicans came surreptitiously up into the wilderness along the Green, and still men like Vasquez and his two renegade Utes delivered bartered or captured Indian slaves to them.

But this day the three were not traveling for slaves, nor did two of the men think often of them. Instead, they were on a bartering mission to dispose of other illicitly gained goods, and the white leader, José Vasquez, felt certain that they stood an excellent chance of success.

So they had ridden for some time through drought-parched country and thick-timbered slopes, cursing the heat. But it was a day for ducks when they finally hit the north foothills, and all thought longingly of the heat they had left behind. All morning, swift clouds with dark, swollen underbellies had scudded across the drab sky. Shortly after their noon stop the rain had begun, catching the men in the open. Two had wanted to find shelter, but José Vasquez, inexorable, absolute, and always sure, had kept them heading east of north into pale, slashing torrents of water that whipped in windlashed gusts against the leaning forms of horses and men. The storm was no brief blow but steadily drenched the high country of the Uintahs, and so they rode it out, the entire half-day siege of it.

Even in high-buttoned slickers over buckskins, the three

were soaked, miserable, and ugly-tempered when, toward evening, a densely-timbered rise of ground loomed ahead and José Vasquez called a halt. They put their horses directly toward the heart of the timbered stand and broke into a wide clearing with a host of deadfalls at the lee end. Vasquez looked around and then dismounted with a grunt of satisfaction. They would be well hidden here, which was all that concerned him. The mutinous, surly grumblings of the others couldn't make Vasquez bat an eyelash. He knew his men, knew they would be lost without him, and knew that they knew it, too.

They made a cold, wet camp—a miserable camp. The rain had only then begun to slacken into a gray drizzle. The Ute called Knife threw saddle, saddlebags, and canvas-wrapped blanket-roll from his sorrel, then lugged them over to the leeward side of a looming granite outcrop. Where the rock checked the blast of wind and rain it was reasonably dry, and he had seen instantly that it was a good place to spread his blankets. With a weary grunt he dropped his gear and sat down, stretching his bony arms. Yet he did not rest long, for shortly Vasquez was yelling at him to build a fire.

Resignedly, the thin Ute rose to his feet and made a circle of the clearing, limbering his legs and arms. Then he chanced to glance at the rock where he had tossed his gear. Limpy, whose Ute name was Bear Who Walks with Wounded Foot, after a wound a giant grizzly had inflicted upon the huge man's foot many years before, but whose name Vasquez had shortened to Limpy, had taken Knife's place behind the rock and was even then kicking Knife's gear out into the wet.

Knife's hands balled into fists, and he started across the clearing, choking on his anger. Limpy, seeing him coming, swung his huge body to face him, with his bubbling laugh showing chalk-white teeth. Then he whipped off his stolen hat, batting the wet felt against the shining wetness of his buckskins, and tossed it onto his other gear. The rain matted his coarse black hair, roached like a mule's mane, and he ran a hand over it in a slicking-back motion, his wide face still laughing.

"Ungh," he growled with malicious glee as he watched his

traveling companion's stiff-legged approach. "The useless one shows his teeth. Does he think to sink them into the great *Queogand,* the great Bear?"

Limpy's speech was Ute, and he referred to himself proudly by a shortened version of his name. For he was like a bear, big, slow of mind, but cat-quick and deadly when cornered.

Trembling with rage, the much smaller Knife circled his mocking opponent for a moment, a gleaming blade suddenly in his hand. Then he dived headlong for the big, mocking figure.

But Limpy made a fluid, side-stepping motion, and the thin Ute burgeoned past, plowing on his face into the littered gear and mud. Instantly he lunged to his feet, whirled, and went after Limpy again, and Limpy backed away, taunting him.

"The useless one's single metal tooth is more useless than is he. *Weitch,* Knife, is a fool's name for such a one as you. Your mother should have called you *Me-poodg-e-Kan-Nab,* Little Willow, and given you a switch to fight with. Perhaps you might have done better."

Vasquez watched disinterestedly as the fight progressed. He knew the two Utes hated each other, and that bothered him not at all. In fact, there were times when he encouraged their animosity toward each other, for he was able to use it to his own advantage.

Knife bored in again, his blade low and swinging upward, and again Limpy easily deflected it. Then Knife's foot skidded on the wet loam — and his feet, aided by the awkward reactions of his thin, bony body, flailed the ground away and piled him on his face again. He lay there, sobbing in torn breaths, while Limpy kicked him hard on the wrist, sending the blade skidding away from Knife's suddenly numbed fingers. Then the big Ute walked away, laughing.

Knife didn't rise immediately, even after Limpy had returned to the rock shelter. Instead, he lay and nursed his hatred, savoring in his mind the bloody end of the larger man that he knew one day was coming.

Finally he pushed himself up on his hands and knees, then to his feet, avoiding the looks of Vasquez. Wet buckskin moccasins squishing as he moved, Knife walked slowly to the wall of deadfalls and living quaking aspens—there hunkering down among them to be alone with his present shame and his murderous dreams. He rested his arms on his knees, set his teeth into the wet buckskin of his shirt, and listened to the rain pock the few remaining aspen leaves above.

From the clearing Knife heard the mild voice of Vasquez, gently chiding the hulking Limpy. "He had a *weitch*. You had him in the grass. Why didn't you *e-i*, kill him?"

Limpy grunted humorlessly. "A waste of a man's time, to kill such an insect. He is *paquy-nary me-poodg-e kan-nab,* a stinking little willow, and one day he will burn in the *coo-nah* of his own hatred."

"Yeah," Vasquez agreed, speaking in English. "And speaking of burning, I want a fire now! Knife! You get the wood and build up that *coo-nah* now, you hear me?"

The gaunt Ute rose to his feet and plunged ahead, heedless of the wet lash of back-whipping branches, till he found a rotten deadfall. With furious energy he kicked out great chunks of its tinder-dry heart. Bending down, he then picked up an armful of the punk, and in his mind he saw himself and the other two men, a sort of vision of the accumulation of all the days that had passed since he had turned his back upon his people to go with the *tsharr,* the white Vasquez.

He hated himself for that, for thinking he could depart from the wise and sacred traditions of his people. And in a way he hated them for expelling him and for forcing him to join Vasquez. But that was *to-edg-e-tish,* a long time ago, and he wasn't certain he could even remember all those traditions or reasons any more. But he kept his hair right, unlike foolish Limpy, and the little rituals of his mornings were as the people did them.

But now the seeing of the more recent past was in Knife's mind, a thousand or more camps like this one, some colder and more wet, some drier and more hungry. Days and often nights of far-ranging, grueling rides in rain, snow, blazing heat, until he would think he had never known anything but the rocking and jolting back and forth on a sweating *kuvah-u,* horse. Seasons stretched into years of hiding in desert holes or mountain hideaways, where boredom hung like a dead weight and there was nothing to do but throw sticks and *ni-a-witch,* gamble the white man's *wah-pana-kar-ra,* money-rock. Ten thousand days and nights in company with the hated Limpy and the more-than-feared José Vasquez who jumped at every sound and was always more than ready to kill. That was the life Knife had somehow, foolishly, chosen for himself.

"Wagh!" he grunted quietly. Why had he done this? Why had he let himself be led along by the white slave trader? Much better that he be back with his people. Much better that he *pe-oh-a,* that he marry, and be making little ones with a warm and comfortable squaw, a woman who would take care of all this woman's work he was constantly being forced to do.

And Knife truly did want a woman. For the past year or so, he had eyed squaws and girls Vasquez had purchased from Ute bands led by men such as Arapene, trying to think of a way he could purchase or steal one for himself. And though several had been possibilities, none had really taken his fancy. Nor, for that matter, had he been able to work out just how he might persuade Vasquez to part with such a possession. After all, women, especially those who were young and thin, brought good money from the Mexican raiders who came regularly to the southern crossing on the Green. And Vasquez loved money—loved it more than anything else. Knife marveled at that, for to him it held little value. So also did he marvel that women seemed to hold no fascination for the trader. In fact, even big Limpy seemed unaffected by them, and Knife wondered at both of his companions.

For him, the supreme happiness of life would be to be part of a *meah-a-bitch,* an encampment of his people, having a squaw or two to do his cooking, and having sons that he might watch grow into warriors. That was his greatest dream, and it was never far from his mind.

His second-greatest dream, he thought sourly as he rose to his feet to return to the clearing, was to see the huge Limpy dead, the man's *pwap,* blood, staining the grass beneath him.

And Knife knew, even as he did the woman's work of carrying the wood for Limpy and Vasquez's fire, that one day he would see the big Ute *e-i,* dead.

But now they were not even after the women and children who could be sold as slaves, and Knife worried at that. Now they were on their way to see another hated white, another trader whose name was Yates. Within the past year, Vasquez and his companions had, quite by accident, stumbled upon a poorly armed caravan of Mexicans, and after treacherously murdering them while they slept, they had found the caravan to be carrying several hundred pounds of gunpowder.

Caching it beneath the heaped-up bodies of the dead Mexicans for future consideration, Vasquez had gone about his other illicit business enterprises, and when word had reached him, only days before, of the march of an approaching army to destroy the feared and hated Mormons, he had suddenly known what he might do with the gunpowder.

Of course, he could not sell the explosive salt-peter and nitrates to the army himself, for his was a known name and face, and that would be too great a risk. But Yates was an old trapping compadre, an honest man who owed Vasquez a mighty favor for the saving of his life, and now would be the perfect time for Vasquez to collect.

Knife knew all this, and it troubled him—not because of the murdered Mexicans or the pack-mule loads of stolen gunpowder or the approaching army did he worry. No, those things mattered little to him. What troubled the gaunt and bony Ute was that there would be no women this trip, no squaws that he might examine and possibly select from. For Knife had decided, in recent weeks, that when the next passable woman was purchased by Vasquez, he would have her, whether he could afford the price or not. For there were other ways of obtaining things than by *nar-ro-wap,* by purchase, Knife thought, grinning evilly. Vasquez had taught him that, and Vasquez had taught him well.

Trudging back to the clearing with an armful of the crumbling punk, Knife dumped it on a dry place under a spreading pine. Setting his face in frustrated determination, he ground a handful of the heartwood between his palms to make a small heap of loose tinder. Over this he built a wigwam of dry sticks he'd gathered from under a nearby log. Then he reached inside his buckskins for an oilcloth-wrapped packet of matches, one of the few white-man things of which he approved. Striking it, he cupped the orange flare in his palms, and then carefully he eased it down to the punk.

Smoke threaded from the tinder, then a spoon of flame that caught the twigs. A brief moment later, when he had secured a steady blaze, Knife piled on chunks of the rotten wood.

Limpy came across the clearing with swinging stride, whistling cheerfully in the disgusting white man's way, carrying the battered coffeepot full of water. Before Knife had time to wonder why the big man was doing a menial woman's chore with such a cheerful air, Limpy reached the fire and bent as though to set the pot close by.

But then it tilted in his hand, and a stream of water gushed over the meager blaze. The fire sizzled and died in a thin mushrooming of steam and smoke, and Knife came to his feet, no uncertainty in him.

"Sar-ich katz-te-suah," he snarled angrily, "dog of a fool! Do you think I do not *pesuds-away,* do you think I do not understand that you did that of choice?"

Limpy's black brows lifted in the blandest motion of innocence. "But Stinking Little Willow, I merely wished to hurry with the coffee — "

And then the giant Limpy was interrupted as José Vasquez strode heavy-footed across the clearing, an emphatic anger visible in his swinging arms. "Limpy," he growled as he bored in, "this time you've gone too far."

The sodden smack of Vasquez's fist froze Knife in position while Limpy somersaulted backward. The big man turned over once, landed on his back, and stared upward into the rain, trying to comprehend what had just taken place. Then he shook his head, his ugly face distorted, and with a grunt he hauled himself to his feet, ripped open his slicker, and clawed for the dead white man's holstered gun that he wore.

Only, through the ponderous haze of red anger that filled Limpy's mind, his eyes suddenly saw the gun in Vasquez's hand, the gun that had arrived there in the magical way that only Vasquez knew. Slowly his own hand dropped from his weapon, and he stood in the drizzle, staring at the feared Vasquez.

One day, he promised himself while Vasquez stared him down, and while the gaunt Knife grinned evilly from the side, one day—

And little did he know that Knife was thinking exactly the same thing about him.

Chapter 11

Cache Cave, to the south of the head of Echo Canyon, was one of the greatest landmarks of the early West. Small and oven-shaped, set in overhanging rocks, it had been used for many years as a shelter for fur trappers and mountaineers, explorers, and the early Mormon pioneers. It looked to me, when I saw it, to be about thirty feet deep, fifteen feet wide, and from four to six feet in height. It was located above a stream called Cache Cave Creek and was an ideal place to hold stock. In addition, it was situated so that it warmed quickly and provided excellent shelter. Therefore, it was an almost perfect camp.

In the cave and on the rocks nearby were carved the names of a hundred or more people who had stopped there as a testimony of the cave's value, and Eph Hanks pointed out to me that those names included many of Brother Brigham's pioneer group of 1847.

It being evening, we took mess with the Mormon troops stationed nearby. These were under the direction of Hosea Stout, who I was told was also a lawyer and an elected officer of the law down in the Valley.

"So you're a lawyer, huh?" old Gideon asked as we sat to eat.

Hosea Stout nodded matter-of-factly.

"Humph," the caustic old Gideon grunted. "Well, lawyers is good for something, I say."

"Which is?"

"They get you out of the kind of trouble you'd never get in if there was no lawyers in the first place."

The rest of us felt mighty uncomfortable, but Hosea Stout chuckled good naturedly. "Well said, Captain Monson," he declared enthusiastically. "May the Lord preserve me from becoming such. Thank goodness we have the Book of Mormon to remind me of the kind of lawyer I never want to be."

Gideon looked at the man with new appreciation, and I was glad that nothing more was said about that topic.

"Well, Ephraim," Stout finally said as we finished the last of the beef and beans, "how are your wives?"

Eph looked up. "Harriet's just fine, or at least she was when I left. But Jane is feeling poorly right now—she's hoping the little one will be here soon. She was not overly anxious that I be gone."

"No, I suppose not. Did Brigham send you out?"

Eph nodded, and his long beard bobbed gently on his chest, causing me to wonder again that any man could grow a beard of such proportions.

"And I suppose that you will go off on your hook?" Stout continued.

Eph nodded again. "Well, Brother Brigham *did* ask Al and me to do what we could to slow Ol' Buck's boys down."

Hosea Stout grinned. "I wish I could go see the fireworks. I'll never forget how you almost single-handedly saved the entire Martin handcart company from starvation."

"The Lord blessed me with those buffalo. You know as well as I do that buffalo don't wander during storms."

"I know that, Eph. I also know you would never have been led to it if you hadn't gone off on your own hook. You recollect all the blessings we gave to those poor souls that night?"

"I do," Eph replied, nodding soberly.

Hosea Stout looked into the fire. "I'll never forget the sufferings and privations of those people. Funny thing, though. Some were merry and cheerful, some dull and stupid, some sick, some frosted, and some lazy and mean. But one thing they all were — elated at the prospect of more speedily arriving in the Valley. Say, Eph, I left the morning after we gave those blessings. Did that feller you raised from the dead continue to live?"

"You mean Brother Blair? He certainly did. Last I saw him he was still singing hymns."

"And what about the Read family?"

Ephraim Hanks grinned. "They're tolerable well, especially young Thisbe Read."

"Yes," Hosea Stout mused, "I recollect her. Right pert woman. She'll make someone a fine wife. By the way, an express came an hour ago from General Wells. I imagine the express passed you."

"He did, but he didn't stop."

"His news, Ephraim, is that General Wells will reach her later tonight, hold a court concerning that shooting, and then take up the march for Fort Bridger in the morning. Are you sure you wouldn't rather wait and accompany him?"

The question sounded to me to be genuine, and so I was surprised at Eph Hanks's response.

"Thanks for the warning, Hosea. We'll mosey along up-trail directly."

Hosea Stout grinned. "I thought that might be how the stick floated. Well, just be sure you don't shoot at everything that moves. Colonel Robert Burton and his seventy-five or so men are out there flanking the army, we have expresses coming and going twice a day, and there are a lot of Mormon folk still at Bridger and Fort Supply. So, do be careful."

"We will. Have you seen anything of a wagon going east? Man by the name of Ben Crost, his wife, and three youngsters? There is also a girl with them, real pretty thing, sixteen or seventeen years old. You seen them?"

Stout nodded again. "I haven't seen them, myself. But I was told they had passed. They took the northern trail and so avoided the cave here. Problems?"

"Some. The young man here, Jons Soderberg, is betrothed to the girl, and he thinks she was forced to leave the valley against her will."

"So you are Jons Soderberg," Hosea Stout said, looking at me. "The miracle worker. So young and yet so famous. Where's the coyote-dog?"

"Uh . . . Lazarus is down with the horses, sir."

"How're that critter and the horse doing? Orson Spencer brought word that they had quite a fight."

"There's truth to that," Al Bagley declared. "I never saw the like in my life, and I missed some of it."

"Spencer told me it was an amazing thing to see."

"The animals are fine, sir," I told him then. "The dog is healing fast, and Perdy is a smooth horse to ride. She acts a little shy without Lazarus around. But since the dog tamed her, she's been gentle as a kitten with me."

"The mare's a good'un," Gideon said then, speaking for the first time. "Plenty of bottom. I would say she could out-distance any of our other mounts. She's been going all day today, and she never even lathered up."

"Hosea," Eph asked, bringing the subject back around, "is there any news?"

Grinning, Hosea Stout stood and walked to the edge of the bluff. "Same old Ephraim. You sure you don't already know?"

Eph lifted his eyebrows in question.

"Revelation, man. You get as much news from heaven, I think, as Brigham does. I suspect I should be asking you."

"Now, Hosea, you know better than that—"

"Know better? I should smile I do. I'll not forget those starving Sioux Indians back on the plains at Ash Hollow this past February, nor the wounded boy you instantly raised up. The rest of you brethren may not know about this, but after the boy was healed, the Spirit of God rested upon Ephraim, and he prophesied that within three days the entire country around the starving Indians would be overrun with buffalo—which traveling of herds, I might add, never occurs in mid-winter.

"Leaving camp hungry the next morning, Ephraim and Feramorz Little, as well as the men they were guiding, found their way lined with thirty of the most prominent Indians—each with a package of the choicest meat to give the elders. Those Lamanite brethren were real impressed with Ephraim's ability to raise the sick and get news from heaven. Thanking them, Ephraim promised to be back later in the season.

"When he returned two months later, carrying word of the coming of Uncle's army to the Saints in the Valley, Ephraim came upon some mountaineers camping near where the Sioux had been camped.

" 'What'd you do to them Indians?' the mountaineers asked when they found out who Ephraim was. 'They've been looking for you for the past two months, and they've been going up and down the country for miles, every day, trying to search you out. And when an Indian loves a white man like that—'

"Ephraim just laughed. 'Have you boys seen any buffalo since I was here before?' he asked.

" 'Yes,' replied one of the men. 'About three days after you left here going east, one of the biggest herds of buffalo we've ever seen passed by.'

" 'And it saved us from starvation,' put in another. 'Our food supply was about gone.'

"Well, boys, the minute Ephraim put in his appearance among the Sioux, he was given the hero's welcome. And he would get it today, happen he was to visit them again."

"Indians are easy to impress," Ephraim Hanks said modestly.

"Well, I'm not," Hosea Stout responded, "but I've heard that tale from forty directions, and *I'm* impressed."

"If you want, I'll tell you another one," Al Bagley stated then.

"Al—" Eph pleaded.

"No, if we're discussing getting messages from heaven, then this is a humdinger. You want to hear it, Stout?"

Hosea smiled. "I certainly do."

"Last winter, scouting across the plains on his way to help rescue the handcart folks, Eph got in a blizzard and wandered off track. Pretty soon he stumbled on a group of Indians, none of them very friendly looking, and they proceeded to give his horses and outfit the look-over.

116

"By pointing and tracing lines in the snow, the Indians showed Eph where the road was. Well, Eph was paying attention to that, but he was just as interested in figuring out some way to scare those Indians so they would forget coming after him and planting him deep for his outfit.

"Suddenly he had an idea. Drawing his hunting knife from his boot-leg, Eph also made lines in the snow, showing that he understood their directions. Then purposefully he dropped his knife, but he continued to talk as if nothing had happened. From the corner of his eye he saw one of the braves kick snow over the knife and then stand on it, and Eph knew his little plan was going to work.

"Acting satisfied with their directions, he mounted his horse and started away. After he had ridden about ten yards, with the Indians watching him closely, he stopped his horse and began to feel for his knife. He searched himself well, then searched his packhorse. But of course no knife could be found. So, turning his horse, he rode back to the watching Indians.

"He then raised his hands high above his head and began to speak, half in Sioux, half in English, to the Great Spirit. Then, drawing his eyes to narrow slits, he dropped his hand and pointed with long forefinger straight at the feet of the man who was standing over his knife. He didn't actually look at the man, but still he held that finger pointed, without moving.

"When he asked them which one had his knife, all the Indians shook their heads and said they didn't know, including the guilty party.

"Again Eph pointed skyward and talked to the Great Spirit. Then, like a shadow on a sundial, Eph's long forefinger dropped, slowly moved, and once again pointed straight at the guilty party, who by then was trembling with fright. And that time, Eph followed his finger with his eyes, staring that Indian right into the ground, so to speak.

" 'You have stolen my knife!' he intoned with powerful voice. 'It is in the snow under your feet. The Great Spirit has shown it to me, and he is angry with you!'

"Slowly moving his finger around the group, Eph then eyed

them all. 'Each of you saw him hide the knife under the snow, and the Great Spirit is going to kill you now. When I lift my finger again, the lightning will come and you will burn on the spot!'

"Well, those braves were all shaking like leaves in a high wind, and so slowly, dramatically, Eph began to lift his forefinger skyward. The Sioux looked at each other, they looked back at him, they shook harder and got more frightened, and finally one of them shoved the thief off Eph's knife, grabbed it up, and, pulling Eph's hand down out of the air, forced the knife into it.

"Needless to say, Eph had no further trouble with those particular Indians."

We all chuckled over that story, and Al Bagley was just unlimbering for another when Eph impatiently cut him short. "Hosea, you were going to tell me the news?"

"So I was," Stout replied with a sigh, "though I would rather hear more of these tales. Abraham Hunsaker and the others have been called in from Carson Valley and the Humboldt, and word has it he's bringing with him about 2,700 pounds of gunpowder, ammunition, and arms. The people are abandoning San Bernardino, and at last report all feel good about it. Samuel W. Richards has gone to England to bring back apostles Orson Pratt and Ezra T. Benson, and I've heard that they're closing the mission to the Sandwich Islands and bringing the elders in from there. I imagine you know the rest.

"Oh, yes, one more thing. We've made our first strike at the army. Porter Rockwell raided some of the soldiers at Pacific Springs the other morning, trying to make off with their mules. They got in and out successfully and nobody was hurt, but somehow the attempt to get the stock failed, and now the army is warned. So be careful, Ephraim. They'll be watching for you. And remember, unlike our forces, Uncle's boys are under no such orders to fight a bloodless war."

"True enough," Eph said as he rose to his feet. "Where are the closest government troops now, Hosea?"

"Last express said they were camped on the Big Sandy, some

twenty miles from Fort Bridger. They're calling the place Camp Scott. But we're also told that they're sending scouts out in all directions, so a man just never knows."

"Well, boys," Eph said quietly as we walked down toward our horses, "what say we make a night of it. I have a feeling that by tomorrow, if we ride all night, we can have us a little fun."

I was ready and said so, though I worried a little about missing Steenie's camp in the dark. But she should still have been most of a full day ahead of me, so I put that out of my mind and did my best to concentrate on the assignment at hand.

Of course, Al Bagley was ready for an all-night ride, and he quickly told us so. Gideon wasn't sure he could handle such an errand at his age. He explained that an aging man lost his dreams, his teeth, and his idiotic follies, in that order. But he further allowed that if we were so all-fired ready to show stupid, then he would have no choice but to ride along and keep us from getting ourselves killed, no matter how it pained him.

Eph thanked him for his magnanimity, and right there I picked up another word for my growing vocabulary. More and more I was sounding pure American.

Lifting my crippled dog up before me, I mounted, and with my little mare moving smooth as could be, I rode with my companions forward into the night.

Chapter 12

"Jons, do you think that dog can hold all the horses?"

I looked down at Lazarus. His recovery was coming along amazingly fast, and he could get about without much trouble. He had no speed yet, but when I removed the splint, that, too, would likely change. And in another day or two I would remove that splint.

We were all gathered in a shallow depression at the base of a high ridge, and it was from the top of the ridge that Eph proposed to make a scout of the country. But he didn't want the horses up there getting skylined, as Gideon put it. So they had to remain behind. That meant either I had to stay with the animals, or Lazarus did. And I was of no mind to stay.

"I think Lazarus can watch the horses, Brother Hanks. I don't know if he's been trained to do that, but if he has, then we should be all right."

"Of course he's been trained," Gideon growled as he started creaking up the hill ahead of us. "The dog did what he did down at Echo because he's been trained, and no consarned idjut is going to train a dog to gentle down a horse without also training him to keep that same horse in line once it's gentled. Don't worry about the horses. I guarantee with that Lazarus dog here, they'll be finer than frog's hair."

Eph grinned and nodded, and so together we started up the rocky, brush-covered slope.

It had been a long ride out of Echo, east across the night-darkened prairies. Eph had kept to the ridges and bluffs in case some of the army might have moved out ahead of the rest and were camped in the bottoms. But we had seen no one during all the long night, nor had we seen any sign of fire—just the vast, empty, rolling land.

During the night, we forded the Bear River at Spaulding Grove—and near daybreak, after riding over what Al called Pine Ridge, we crossed the Muddy and stopped for a bait of breakfast. Eph built the fire while I rubbed down the horses, and poor old Gideon stretched out on the ground and never even moved. His ailments were paining him fierce, and I felt bad for him. But he would have none of my sympathy, and so I had to leave him alone.

With daylight we were in the saddle again, climbing the side of a long ridge, and off to the south I could see some high mountains. I had seen them coming west, but for some reason I hadn't learned their names. Now I learned that they were called the Uintahs. On top of the ridge, which for some reason was called Aspen Mountain, the ground stretched away almost level, and it was covered with sage and very little else. Oh, we had passed small pockets of aspen and cedar or juniper, but other than that, the country seemed mighty desolate.

We took another rest at Mussleman Creek, and then Eph steered us across Bigler Bench, then south of Bridger Butte and around Fort Bridger, crossing Black's Fork and Ham's Fork of the Green a little to the south of the fort. Fort Supply, another Mormon outpost, was five miles to the south of us, but we didn't go there, either. Ephraim Hanks had one thing on his mind, and one thing only. He wanted to come up with the army in a hurry, and he didn't want to be interfered with while he was doing it.

The ridge we finally climbed on foot was far to the east of the Green River, Yates's trading post, and even Big Sandy Creek. It was about three miles from what Eph called Seeping Spring, and it was like most other ridges in that Wyoming country. The rock was basaltic, and except for sage and cedars and sparse bunch grass, the rise was barren.

121

Until a person has seen those wide, western, high-country plains and low flat-topped ridges, they can have no true understanding of the vast and empty land we were in. Of course, along the rivers were stands of cottonwood and willow, but other than that, the scattered cedars, and the endless sagebrush, the country was strangely empty.

For miles it stretched away, appearing flat and monotonous, though actually cut to ribbons with arroyos and draws and lifting volcanic drifts like the one we were on.

And the sky—the wide, eternal sky. Who can imagine such a sky who has never seen it before, stretching like a vast canvas from low and distant horizon to low horizon? And the Lord seemed to use it as a canvas, too. Where we crouched it was sunny, with the hill dropping away in golden hues below us. But off to the north and east a storm had set in, and the clouds were billowing in dark shades of blue, purple, and gray. Here and there streamers of rain slashed down like waving curtains, sweeping the hills and valleys before them, with others staying high and never coming to earth. We could also see occasional flashes of lightning, but it was so far away that the sounds of thunder never did reach us.

The land was inhabited by no one, used by no one but the Indians. And it was useful, as Al Bagley said, for nothing more than to hold the rest of the world together. Of course, the wildlife was there, herds of swift-running antelope and high-bounding muley deer. There were also crows, magpies, badgers, prairie dogs, hawks and eagles, and snakes, though it was so cold that we didn't see any of the latter at all. But I never tired of watching the antelope, their white rumps showing for miles and miles as they fled from us, returned to stare, and then fled again.

Finally reaching the ridgetop, we looked out over the land—and to my surprise, we saw a group of perhaps a hundred horsemen, with packs. They were upwards of ten miles away, but after a time we determined that they were coming somewhat in our direction. So we waited to learn who they were, as Eph felt they would come to us, and I occupied my time with watching a group of a dozen antelope that were grazing down below.

There was one huge buck in the bunch, and I was watching him in particular when Al Bagley interrupted my thoughts.

"A year or two back," he said quietly, "Eph roped a buck like that and dragged it home for dinner."

"Roped him?" I asked, amazed.

"That's right. He lassoed it with his rope and dragged it into camp for the men to eat. George Washington Bean told me about it. On that same trip, Eph killed a mother griz and roped her two cubs, which he carried into the valley and sold for a good profit. I've also been told that he has lassoed buffalo many times, for dragging them to camp alive is much easier than cutting them up and hauling the meat in."

I looked over to where Eph was reclined in the midst of a tall sage, relaxed as if he had been in the most comfortable easy chair in the world. He was watching the distant horsemen but did not seem bothered in the least that they were coming toward us. What manner of man was this, I wondered? Could any human possibly be so strong?

"Does he never feel fear?" I asked.

"If he does, I've seen no sign of it. I've seen him jump on buffalo and ride them until he tired of the sport, then jab them in the ponce and continue riding them until they fell, paralyzed. I've seen him ride alone into villages of wild Indians and come out again unscathed. I've seen him taken advantage of in trades and yet always manage to come out ahead. I even saw him shave off his long beard one night, at Brother Brigham's request. Everyone else scoffed at him for doing it, but Brigham was impressed by Eph's obedience, and in the years since, no one has been more trusted by the Prophet than Ephraim Hanks. Why, Eph has crossed these same plains on missions for Brigham all the way to the states and back, at least fifty times. And single-handedly he took in the first food to the stranded and suffering Willey and Martin handcart companies a year ago, having been impressed by the Spirit that they needed him to hurry."

123

"By jings," declared old Gideon, who had also been listening, "he's enough to make a good man feel like a sinner."

"What do you mean?"

"I mean," the old man said easily, "that few things are harder to put up with than a good example. Too confounded intimidating. Sort of makes us normal folks feel like throwing in the towel and giving up."

Al shook his head. "That's the funny part, Captain. Eph is so normal in every other way, it's scary. And *he* thinks he's normal in spiritual things, as well. He says there isn't a man or woman alive who can't enjoy the same spiritual freedom, or have the same spiritual courage, that he does."

Again I looked at the distant, silent scout. "How does he do it?"

"Well, he says that he wants to be close to the Spirit more than he wants those favorite little sins that most of the rest of us hang on to. Because he's willing to give them up, he's blessed with unusual protection. This is real personal, and I'm not sure at all that I understand what he's saying. But he has told me on occasion of a man in a gray tweed suit who has promised to watch over him. Eph doesn't know if the man is a spirit of an ancestor, or just who he is. But several times he has seen him, almost always in precarious situations, and never has Eph been injured. That is at least part of what gives him his courage."

Well, again I cast my eyes at the reposing man, and I found myself wondering, as I sat there, if I had such a guardian. I had never seen such a character, but then, I hadn't been overly spiritual in my young life and probably hadn't been worthy.

However, then and there I determined that I was going to become spiritual. I wanted angelic help like that, and I knew it wouldn't come until I was worthy of it.

Towards evening, to everyone's amazement but Ephraim Hanks's, the hundred horsemen reached the base of our hill and established camp at a small spring that bubbled there. We watched as they picketed their horses, set up their tents, and built cooking fires — and I realized that my heart was hammering with excitement as I gazed down at them. They were the army, all right, a company off on some scout. And there we were, four of us, to fight the whole bunch of them. As Gideon grumbled, it was enough to give a man the fluttering fantods, for sure.

After dark, Eph spoke. "Brethren, we've got to go down among them, find out what they're up to, and create a little havoc with their livestock. You all up to it?"

"I am," I said, feeling tremendously excited about the prospect.

"You know me," Al Bagley said quietly.

Gideon pulled himself to his feet. "Well, you know me, too," he said, his voice scraping low like a burro with a bad cold. "When there's heroin' to be done, some coward besides that crippled dog has to hold the horses. I'll be waiting there for you."

Well, all of us knew he was withdrawing on account of his age and slowness, so we chuckled at his humor and watched as he started hobbling down the backslope. Then Ephraim, Al, and I crept down and entered the camp of the enemy.

Al went one way, and I followed Eph the other, until we were crouched beneath the bushy boughs of a huge cedar. We had hardly gotten settled, though, when the crunching of boots warned us that a man was near.

"Sure," an Irish voice boomed from so close I jumped, "an' if the Mormons come tonight, we'll be ready for 'em."

The man stretched his long arms, breathed deeply, and spoke again. "Faith, boys, but it's a lovely land this is. Do ye smell the air of it, the cleanness and the sweetness of it? It's right glad I am to be here."

"You won't be so glad, Patrick, if one of those long-bearded Mormons should get the drop on you."

The man called Patrick laughed. "It's blarney you're blatherin', man. There won't be a Mormon in fifty miles, and if there is, he'd best be watchin' out for the swingin' mits of Patrick Mulhavey."

Several men laughed, and Eph and I listened as the men then talked of their mission, to find a road to the valley somewhere to the south of Echo Canyon. I grinned at that, knowing

125

that there was nothing passable that would admit of wagons. Horses and men, yes, but wagons and team? Not without a lot of work would they find a road through.

Of course, I suddenly thought, maybe there was some open canyon that the Mormon explorers had missed—

With a gasp I realized that the Irish soldier had spat, and what he had unloaded had hit me squarely on the forehead. I wanted to move but couldn't, and so I suffered in silence, waiting for the soldiers to return to their camp.

"Ahhh," he sighed as he returned to the fire, "I did na' think, when Donegal passed behind me, that I'd see another land so fresh and clean. 'Twas my wish to go back to Ireland a rich man, and to have the pick o' the lasses there. But now it's off to fight the Mormons I am, and maybe a wee pretty thing will be found amongst the lot o' them heathen scuts."

"You're dreaming, man," another soldier said as I desperately attempted to wipe myself off with a sage bough. "How can a woman with horns in her forehead be beautiful?"

"Horns? Go on with ye, mon, there's no such thing, even if they *are* Mormons."

Not waiting to hear the rest of that amazing discussion, we crept to the herd grounds, where we met up with a crouching Al Bagley. Both he and Eph Hanks had a good snicker over my recent misfortune, and I didn't blame them, though at the time I didn't see much humor in being spat upon.

As soon as the pickets had gone back to the fires for some supper, we stood and walked among the restless horses, removing the picket ropes, hobbles, and bells. Then, silently mounting some gentle-looking mares, we were off—walking slowly, taking the entire herd of horses and mules with us.

We rode west, far around the ridge and back to where Lazarus and Gideon were tending our horses, and there Eph dismounted and lashed his pack to a government animal. Al did the same, and then they both turned their own horses loose, knowing that their mounts would lead the entire band back toward the Valley, where the Mormon boys could gather them up.

With daybreak we sat on the hill again, watching the soldiers searching everywhere for their missing horses, and we all enjoyed a good chuckle over their discomfiture. Of course, their mission was now concluded, and they would have a long walk back to the place they were calling Camp Scott.

Suddenly the colonel of the group below walked straight toward the hill we were on, and straightway he climbed toward us. I watched him come from the bush I was behind, and I wondered why we didn't get out of there. But Eph Hanks, who was behind a tree, stood still, and the man came on.

Finally, when less than ten feet separated them, Eph stepped out with gun leveled and cried, "Halt!"

"Who're you?" the soldier asked as he raised his hands in surprise.

"We're a platoon of your long-bearded Mormons," Eph replied easily, fingering his own beard as he talked.

"Mormons? We were told they were all to the north and west of here."

"Just goes to show you can't believe all that you're told. Now Colonel, you might just as well call your boys off their search."

The man looked startled. "What? But they're looking for our horses. That's why I came up here — "

"You won't see them, even from here," Eph said. "The entire herd of livestock is well on its way to Great Salt Lake City, where it will be held safely until these foolish hostilities between your people and ours are concluded."

"Great Salt Lake City!" the man stormed. "Man, you can't *do* that! My men must have those mounts, and . . . and . . . by thunder, I'll sing out and the boys will have you surrounded in no time. Now drop that weapon, Mormon, and submit yourself to arrest."

"He'll not do it," Al Bagley said as he rose to his feet some fifty feet away. "You're the ones that are surrounded, Colonel. These woods are fuller of us long-bearded Mormons than a dog is of fleas, and if your boys have any respect for their lives, they'll be hoofing it back to their army post right *pronto*. Being mountaineers, we're real good at shooting down from heights such as this, and few of us are ever known to miss."

For emphasis, old Gideon stood up with his Henrietta pointed loosely at the man — and finally catching on, I stood up, too. Of course I had no weapon, but as it turned out, that didn't matter. The Colonel looked at the four of us and saw four hundred armed and hidden Mormons. He then turned tail and scooted down the slope, and in less than an hour the soldiers had packed up food, blankets, guns, and ammunition and were on their way to their distant post, moving double-quick on their shanks ponies.

And us? We spent the rest of the day gathering up saddles, pack bags, and other equipment, and hauling it all to a safe cache a mile or so south of our ridge. Altogether, it had turned into a dandy sort of encounter with the enemy.

Chapter 13

The next twenty-four hours seemed to me like one continual round of adventure. I didn't have time even to think of Steenie and where she might be, and I was so tired that I could hardly see straight. But except for a couple of quick cat-naps, Ephraim Hanks kept us on the move. We set several fires to burn animal forage so the government troops would have a more difficult time passing by. We hoorawed a couple of small units from the ridgetops, shooting in the air and riding our horses around and around to raise a dust like we were more than we were, thus throwing the fear of the Mormons into the poor souls and sending them scurrying back to their outfits. And, finally, we drove off a couple of herders and picked up fifty head of government cattle which we delivered to some of Colonel Burton's men.

But now it was night again, and we we sprawled out in a spring-fed, grassy swale about twenty miles east of Green River. I was doing my best to stay awake, and Lazarus was helping me by thumping me now and again with his bushy tail. Old Gideon had no dog, however, and he was sound asleep, his soft snores adding a gentle rhythm to the night.

The horses were cropping grass nearby, and every few moments Perdy would raise her head and look in our direction, making certain that the dog and I were still there. Satisfied, she would drop her muzzle and chomp down on more of the delicious feed she had found. Altogether it was a peaceful scene, and it was hard for me to keep in mind that enemies might be near and might even come upon us unawares.

"Al?"

Al Bagley rolled over and grunted at Ephraim's inquiry.

"Al, is it your turn to fix the grub, or is it mine?"

Sighing, Al laid back and closed his eyes. "Yours, Eph. I cooked it the night we picked up Captain Monson and the boy."

"You mean we haven't eaten a decent meal since then?"

Ephraim sounded shocked, and I grinned. I knew he was funning, but my stomach had been growling all afternoon, and now that I was no longer riding, the hunger was truly upon me.

"No, Eph," Al replied, "I didn't mean that. Hosea Stout fed us just forty or fifty hours ago, and that ought to be enough to last a good Mormon elder like you for two or three days, at least."

"Then I'm certain going to need to repent," Eph growled as he sat up. "I'm hungry enough to eat my pack, buckles and all."

"You may have to," Al said quietly.

"What do you mean?"

Now Al sat up. "I mean, I got to looking for our provisions this afternoon, thinking about supper. And unless you have them in your pack, they're gone."

"I don't have them, Al. You were to carry them."

"Then they're lost," Al Bagley sighed.

"Lost," I said, sitting up with the rest of them. "Where did we lose them?"

"If I knew that," Al muttered, "they wouldn't be lost, only cached, and I'd go back and pick them up. When I thought to check my pack this afternoon, I found that it had come open. I reckon our grub is scattered all the way back to Butcher Knife Spring."

Groaning, I lay back down — and Lazarus crawled to me and laid his head across my body. I scratched his ears, feeling bad about our hunger and feeling worse that it couldn't be solved. I was also feeling bad that the search for Steenie had sort of been swallowed up in the bigger issue of the war. I had no idea anymore where the emigrant trail was, or even for certain where *we* were. Nor had I talked to a single person all day who had seen Ben Crost's wagon. He might have been behind us, or he might have been ahead of us, I didn't know. For that matter, he might be camped directly across the next low ridge, and we would get up and move on, and I would never know of it. So, the uncertainty was there, and I was feeling pretty low about it.

But the hunger made it worse, it surely did.

"What you pilgrims intend on doing about it?" Gideon suddenly asked.

"What?"

"About supper, you consarned idjut! You young fellers may be able to go on forever without fodder, but old relics like me have got to eat."

"Same for us young relics," I said softly.

"All right, all right," Al muttered as he struggled to his feet. "I'll go out scouting. Maybe by morning I can scare up something to wrap our bellies around."

"Go west," Eph said quietly.

"What?"

"I said, go west. You won't need to go more than a mile. Then come back and tell us what you've found."

Shaking his head. Al saddled his horse, mounted, and rode away into the darkness. Gideon and I looked at each other. I shrugged, and he nodded knowingly—and then he laid back again and closed his eyes.

"Jons?" Eph suddenly spoke, his voice low and quiet.

"Yes, Sir?"

"You'll be wondering about Christena."

"I ... I have been, sir. Do ... you happen to know where she is? By inspiration, I mean?"

Eph shook his head. "I don't, Son. Wish I did—for I think the world of that girl, and of you, too. But maybe that sort of information isn't for me to know. However, the Lord has told me something, and you need to know it. I don't think you are going to find the girl, not galavanting around the country with

Al and me. I think you and Captain Monson had better take off on your own hook, heading back west — if you get my drift."

"You can't help us?" I asked.

"Not while I'm on a mission for the Prophet. But you won't need me, either. You'll see."

Stunned, I lay back and stared up at the darkness that I knew was lowering clouds. I was pretty sure that it was going to rain, but for some reason that was the furthest worry from my mind. I had truly come to depend upon Ephraim Hanks and Al Bagley, and I had felt certain that with their help, Gideon and I would have no trouble finding and getting Steenie back again. Now we would be going separate ways, and suddenly I felt lost and alone.

Somewhere in the distance, thunder rumbled, and the entire night felt heavy and ominous. I had seen no lightning, but again I heard a distant rumbling. Lazarus stirred next to me, then rose to his feet and whined. Seconds later, my Perdy mare came to us, and after she had touched noses with the dog, she lifted her head and stared off into the darkness.

"Horses are better than dogs for smelling trouble," Ephraim said quietly.

"That's so," Gideon agreed, "especially these little wild mustangs like your mare. What do you think she smells out there?"

"Or hears?" Ephraim added.

I didn't know, but by then even Lazarus had his head up and his hackles lifted. I sat tensely, waiting, not even realizing that Gideon had once again disappeared.

"Yo, Ephraim."

The voice was low, and with a sigh of relief I recognized it as belonging to Al Bagley.

"Here, Al."

A moment later the dark shape of Al's horse materialized out of the night, and with a grunt he dismounted. "Boys," he said as he leaned against his saddle, "I must be getting too old for this chasing around the country night and day. I got saddle-sores and a sprained finger, and my eyes hurt something awful.

132

My belly is growling out a Captain William Pitt's Brass Band marching tune it is so empty, and my head is pounding enough to add the whole percussion section to it. The sum of it is, I am tuckered plumb out, and if I wasn't so doggone hungry, I'd unsaddle and go to sleep right now."

"Hypochondriac," Gideon muttered as he stepped back into sight.

"What?"

"You can always tell it," replied the old man. "When a hypochondriac has measles, he spends all day telling you how many."

"Hummph," grunted Al Bagley.

"You must have found some food," Ephraim said, grinning.

"I did. Plenty. The trick will be getting it."

"You speaking of the army?" Eph asked.

"As ever was. I think we could sneak in there and steal it, but I didn't want to try it without I should tell you first. Besides, you said to come back and report, so here I am."

Ephraim thought a moment, then broke into a wide grin. "Better than stealing it," he said, sounding pleased as punch, "why don't we get Uncle's boys to give it to us."

"Eph, you know full well that the U. S. of A. Army isn't about to give their food supplies away to a bunch of rebellious Mormons. So what do you have up your sleeve?"

"You still remember any Sioux or Cheyenne, Brother Al?"

"Some, but more Cheyenne than Sioux."

"Good," Ephraim grinned. "Then let's stage us an honest-to-goodness Cheyenne uprising."

"You mean . . . "

"That's right, Al. You be the chief. You've got the nose for it, the dark eyes and the color, too. Besides, it won't take you but a minute to shave off that puny little growth you call a beard."

"Shave off my beard! I wouldn't shave—"

"Up to you, Al. But if I was as hungry as you say you are . . . "

Well, Al Bagley fumed and fussed, but in not much time he had a tiny fire built and was shaving off his beard. He was already

133

in full buckskins, so Ephraim added a mort of feathers out of his pack and then painted him with charcoal and white paint.

"Lawsy," Gideon said as he watched in wonder, "you do look like the genuine article."

"He can act the part, too," Ephraim said easily as he added some finishing touches. "Al spent a little time with the Cheyenne — two, three years ago. As I recollect it wasn't an intentional visit, but it turned out to be highly educational for both parties. Al got rid of a little extra blood, and old Roman Nose was surely pleased with those two copies of the Book of Mormon he ended up with when Al disappeared.

"All right, Chief. You set?"

"Ungh!"

I grinned, and Gideon clapped me on the back. "Watch close, Bucko," he said. "These pilgrims will either be teaching us a few tricks tonight, or they're about to learn a few new ones themselves. Whichever, I'm mighty anxious to go along and take me a looksee, for I ain't certain this will work."

"You're welcome along," Eph said as he saddled his horse. "Fact is, we might need a few extra 'braves' just outside of the firelight. For effect, of course, and not for any direct action. And don't you fret about whether or not this will work, either. George Clawson and I did this same stunt one night back in '53, and it came off like a charm. Besides which, the impression is powerful that it will work again tonight."

"Well, I haven't heard no Spirit say anything," Gideon said. "All the same, I hope you're right. Of course, I've learned that you can't tell how far a horse will run by the color of his hide. Maybe the same eternal principle applies to made-up Cheyenne chiefs."

"Maybe so," Eph replied.

"On the other hand," the old man continued, "I learned years and years ago that if a feller gets the drop on you, then the best thing to do is to smile and walk away. There's plenty of time to look tough when you're out of sight."

"Meaning?"

"Meaning maybe I'm overly cautious. But some men are so

stingy they'd skin a flea for the hide and tallow. If those soldier-boys don't want to part with their food and start lifting weapons, then I don't recommend pressing the issue."

"Sage counsel," Ephraim said softly. "However, I'm certain that all will be well. Should it turn out otherwise, we'll do as you say."

"And do it *pronto*," Al Bagley agreed.

After Gideon and I saddled up, we all mounted. Ephraim was then given hasty directions to exactly where he had told Al that he might find food, which was less than a mile to the west — and while he went off alone into the darkness one way, Chief Al Bagley, Gideon, and I went another.

We followed a deep ravine that led to the hills some distance above the soldiers' camp, and then we swung toward the camp and halted. Meanwhile, Eph, looking for all the world like an old mountaineer, and armed to the teeth with every weapon he had on this earth — and all of them showing plainly — followed the same ravine down the other way until he came to the trail the soldiers had made heading into camp. Then he turned and, sinking spurs to his horse, rode wildly up the trail and into their firelight.

From where we sat, we could see plainly the commotion he made, with the sentries stopping him and the soldiers spilling out from tents and jumping up from fires to surround him. Finally the commander of the men emerged from his tent to meet the stranger, and at that, Al urged his horse forward.

We pulled up several dozen yards outside the light, and while Al grinned, Gideon and I listened in amazement to Eph's windy tale of the heathen Cheyenne savages that the soldiers had spread camp right in the hotbed of.

"This ol' son's tellin' you pilgrims the gospel," Eph shouted. "Them bloodthirsty Cheyenne dog soljurs would think no more of peelin' scalps from you poor ignorant souls than they would of eatin' a chunk of raw buffalo liver after a hard day's hunt. And boys, raw liver is to them misbegotten heathen Injuns a purr-dee wondrous delicacy."

Right off men started running after rifles and Yeagers, and

135

the commander started putting more men out on perimeter patrol. But Eph stood in his stirrups and shouted them back in, and he yelled and cussed and kicked up a storm until every man was back listening to him.

Then he started in again to gussying things up, making conditions sound worse by the minute, until that whole entire camp was like a stick-swatted hornet's nest.

"You blinkin' idjuts," he raged. "Don't you know nothing about fighting Cheyenne? Get those rifles out of sight, and do it *pronto!* They get the idea you want to fight, and you'll all be dead. These braves is on the warpath, and they've swore the blood oath not to come back alive if they happen to run into anybody who is hankering for war. Now go on! Get them rifles under cover. You'll all be deader'n the last century if you give them Injuns the idea you want to fight!"

Without a word, every soldier hurried to restack his rifle, even as Eph had cautioned them to.

"That's better. Now listen to me, and listen good. According to the Cheyenne, you're trespassin', plain and simple. This exact spot is sacred ground, and the man who chose it for a camp ought to be whipped good and double-cursed by the meanest Cheyenne medicine man alive, who it so happens is right out there with another two or three hundred other unrighteously wicked warriors."

"Two or three . . . *hundred?*" several gasped.

"Aye, maybe four hundred, the way you boys is spending so much time augerin' with me. And now you pilgrims are starting to get my drift. Why, if you ain't packed up and out of here faster'n chain lightning with a link snapped, then I don't hold out no more hope for your sorry miserable lives than —"

"Oh, no. Oh, my merciful heavens, *no!*"

"What . . . what is it?" the commander asked, looking around.

"Hoofbeats, consarned it. I . . . I . . . Well, boys, that cuts it. It's been nice knowing you."

"Wait a minute!" the commander shouted. "What is it? Who —"

Eph swung his horse back impatiently. "You poor, sorry fools, that's Chief Ugly Face's horse I hear. Now I got to git—"

At that very instant, Al kicked his horse—and with a series of high shrieks and barks, he left my side and galloped down the hill at breakneck speed, letting out yells that would have done justice to a whole nation of Cheyenne warriors.

When he reached the camp, he slid his pony to a halt and began to harangue the bystanders in regular Indian fashion, at the same time swinging his arms and pointing to the mountains, hills, and plains.

By now the whole blue-coated outfit was standing open-mouthed, watching—and the commander, with flushed face, was wanting to know what the Indian wanted.

Reluctantly stating that he would find out, Eph rode forward and began talking with the "chief," using sign-language as well as Cheyenne. Finally he nodded, satisfied.

"Captain," he declared, turning his horse away from the disguised Al Bagley, "he wants you to understand that he owns this whole country as far as the eye can see—the land, the rocks, the rivers, the brush and trees, the birds and animals, and everything else that he can't think of at the moment. Further, he wants you to understand that you will have to pay dearly for the sacred bunch-grass your hungry animals have been devouring—not only tonight, but for the past five sleeps. Otherwise, he will give his five hundred men the word, and you will lose your scalps, just as sure as his name is Ugly Face."

"Andrews," the Captain shouted into the darkness, "are there others out there?"

"There sure are," a man shouted from so near Gideon and me that we both jumped. "There's at least two dozen right over here, and I can hear dozens of others all over the place."

Muttering, the captain shook his head, while Gideon and I both stared at each other, wondered who besides us the man had seen. We both breathed a sigh of relief.

"All right, Mister," the commander asked of Eph, "what does the chief want as tribute? I'm willing to pay anything within

137

reason, for we can't afford to get in a shooting war with the Indians. We're too busy fighting Mormons to let that happen. So find out, and we'll see what we can do."

After the "chief" and the "mountaineer" had had another spirited talk, Eph turned around again.

"Captain, I reckon you're getting off lucky. He says his people are hungry. All he wants is some flour, bacon, beans, coffee, tea, sugar, and tobacco. A good bait of all those items ought to do the trick."

The captain ordered the commissary to bring forth the desired supplies, and the order was immediately filled.

Suddenly, however, the "chief" began to jabber again, at the same time rubbing his stomach and making all sorts of horrid faces.

"What in the name of common sense is the old cuss kicking about this time?" the captain growled.

Eph grinned and explained to him that the wife of Ugly Face was very sick, and he wanted some good brandy to rub on her stomach. And, oh yes, he also wanted a little candy for his children.

Well, there was another order, a government horse was brought forward and loaded with a good U.S. Army issue pack, which was in turn loaded with the mound of foodstuffs, and in a short time we were all sitting less than a mile away in our little camp with everything our hearts could desire for a delicious meal. We cached the liquor, coffee, tea, and tobacco for possible trading later on, and then commenced to eat and laugh, feeling thankful for U.S. Army vittles.

Meanwhile, the captain and his men were also happy and busy congratulating themselves over the clever manner in which they had concluded the deadly threat they had faced.

"Brother Hanks," Gideon said as we cleaned up the last of the bounteous supper, "a lot of folks would do more praying if they could find a soft spot for their knees. But from now on, I ain't waiting for such luxuries. I aim to repent right along, until I get to where I can hear like you do. Why, that little drama was a pure delight to behold, and I thank you for the privilege."

Ephraim smiled. "You're welcome as you can be. What do you boys think you'll be doing tomorrow?"

Gideon looked at me and nodded, saying by his expression that it was my decision. So right there I made it, pure and simple. "We'll be moving on," I said. "I hate to do it, for this has been a wondrous education. But I've got to find Steenie, and I'm not going to do it chasing the army all over creation."

"You follow the Spirit, Son, and you'll find her sure as coyote-dogs growl."

And as Ephraim said it, I suddenly knew with all my heart that he was right. If I could just get in tune, the Lord would lead me to Steenie, and then tell me what to do when I got there.

Chapter 14

When I awakened the next morning, just as light was breaking in the east, Ephraim Hanks and Al Bagley were gone. Rolling over with a groan I sat up, put on my hat, stomped into my boots, and set about building up a fire. Gideon was still asleep, but Lazarus was at his tail-thumping best, whining as though he couldn't stand not being able to tell me good morning. And even my Perdy mare stood close in, tossing her head and blowing joyfully with the light of the new day.

I felt good about the day, too. Even with the two Mormon scouts gone, I felt good. I didn't know where we were going to find her, but somewhere roughly south and west of us had to be Ben Crost's wagon and my sweetheart, Steenie Bergman. No one in the other direction had seen any sign of them. So, given a little luck and a lot of the Lord's blessings, right soon she and I would be together.

Surprisingly, it hadn't rained during the night, but the sky was still threatening, and so I knew it was only a matter of time. Meanwhile, the overcast made things warmer, which helped, and I had no trouble finding dry wood—which also helped. By the time poor old Gideon opened his eyes, I had a cozy fire going, and breakfast was sizzling and smelling wondrously.

"Morning, Gideon," I said cheerfully. "Arise and shine. Daylight's burning out here."

"Looks more like she's ready to drown," Gideon grumbled as he stared skyward. "Friend Jons, I feel somewhat like I've been trod upon by a herd of stampeding buffalo. My pappy always used to tell me that if I woke up feeling halfway between 'Oh, no,' and 'My lawsy,' then I had overdid it."

"It was a tolerable long day, with an adventurous night," I agreed.

"Ummph. You maybe had ought to leave me here to go to my eternal reward, for I surely think the crossing of the River Jordan is close upon me."

Looking quickly at him, I tried to tell if he was being serious. "You truly feeling poorly, Gideon?"

"Worse than a calf with the slobbers. Trouble is, I don't reckon the good Lord is going to let me pass away without I should finish up my job getting that little gal back to you. So spread the table, for I'm about to be getting up."

Gideon dragged his blanket and tarp aside, revealing his bony old body in its patched underwear and scraggly socks. Me, I slept in my clothes, but Gideon wasn't of a mind to do that. He told me time and again that my body couldn't get a good sleep unless it got uncovered as a recognition that it was time for rest.

He lay still a moment, gathering determination. Then he propped himself up to a sitting position with arms behind him, and gently he eased his thin old legs off the side of the bedroll. Reaching to a nearby bush, he took his floppy wide-brimmed hat and settled it on his head—and I couldn't help but grin. At night he undressed from the bottom up, and in the morning he dressed from the top down. He told me when I asked him about it that no true man would get dressed or vice versa any other way—so I was trying to make it a habit of my own. And I was making some very minor progress, at least in that area.

Next Gideon took his frayed khaki shirt and fought the stiffness in his arms and shoulders to get it on, and then he fought again with the buttons of it to get them through the right buttonholes—his arthritis being a major obstacle to that endeavor. Next came the greasy leather vest, and with the aid of various snorts and grunts he finally shrugged into that. And only then did he roll over to his knees and slowly push himself to his feet.

I wanted to help him then—with all my heart I wanted to reach in and give the old man a hand. But I had tried it once, and he had snapped at me like a trapped weasel, letting me know in no uncertain terms that he could do this himself. So from then on I let my aging friend alone. But still I ached for him, I truly did. I had come to love Gideon Monson as I loved my own father, and it hurt to see him in pain.

Small things, like still managing to struggle into a shirt or pair of pants, were what gave him pleasure, though, and so I would not offend him by offering my help again. No, I knew that when he needed it, he would ask.

But his struggles also made me proud, too, for the old man was a fighter. And I knew that if he wouldn't give in to the miseries of life, then, by jings, neither would I.

Reaching his arms up and out, with me hearing—but not hearing so much as feeling—the creakings in the joints of his brittle old bones, Gideon stretched. Then carefully he took up his pants and nearly toppled trying to get his right leg in.

With a mumbled oath he hobbled to a convenient rock, sat down, and began to work the pantlegs one at a time all bunched over his feet and around his thin shanks. Then finally he could stand and pull them up into position. Giving a grunt of satisfaction, he tightened his belt. He then fastened the battered silver buckle that looked like it was of home manufacture but that, he had told me, had been given to him by a Cherokee Indian girl back in his younger days. For all I knew of his age, this could have meant before the Revolutionary War.

"I surely ain't so young like I once was," he grumbled while he battled his boots, stomping to push his heels all the way down inside them. "But I can still make it, friend Jons. Now, what's for breakfast?"

The next few moments we spent in silence—silence, that is, except for the lip-smacking time we each had downing those government vittles. I was beginning to think of myself as a westerner in every way—and judging by my new eating and speaking habits, as well as the increasing bow I was getting in my legs, I wasn't far off.

After we had eaten, Gideon looked down at Lazarus. "Jons, you reckon that wolf's ready to go it on his own?"

"It's hard to say," I answered. "But I'll tell you this. I think that *he* thinks he is. Come here, Lazarus. That a boy. Now, let me see that leg . . . Gideon, take a look. He doesn't even flinch when I pinch or twist it. And the wound is no more than a thin red line. Is it possible that he's healed so soon?"

"Well, Son, it's been four, nearly five days — and Eph Hanks did prophesy that the critter would heal fast. I'd say you should take the splint off and see how he does."

I did as instructed. Lazarus trotted off into the sage and back again, and some six hours later he was still going strong, acting as if he'd never even been shot in the first place. So, with my miracle dog ranging before us, we rode south and west across the wide and lonely plains. And as we rode, we saw more and more smoke from grass fires spotting the distant horizon, confirming our suspicion that Mormon patrols were still busily engaged. Then we topped a ridge and learned how truly unlonely the plains of Wyoming really were. For there, angling toward us, were a patrol of twenty or more long-bearded Mormon soldiers.

We all pulled up and eyed each other, and finally the leader, a lean young man with wide hat and twinkling eyes, spurred forward.

"Boys," he said, "if you aren't Mormons, then the Good Lord has led you into a heap of trouble — for you have been delivered into our hands."

"The Lord has preserved us then," I replied, grinning. "I'm Jons Soderberg, lately of the Valley, and this is Captain Gideon Monson, of the Battle of New Orleans fame. Perhaps you've heard of him?"

"Don't allow as I have," the other said.

"Uneducated pilgrims," Gideon muttered from behind me.

"And who might you be?" I asked.

143

"Major!" somebody in the rear suddenly shouted, interrupting us, "lookee there!"

We all turned to see where the man was pointing, and there was Lazarus, squatting in the sagebrush behind us, eyeing the group of men with skepticism.

"That your wolf?" the leader asked as Lazarus then trotted up and lay down beneath Perdy's nose.

"That's an often-asked question, and the answer is no. He stays with us of his own free will, which we appreciate. Besides which, he's a dog, not a wolf."

"Could've fooled me," the man grinned. "But he's acting like a dog, so I'll let it ride."

"That's awful kind of you," I said easily, with just a trace of sarcasm directed at his condescending attitude.

The man grinned again. "You're a strange kid, but well said. I'm Major Lot Smith, lately of Fort Bridger and headed back from the Big Sandy on a mission that accomplished a little pillaging and burning of the enemy's supplies."

Well, to me it was astounding to learn how many of the brethren were out and about on the plains, doing their own small parts to throw sand into the machinery of the army, thus grinding its progress to an early and winter-catching halt. And the amazing thing was how small most of the bands of Mormons were. This bunch of twenty was the largest I had seen, and yet they were just as confident as if they had been two hundred. That was, of course, because to a man they were convinced that they went in the strength of Israel's God, and that He would fight their battles for them.

"Until this morning," I told Major Smith, "we rode with Ephraim Hanks and Al Bagley, doing the same."

"So ol' Eph is already out. I wondered if he would be. Who's he working under?"

"As far as I know, he's ranging free under President Young's direction."

Lot Smith nodded. "Yes, that would be so. Why aren't you together now?"

I looked at Gideon, but he only blinked a couple of times,

leaving it all up to me. So I told it all, about Ben Crost and Steenie, and about our quest to find them and return her to the Valley.

"That's a tall order, Son. You met anybody who's seen them?"

"Not since Cache Cave. But I figure they have to be on the emigrant road, so Gideon and I are going to ride backward down it. Given time, we'll find them."

"Major Smith?"

Lot Smith turned toward his men. "Yes, Lewis?"

A man rode forward to side with the major, and for a moment or so they spoke in tones too low for me to hear. Finally Lot Smith turned back to me.

"Son, this is Brother Lewis Robison. He's quartermaster-general of the Nauvoo Legion, and he saw something you might be interested in hearing about."

"That I did," the man said quickly. "Lot and I had delivered Governor Brigham Young's message to Colonel Alexander at Camp Scott, forbidding either him or his army from coming any closer to the Valley — and commanding them to surrender their arms and ammunition to me.

"The Colonel declined the Prophet's order," he continued, grinning, "and he said so in a letter we were ordered to return. On our way back to General Wells with Alexander's reply, we rode within a mile of Mister Yates's trading post, down on the Green. Because I'm quartermaster-general, it's my duty not only to requisition supplies for the Legion, but to see that other supplies don't get into the hands of Uncle's army.

"Mister Yates is not a Mormon, but he's been friendly to our people for several years. So I stopped at his post to see if he had any gunpowder and to secure a promise from him that he would sell what he had to us. He was supplied with a few dozen pounds, which I bought all but a little of — as well as two Sharps rifles, which I also purchased. It was while I was leaving that I saw the wagon."

"Wagon?" I asked quickly.

"That's right, Son. It was a civilian wagon, camped down

145

on the river behind the post. I had the feeling that the folks might be runaway Mormons, so my horse 'accidentally' got real skittish, and before I could get it under control, it had pranced and sidestepped and bucked its way back and forth past their encampment. Sorta gave me a better look.

"But the point is, Son, that I believe they are the people you're looking for—man, woman, young family. There was a young lady with them, too, a right pretty thing. And I noticed that she watched me the entire time I was there, like she wanted to say something but didn't dare."

"Dark hair?" I asked hopefully.

"Dark, but sort of reddish. Real fetching color—and she wore it loose, not up, so it was easy to notice."

Well, my heart was pounding like I had just run ten miles. "It's her!" I breathed. "It's Steenie. Sir, where exactly is their camp?"

"It's on the Green, Son. But you can't go there alone."

Shocked, I looked from Lewis Robison to Lot Smith and back again. "But . . . but . . . I must, Sir! She's been abducted against her will, and she's depending on me to rescue her."

"Besides which," Gideon growled from a little way off to my side, "he ain't exactly alone."

For the first time, Lot Smith and Lewis Robison noticed my companion—or rather, for the first time they noticed my companion's rifle Henrietta, which was easily covering both of them with her single dark eye of death.

"So that's the way the stick floats?" Lot Smith asked, watching Gideon carefully.

"No, it isn't," I declared. "At least it doesn't need to be. After all, we're on the same side, and if you are as you call it, pillaging and burning, then Gideon and I are rescuing. It seems to me that we're both after the same thing—disrupting the army and protecting our own."

"And you say she asked for your help?" Lot Smith asked.

"Yes, Sir." I then pulled the slingshot from my rear pocket, ignoring the men's grins as I did so. That little elm-crotch sling-shot was *not* a well-respected weapon.

"She wrapped the note around the fork of this slingshot," I said, holding it up. "Fact is, I have her note right here, if you'd like to read it."

Smith nodded, so I put the old slingshot back, fished the note from my breast pocket, and handed it to him.

"It's a request for assistance, all right," Lot said as he read it. "Thing is, how do we deal with it?"

"You don't," Gideon said quietly. "She's our job, and we'll do 'er just dandy. You brethren have enough to worry over."

Lot Smith looked over at Gideon. "Feisty old cuss, ain't you? You sure you don't want to join my men in our fight with Uncle? You could do the Lord's cause a powerful lot of good and maybe wrap this entire war up by your lonesome."

Gideon merely looked at him.

"Well?"

"After some folks tell you all they know," the old man growled sarcastically, "they keep on talking. You fit the bill, Brother."

"Oh?"

"That's right. In the midst of all that verbal lather you've been whipping up, I said that I figure the boy and me are already in the Lord's cause."

Lot grinned at Gideon's response and turned back to me. "Son, wherever you got this old coot, you hang onto him. He's worth his weight in gold. Now, it seems to me that the best way to solve this dilemma is to work together. You try to ride from here to that camp on the Green alone, with all the government's boys out and about, and you won't have a prayer. But if we combine forces and put our noggins together, why, I think we can get that little girl back for you without much trouble. Either of you interested?"

"If we aren't?" Gideon asked.

"Then likely we'll all have a few problems."

Gideon's head came up. "That a threat?"

"Not hardly. We won't harm you at all. But Uncle's boys aren't very friendly, and what my men and I propose to do between here and Camp Winfield, which is near Yates's post, won't help pacify them at all. On the other hand, if we throw in together, we'll be moving fast enough that the word won't get out ahead of us, and we can lead you directly to their camp. Plus we'll be nearby to help you—that is, should you need it. What do you think?"

Gideon looked at me. "Son, the switching tail is always the one to catch the cockleburs," he said quietly as I looked at him. "The more you keep on joining up with every tomfool scout traipsing about on these miserable plains, the more likely you'll be heading for trouble. Howsomever, it's up to you."

Well, I knew that. And I knew, too, that my decision had better be right. Quickly I pleaded in my mind for the Lord to impress me with what I should do. I waited but nothing happened, nothing except that the more I thought about it the more it seemed like joining up with Major Smith was a smart thing to do. I didn't know if that feeling was an answer, but it was the closest thing to one that I was getting, so I decided to go with it.

"Major, we'll ride along. And Gideon and I will truly appreciate all the help you can give us."

"Good enough," the Major declared. "All right, men, let's move out. We've got work to do."

And so once again, Gideon and I were caught up in the maneuverings of the blossoming Utah War. But at last and at *least* we were finally doing it in the right direction again.

Chapter 15

It was dark, and the smell of rain was on the dusty land. There had been showers, two or three, though not enough to really complain about. But they had left the clean, fresh smell of newly fallen rain behind them, and I breathed deeply of it.

"Ol' Lazarus is doing mighty well," Gideon said quietly from beside me, where we sat on our horses in the darkness. "The Lord surely must have had a hand in the healing of his leg."

"It's hard for me to imagine that the Lord heals animals," I said.

"Why's that? They're his critters too, ain't they?"

Well, Gideon had me there, and I mortared up another stone of gospel truth in my shallow well of knowledge. Actually, I'd never thought of such a thing—but now that I had seen it for myself, it truly made sense.

"Friend Jons," he said then, "this is purely a risky business we're in the middle of. You sure you were following the Spirit when you agreed to throw in with these brethren?"

"No," I replied honestly, "but I was surely trying to. Until I get the hang of it a little better, that's about the best I can admit to."

"Well, I do hope you were right. Trouble is, I have this pain high up between my shoulder blades, and that has me worried. Of course, it might be my bursitis, but I can't tell. I'll say this, though, friend Jons. You and I had better be carefuller'n a couple of chickens on a fox run, or any help you can give that little gal might be nothing more than old wishes."

Nodding nervously, I looked off across the wide, dark land. There was something nagging at me, too, some awful dread that I couldn't place. Maybe it had to do with Steenie, and maybe it had to do with the raid we were about to make. I didn't know, but I was sure tight inside. Of course, like Gideon had said to me maybe twenty times in the past week, "If you don't have a choice, be brave." So I gritted down on my fears and did my best to get ready for whatever was coming next.

"All right, men," Lot Smith said quietly, "these teamsters are drunk as skunks, but the scouts say they have settled down some. So here's the plan. We'll ride forward until we're somewhat in the light, and then I'll do the talking. Questions?"

"Aye," a man called Big James said. Big James was an Irishman, and I had learned that he wasn't Mormon. He just happened to believe in the same ideas of freedom that the Saints did, and so he was fighting with them.

"Sure, an' ye've got a head count, Major, but in case ye've forgotten, it's outnumbered that we are."

"You're right, James. I thought there were twenty-six wagons, but it turns out there are fifty-two. I'd say, with the help of the Lord, that still puts the odds heavily in our favor. Wouldn't you?"

"It's a poor joke ye be telling us, Major."

Lot Smith looked right back at him. "This is not a time for joking, man."

James grinned widely. "Sure and you Mormons are blatherin' idiots, but it's ready to follow you I am. And if it's the Lord ye see fighting beside ye, Major, then tell him hello from Big James of County Cork."

There was a quiet chuckle from the men, and without another word Lot Smith spurred his horse forward toward the blazing fire near the center of the wagons.

"Who goes there?" a man standing with his back to the fire shouted as the column drew close.

150

"We're here to see the captain of the train," Lot Smith declared quietly. Then he signaled the column to halt.

"I'm the captain," another man said, stepping forward. "Name's Dawson. Who might you be?"

"My name is Lot Smith, Mister Dawson, and my boys and I have a little business with you."

"This is a passing strange hour for business, Mr. Smith. State the nature of it and then be on your way."

Lot grinned. "Very well, here it is. You are ordered to get all your men and their private property out of the wagons as quickly as possible, for my boys and I mean to put a little fire to them."

"For God's sake," the wagon-master exclaimed, "don't burn the wagons!"

"It's for His sake that I *am* burning them," Major Smith replied coolly. "Stack your arms over there, and then come back and stand here—all of you in a group.

"Lee Kimball and Jim Hewlett," Major Smith then ordered, "come guard these men. Bishop Steve Apple, you take a ride down toward Little Mountaineer Fork and set a scout there. Three rounds fired fast will let us know there are people coming. Four rounds will tell us they are soldiers.

"Mister Dawson," Lot then said, turning back to the teamster captain, "are your men making haste?"

"Yes, Sir, they are that."

"Well then, tell them to be double-quick about it. I have little patience with dawdlers and would just as soon burn personal property as otherwise, if it be in the way."

"Men," Dawson shouted anxiously while I grinned with the pure joy of watching this event unfold, "hurry faster. They're going to fire the wagons! Billy Cody, you and Bill Hickock get help with your wagons. You boys can't work fast enough for these Mormon fellers.

"Those two are just youngsters," he said by way of explanation to Major Smith, "but on that wagon bench they're mighty fine teamsters and can move a team with the best of 'em."

There was anxious scurrying then, and we were all watching

151

that, when from nowhere a mounted blue-coat rode up to the fire from a direction that Major Smith hadn't covered.

"Who's in charge here?" the young soldier asked.

"I am," Major Smith replied as he rode forward. "If you have dispatches, hand them to me."

"I have them, Sir, but they are verbal."

"Well then, sing them out. And remember, Son, if you lie to me, your life isn't worth a straw in a high wind."

The poor soldier, suddenly terrified, for he belatedly realized what was happening at the train and to whom he was speaking, began to shake and his jaws to clatter. And as Major Smith later said, it was from considerably more than the cool weather.

"Big James," Lot Smith then ordered, "take his man's mule and arms, and if he moves, even a little, shoot him on the spot."

"N-no . . . please . . . please don't kill me," the man sobbed.

"Sure and it'll be doin' ye no good to whine," Big James growled as he gave the man a poke with his pistol. "Soldiers' lives are worth very little around here. It'll be only the bull-whackers who get off easily, so stop bawling and stop quivering, or it'll be escaping I'll think you're up to."

The man dropped to his knees. "I'll . . . I'll give my dispatches, please, only d-don't shot me."

"And what are they, man?"

"I . . . I'm from Winfred, and . . . and I'm to tell the teamsters to be on the watch for M-Mormons. The . . . they're . . . *You're* in the field, and the . . . the bull-whackers are to put out g-guards. In the morning there will be . . . four c-companies of cavalry and two pieces of field artillery to . . . to protect them."

There was a round of laughter from the men behind me, and I joined with them. The poor man was so pitiful that he was funny, and knowing that he was actually safe from harm, I couldn't help but enjoy his discomfiture.

"Say there," another man said as he strode into the firelight, "what goes on there?"

Quickly swinging his rifle upon the surprised man, Lot Smith identified himself. "Now mister," he ordered, "where are you from?"

"The . . . the other train," the man responded.

"Then you get back to your train and don't move from there," Lot told him. "Don't do one single thing but wait, and I'll be up directly to take care of you."

The man took off like a shot, and then Lot Smith scattered a few of the men to make certain the first train was ready to burn. While they were doing that, the Major herded the frightened Mister Dawson ahead of him, and another group of us followed the two of them through the sage to where the second train was halted.

"Well," Lot said to the quaking man whom he had sent running a few minutes before, and who was still squatted down next to the closest wagon wheel, "you were wise to be obedient. Now step lively here, up beside Mister Dawson."

Nimbly the man sprang to the side of the captain, and shortly the two teamsters, with several of us lined out behind them, came to the wagon of the sleeping captain of the second train.

"Bill!" shouted Mister Dawson as he furiously shook the wagon. "Confound it man, get up, or you'll be burned to a cinder in five minutes!"

Bill suddenly displayed remarkable activity. He came boiling out of that wagon like it was already in flames. Major Smith then introduced the same program to him that had been introduced to Captain Dawson, and in a short time the arms of the second wagon train were in a pile and the teamsters and others were huddled under guard several yards away.

"It's amazing," Lot said then, shaking his head at Gideon and me. "Our boys appear to have dwindled to a mighty small body, but these sixty or seventy prisoners don't seem to notice it. General Wells prophesied that our numbers would be multiplied in the eyes of the enemy, but I never thought I'd see such a literal fulfillment.

"Captain Dawson," the Major then continued, "what sort of loading do you have? I have need of overcoats and gunpowder and would hate to see such items go up when I fire the wagons."

153

Hastily Dawson produced his bills of lading, for he truly didn't know what he had.

"Hunt the stuff up, yourself," Major Smith told him. "I'm somewhat busy at the moment."

Diligently, Captain Dawson began searching by the light of the fire, and in not more than a minute he announced that he had found large quantities of saltpeter and sulfur, which he claimed were not less dangerous than powder.

"Well," Lot said, shaking his head, "we'll have to take the risk of injury from it, for we can't separate it, and the train must be fired now. Any overcoats?"

"Not a one."

"Then fire it up!"

"Oh, please, Major, don't make me fire my train," Mister Dawson pleaded. "I've been sick and am not well yet, and don't w-want to be hurt."

Suddenly I became aware of a deep growling, and, looking down, I saw Lazarus staring off into the darkness, the hackles on his neck raised straight into the air.

Gideon, who could somehow see better in the dark than I ever could, was fingering his rifle as he watched in the same direction that Lazarus was pointing. And then, suddenly, he grinned.

"Major," my elderly friend interrupted as he signaled me to quiet my dog, "look smart, now. Here's a fellow coming up that's been afflicted with Saint Vitus' dance or some such malady, he's shaking so badly."

We all looked, and at last the poor soul moved into the firelight, gazing wide-eyed around him as he stumbled forward. "Why . . . why am I bringing in the oxen so early?" he asked with quavering voice. "Are we hitching up the t-train already?"

"No, sir," Major Smith told him, "we're *burning* it already. The oxen won't be needed here any longer, so we'll be taking them with us when we depart. Just bring them up and leave them with my boys, and then take your place here under guard."

"You . . . you're *Mormons?*"

"That's pretty near the truth."

154

"Well, then I d-don't think much of your methods. I should think you would have c-come sooner, and not waited until I was in bed and asleep and liable to be burned up."

Big James laughed. "Sure and it's a lucky mon ye be, old son. It's busy we are, and the luck of the Irish is with ye that ye even got called up at all."

The man stared, wide-eyed, looking from one of us to the other. "M- Mormons," he gargled in a strange sort of way, "real, honest-to-goodness Mormons. I . . . I never thought . . ."

Suddenly Lot Smith reached up and swept off his hat. "Since I'm bald," he said, grinning at the quivering fellow, "you can see that I have precious small horns. But they're there, none-theless, and I'm doing my best to make 'em grow. Now, shoo, before I butt you!"

The man, with a squeal, turned and ran, and I stared after him, astonished that he could believe such nonsense. But he did, that was evident, and I realized that he wasn't alone on this earth. There were many who were willing to believe almost anything, no matter how preposterous, so long as it pushed along their own preconceived but false notions of truth. And suddenly it was crystal clear to me why it was so all-fired important that a person learn to go to the source of all truth, to God Himself, to obtain answers. Only from the Lord could a man believe everything he was told and rely on it eternally. And only by relying on the Lord's information to him could a man ever hope to regain God's presence.

Soon everything was prepared in both trains, and we were getting ready to fire them when three shots in rapid succession came from Bishop Apple, down toward the Mountaineer Fork. Tensely we waited, and soon an Indian, a Ute brave, came riding alone into the firelight.

Since we were all awake, he was seeking presents—though I imagine, since Indians don't usually make social visits at such an early hour, that he would have taken what he wanted by grand theft had everybody been asleep. But Major Smith was feeling generous, and the brave went away elated with some flour, some soap, and two wagon covers for his lodge. Nor did he have to fracture the seventh of the great commandments to get them.

And then the major lighted his torches.

"Come, James," he said as he rode toward the wagons. "It seems fitting and proper for the Gentiles to spoil the Gentiles."

Laughing gleefully, Big James took up another torch. Then the two men rode from wagon to wagon in both trains, setting the covers afire. Meanwhile, a couple of the Mormon boys had several of Dawson's men separating two wagons from the rest and filling them with supplies.

"The boys down below will like this," one of the Mormons said, giving the hint to Dawson and the others that we were accompanied by an entire host of others who were camped nearby.

Soon teams were hitched to the wagons of supplies, and the other fifty wagons were sending a bright glow into the Wyoming night.

"By Saint Patrick, ain't it beautiful!" Big James exclaimed as he looked on in awe. "Sure and I never saw anything go better in all my life."

As I watched the billowing flames, I had to agree with him, though it seemed unnatural for the Lord's army to be wantonly destroying government property. However, I knew that our mission was simply to put time and distance between Uncle's troops and the Valley—and that by crippling their progress, so to speak, the hot air they were blowing would naturally cool down.

But now it was on to Steenie, and I couldn't have been more anxious, knowing that every hour of every day could possibly mean the difference in whether I succeeded or not.

Chapter 16

"Vasquez, I won't do it!"

Yates glared from behind the barrels and planks that served as the counter in his low-ceilinged, sod-walled trading post. It was not a large post, and it was overly full of hides, furs, traps, saddle tack, barrels of salt pork and onions, and just about anything else that someone crossing the great American desert might find use for. In short, it was a typical, side-bulging western trading post.

In the corrals down on the flat were a motley herd of horses, oxen, and mules, taken in trade because they were too jaded and worn to make the trip over the mountains to the west or the plains to the east. But Yates was feeding and resting the beasts, and in time most of them would regain their strength. For above all else, Yates was a connoisseur of animals, and he loved and took under his protective wing even the worst possible cases of travel-abused carcasses that came along.

But as if to prove to the world that he could also spot the good ones when they showed up, Yates kept in a separate corral, butted against the post itself where he could keep his eye on them, two horses of an entirely different sort than the beaten-down trades that were down on the flat. These two horse were tall, long-boned and long-bodied, well muscled and well bred. One was a Morgan and Standard cross and the other a Thoroughbred and Hambletonian cross. They were beautiful animals, rare animals, and they were born to run and race. They were also the pride and joy of the trader.

Only now it was not his two prize horses that he worried about. No, now it was the singularly dirty man who stood before him, as well as the two renegade Utes who stood back and behind. These three worried the trader Yates, and they worried him badly.

"You'll do it," Vasquez said quietly, his voice filled with malicious venom. "You owe me, Yates, and I'm collecting."

The man sighed and stared at the floor. "All right, all right," he agreed reluctantly. "But I'll be seen in blazes before I sell the powder to the army. They've got no business here, and they know it. Besides, I already promised the Mormons that I'd sell what I had to them."

"*Promised?* Since when did a promise to a Mormon mean any more than a promise to an Indian?"

Vasquez laughed at his own joke, but the other men remained still. So he grew quiet again, and, picking up a fox pelt, he began caressing it between his dirty fingers.

"So, how will the Mormons pay you? In scrip, or in trade?"

"Trade, I reckon. They're an honest folk, and I don't care how many pounds you have to sell, they'll make it good."

"At how much a pound?"

"I sold them a few pounds day before yesterday at two bits a pound."

"Cash?"

Yates shook his head. "Course not."

"Then it won't wash with the Mormons—neither the price nor the method. You take that train of mules outside and take it to the army today—and don't bother to come back without you have a dollar a pound, gold money."

"But . . . but I can't leave here," Yates protested.

"I'll mind the store," Vasquez grinned. "And Limpy and Knife will feed your animals. Oh, by the way, there's eight hundred pounds of powder out there. That means I want eight hundred dollars. But I'm a generous man, Yates. Anything beyond eight hundred dollars that you can get, we'll split fifty-fifty. So, do your best."

"And if I can't get a dollar a pound?" Yates growled.

Again Vasquez grinned. "Well, then, since you'll have our mules and powder, we'll have your store, and your two pet racers out back to boot. I'm sure, ol' Son, if we lumped everything in here together, with your pet horses tied inside here against the wall, it might be worth eight hundred dollars. Especially if we poured coal oil over the whole shebang and struck a sulfur match to it."

"You wouldn't dare."

Now Vasquez laughed outright, and the two Indians behind him joined in. "*Dare*, Yates? Don't even tempt me. Now, go on. You have until tomorrow night to be back here with the gold. Otherwise, the boys and I will warm ourselves by a nice fire and eat a hearty supper of roast horsemeat. And you can start hauling goods by stolen Mexican mule train again, just like we did fifteen years ago."

Yates shook his head in anger and frustration. But there was nothing he could do, and he knew it. He feared Vasquez, feared him with all his soul. The man was as cold-blooded as any man Yates had ever known. Nor were the two Indians hardly less so. But toward them Yates carried no animosity. They weren't of his culture and could not be expected to think as he did. But Vasquez, who murdered as easily as he took a drink of water —

"Mister Yates . . . "

All three men whirled to the startlingly clear, feminine voice that came from the doorway behind them, and Yates felt his heart sink. He had forgotten about the runaway Mormon family down on the river, and he had forgotten most especially about this lovely girl who was traveling with them. But now Vasquez and his men had seen her, and, as Yates watched the leering expressions on the faces of the three renegades, his heart turned cold as winter ice.

"Well, well, well," Vasquez said as his eyes burned into the girl in the doorway. "Do come in, honey-child."

"Thank you," she said spiritedly, "but I will wait out here until you are finished. Then I will speak with Mister Yates."

Vasquez laughed. "Then you will have a long wait, little sister. Mister Yates is just now leaving on a mighty long journey."

The girl turned back, confused. "But . . . but . . . "

"Christena," Yates said as he came hurriedly from behind the barrels and planks, "you go down and wait with your family. I'll be back from delivering this gunpowder to the army by tomorrow night, and then you and I can conclude our discussion about the young man with the slingshot."

"Slingshot?" Vasquez laughed derisively. "Is some young sprout coming to protect her with a slingshot? Or to fight the army with it? Ha, ha! A slingshot . . . "

"Don't mind him," Yates said as he stepped out through the low door. "You just wait down below with your family, and I'll be back as soon as I can get here. And whatever you do, stay away from those men in there."

Steenie smiled and then beat a hasty retreat from the men inside the post. But as she walked away, her skin crawled, and she knew to the depths of her soul that she had been in the presence of evil men, men more wicked than any she had encountered before in her life. Oh, if only Jons were there . . .

"Well, boys," Vasquez said as Yates rode away with the string of loaded mules behind him, "by tomorrow night we'll be eight hundred dollars richer."

"Unngh," grunted Limpy, "and the little *tsharr* squaw?"

"Ah, yes," Vasquez said with an evil grin as he turned inside the room, "the lady. A likely looking creature. In Taos or thereabouts, she might fetch upwards of two hundred dollars. But I've a feeling that she's worth more than that, much more. If Arapeen, or Hunkootoop even, got a good look at her, well — I'd give my best saddle if one of them redskinned heathens wouldn't give five hundred American dollars to make her their *numero uno* squaw."

"What of the squaw for today?" Limpy asked hopefully.

"Until we get her to the *kibah*, to the mountains."

160

"You don't touch her!" Vasquez ordered. "Not either one of you. Not until we are ready to go tomorrow night. You hear me, Limpy?"

Bear That Walks with Crippled Foot nodded agreeably, for he knew what came of arguing with his white boss. But neither did he worry overly much about his commitment. There was time, and there were ways . . .

Knife, on the other hand, said nothing to either of the others. But his dark eyes were glued to the place out in the sage where the girl had disappeared over a small rise of ground. And he noticed, as he stood there, that his breath was coming much more rapidly than it had in years.

At long last, he knew, he had found the squaw he had dreamed of for so many difficult seasons. She was not exactly as he had pictured her, true. But this white girl with the fire of sunset in her hair took his breath away. Further, she left him with a deep longing in his belly that was like nothing he had ever before known. Yes, he would have her, and with her he would disappear into the mountains far to the south, where he would return forever to the true ways of his people.

"Knife?"

Without turning, Knife grunted that he had heard.

"I mean it," Vasquez growled. "The girl is mine, and I want full value for her when I *nar-o-wap*, when I trade her. Touch her and you're *e-i*, dead. Now get out there and see that our horses are fed and watered."

"Oh, Stinking Little Willow," Limpy added scornfully in Ute, "remove the *timbi-up* and the *carri-nump*, the bridle and saddle, from my pony before you take care of your own. Then make haste to see that my pony is happy with grain and a good rubdown. Afterward you may care for your own. *Pe-nun-ko*, in the future you will do this always, for the ponies of squaws are always taken care of last."

Limpy laughed. "Do otherwise, Stinking Small Willow, and *Tabby* will smile down on an *e-i* fool, a very dead little willow."

Without a word Knife went out the door. But in him was a burning hatred, and anger that startled him with its intensity.

161

No longer was he one with those two in the white trader's *paquy-nary* wickiup, his stinking lodge. Now it was just he, himself, *towats*, a man of the Southern People, who with his *tsharr* squaw, his white woman, would go off into the mountains to dream his happiness.

From where he stood trembling with anger and determination, Knife could not see the girl's camp. But that did not matter. He knew where it was, and he knew also that before *tabby-moushy*, before sunrise, he and she would be gone. And if that meant that Limpy and Vasquez would have to die, then so be it. He would see to that, and see to it with pleasure. Nor, he decided as he broke into one of his rare smiles, would they die easily. Neither of them deserved that privilege.

Of course, Knife thought as he drew his blade in a motion swift as thought, it would be the one called Limpy who died first. That went without saying. His eyes flashing, the scrawny little man drew his thumb along the razor-sharp blade of the Spanish knife, feeling the narrow slice of it into his flesh.

In his mind he could see the big oaf called Limpy, staked over an anthill and sobbing silently, tonguelessly for mercy as his flesh was sliced and peeled. The mental image felt good, better than good, and from that instant Knife began to plan.

Chapter 17

Trying not to worry about the men she had seen at the post, Christena sank to the wagon tongue. Ben Crost was off looking for a stray cow, and it had been her first real opportunity to get away from her bed and finish her talk with Mister Yates. Of course, he had come to doctor her when they had first arrived, and knowing that a real illness couldn't be faked, she had confided in the trader, explaining to him what she was trying to do.

He had winked in response, told her not to worry, and then had told Ben and Maria Crost that "the poor little thing" shouldn't be moved for at least three days. So for three days Christena had been "recuperating." But now Mister Yates was gone, and Christena felt a deep foreboding about the men up at the post.

"Steenie, what's the matter?"

Christena looked down at the small boy who had spoken. Maria was down on the riverbank, washing clothes. The two younger children were with her, and so Christena and Daniel Crost, Ben and Maria's eldest son, were alone at the wagon.

"Nothing's the matter, Danny."

"Are you all better now?"

Christena smiled. "Yes, I am feeling much better, thank you."

But then, when the boy's face showed his great relief, she sighed. Of all that had happened, this was the worst for her, the guilt over fooling poor Maria and the children. They were so sincerely sympathetic, and they treated her so nicely, that it really hurt her to carry on her charade. Yet there was no other way, for none of them knew of Ben Crost's threats against her, or of his lustful desires. So it was him she was fooling, him she was holding off until such time as Jons would be able to rescue her. Then, when she was free, she would tell the rest of them, and all would finally be right.

For the hundredth time she scanned the horizon to the west, hoping to see Jons riding up to get her. But the land seemed empty, devoid of life, and sighing with discouragement Christena turned away.

"See this?" Danny asked as he held out his hand.

"What is it?"

"Arrowhead."

"Can I see?" she asked.

Danny held it out in his open palm.

"Christena looked, amazed. "That's pretty. Where did you get it, Danny?"

The child waved a hand toward the hill rising north and east of the bluff. "Yonder. There's more of them there, too."

"Could I find one?"

"Maybe, if you look sharp, and if you're lucky."

Feeling unaccountably bored, and certain that Ben wouldn't be back for some time to catch her in such a healthy state, Christena smiled at the boy. "Will you take me there and let me look?"

"I don't know. What would Ma say?"

"She wouldn't mind. It isn't far, is it?"

The boy shook his head. "But you'd be scared, I bet."

"Scared? Danny, what's there to be afraid of?"

"Ghosts of dead Indians that these arrowheads killed," the boy responded seriously.

"Did you see a ghost?"

"No, I never. But that doesn't say they ain't none. You really want to go?"

Christena nodded.

"Okay, and you don't have to be scared. I'll take care of you."

"I'm *not* scared," Christena declared, smiling at her pint-sized escort.

Walking together, the two started up the bluff, toward the sharp-rising hill. Climbing it, they followed the top, descended a narrow draw that headed toward the trading post, and came to a bare level place in the midst of some brush, part way down the slope.

"See," Danny said, indicating a circle of fire-blackened stones almost covered with dirt and sand. "This was where they roasted each other, I bet."

Christena giggled. "Indians didn't do that, silly. You're thinking of headhunters or cannibals. But I'll bet this was a real Indian camp, just the same. Have you come here a lot, looking for arrowheads?"

"Naw, just once. I found some old bones, and I was looking for more."

"Bones?"

"Yeah. Mister Yates told me there were old elephant bones up here, buried in the bank. He even has a big, yellow tusk down at his post, and a picture of an elephant, to show what it looked like."

"An elephant, Danny? There aren't any elephants here."

The boy looked seriously at her. "I know, not anymore. Mister Yates says they lived a long time ago, before even you or he were born. He says they are ex . . . ex . . . well, 'ex' something. It means they are all dead now, like the ones I was looking for. He said a man offered him eighteen whole dollars for that tusk, but he didn't want to part with it."

Danny stopped suddenly, picking up a piece of stone almost as large as a man's fist. It had been chipped along one edge and was quite sharp.

"See this? I'll bet an old Indian made this, too."

Christena looked carefully at the stone. "You're right, Danny. I'm sure that was a scraper, something the squaws used to scrape the fat off a buffalo hide. Ephraim Hanks told me about that. Just think, years and years ago, a busy young squaw knelt right here in this exact spot and scraped a robe, getting it soft and ready for her new husband. It was the first buffalo he had killed since they had been married, and so she was doing her best to make it perfect, just so he would be happy. And I'll bet he was real happy, for she was the prettiest and sweetest maiden in the whole tribe. She was also—oh, look, Danny! I found an arrowhead!"

Christena held it up for young Danny's inspection.

"By golly, you sure 'nuff did. Come on, let's see if we can find some more."

Eagerly the boy began to search, his head down, his attention fixed upon the earth at his feet. Christena, almost as excited, followed suit, and for several minutes they cast about the camp, moving in ever-widening circles, looking for the next arrowhead.

Christena never knew what made her suddenly look up, but when she did, her heart almost stopped. There, not a dozen feet away, his eyes boring into hers and a fiendish grin on his face, was the huge Indian she had seen earlier in Mister Yates's post.

"Unngh," the man grunted, "good for little squaw to come to Great Bear. Save him trouble."

"Danny," Christena whispered, trying to calm her terrible fear.

"Yeah, I . . . Gosh, Steenie," he gasped, "look! A real Indian."

"I . . . I know, and he isn't a nice man, either. When I give the word, Danny, run up the hill and then around and down to the wagon, just as hard as you can. We can run uphill faster than him because we're smaller and lighter. You ready?"

The boy, three or four feet away, his eyes wide with fright, nodded slowly.

Christena took one step backward, and with a gruff roar the big Indian leaped forward. Only he staggered because of the old wound in his foot, and that momentarily slowed him down.

"Run," Christena shrieked, and then she and Danny were off like rabbits, running up the steep hill, dodging past brush and rocks, and straining for the top. Behind her, though Christena feared to look back, she could hear the man's big feet scratching the gravel, she could hear his labored breathing, and she knew that he was coming on.

Off to her left, Danny was also scrambling upward, seeking the top of the steep ridge. He darted past a large boulder, and suddenly Christena had an idea.

"Help me!" she called frantically to the boy. Then, scrambling, she got behind the boulder and started pushing. After a few seconds, Danny joined her, and together they pushed, pushed, pushed—

The rock moved, tilted, and finally began to roll, a slow, ponderous roll—then it fell free and started downhill, leaping and bounding, right at the huge Indian.

He heard it and looked up, eyes bulging, and then he gave a great and twisting leap to one side and hit the scrabble rolling. Down he went, the boulder narrowly missing him as it crashed past.

The Indian started to rise, staggered, and fell again.

"Quick," Christena cried, "another one!"

Scrambling after her, the two got behind another boulder and shoved and pushed. Down it went after the other one, leaping and bounding, followed by a torrent of smaller rocks, some of them flying high as they fell—all of them cascading about the fallen Ute.

"Come on," Christena shouted without looking to see what damage they might have inflicted, "let's run!" And they did, scrambling up the hill, sprinting along the top and sliding and tumbling down the far end. Sprinting, though out of breath, they ran across the flat to their wagon—and there they were greeted by a surprised Ben Crost, who had just ridden up.

"Pa," Danny shouted, "Pa, help! Steenie and me was attacked by an Indian, and he's still a'coming."

"Sounds like a fun game," Ben Crost replied, never taking his eyes off a breathless and absolutely-surprised-to-see-him Christena Bergman.

"Feeling better?" he asked. And then, before she could

answer, he turned his horse away to stake out the recovered cow.

"Good," he then said over his shoulder, responding to her silence. "That means we can pull out with first light. Be ready."

Christena stared, the new horror compounding with interest the one she had just escaped — and with a sigh and a sudden gushing of tears, she slumped back to the tongue of the wagon.

What would she do? Mister Yates was gone. Jons was not there, and it didn't look like he would make it before morning. Could she stall longer? Or would it be better if she just allowed herself to be taken farther eastward, hoping against hope that Jons would travel faster than the wagon and ultimately catch up with her?

Christena didn't know the answers, but she was pondering the issue so deeply that she didn't see Ben Crost, standing by the tethered cow, staring at her with haunted eyes. Nor did she see, back on the slope of the high hill, the smaller Indian called Knife. He was bending quite joyfully over the unconscious form of his huge, former, and hated companion, and he had some rope and his razor-sharp blade in his hand.

To say that he had expected the huge Bear That Walks with Wounded Foot to be so summarily delivered to him would have been an untruth. But to say that he was not prepared to act immediately upon Limpy's unconscious condition would have also been false.

"Unngh," Knife grunted in great satisfaction. "It is a fitting end to my *no-ni-shee*, to my dream." And then, haughtily, he looked off in the direction of Ben Crost's camp, where his other dream slumped on the wagon tongue.

"Get ready, little white squaw," he breathed, "for I will very soon finish what must be done here. Then I come with the darkness and the two big horses from behind the post, to take you to my *put-te-ent*, to my home. Truly you will make a fitting wife for the great Knife. *Poo-suds-a-way-ah?* Do you understand?"

Chapter 18

"Son," Gideon said from where we sat our horses on the rise above the small trading post, "It looks mighty quiet down there."

"Do you think something's wrong?" I asked quickly.

"I reckon. You see the wagon out there on the flat?"

"I see it."

And I did. Not only the wagon, but every detail about it, including the fire-blackened bows and the breeze-flapping remnants of burnt wagon cover. I also saw, in the late afternoon light, that it looked hopelessly abandoned — and I knew in my heart that I had arrived too late.

"Go easy," Gideon called as I spurred my Perdy mare down the hill, but I wasn't interested in going easy. I had the worst feeling in the pit of my stomach, and it was all I could do to hold back the tears. I knew that wagon had belonged to Ben Crost, and the fear was rising in me that I would find him and his wife and children, as well as my Steenie girl, dead.

With Lazarus running beside us, my mare pounded past the sod trading post, past the eerily silent corrals, and over the side of the low bluff that dropped to where the wagon stood, mute and alone. Sliding to a halt, I was off and running around the wagon, looking for something, *anything*!

Only, I found nothing but ruin and desolation. The wagon, with the name Crost carved into the tailgate, had been burned where it stood, and it had been burned long enough before that the fire was out and the charred wood had turned cold. Some of the Crost family's belongings had been scattered about—but most had not, and had burned and smoldered inside the wagon. Still, there were no bodies, no evidence anywhere as to the fate of the family.

In pain and frustration, I kicked the charred wheel spokes, and then the tears finally came and I sank to my knees while Lazarus came forward and rested his head on my lap.

Why had I taken so long? Why had I thought that by coming with Lot Smith's men I would be better off? I *couldn't* have been inspired! Not seeing what had happened here around me. Oh, if I had only come straightway from the Sandy—

"Jons?"

Gideon's cracked voice caused me to look up, and I saw him sitting on his horse back on the low bluff, a little to the right of where I had jumped Perdy over.

"Boy, you'll want to come take a look."

I knew that Gideon had found the bodies, and with heavy heart I pulled myself to my feet and stumbled across the flat and up the bluff. But when I got there, I found I had been wrong, and for the first time I began to feel a little hope.

The single fresh grave was marked with a simple board, and on it was only one name, that of Ben Crost.

"That your man?"

"He was Steenie's uncle," I replied woodenly.

"Then we may be in luck, Son. White folks buried him, which means they didn't all die."

"Yeah, but Ben surely did. I . . . I . . . "

But I couldn't say any more. All I could do was stand there, with silent tears in my eyes, and think of Ben Crost. I had come mighty close to hating him, which Ma had warned me against but which I hadn't been able to stop. I had wanted to beat him, to pulverize him, to make him sob out his apologies to me and to my Steenie. I had even thought of killing him, or at least I had wondered if I could. But now he was dead, gone, and all I wanted to do was cry. It was like a big, empty place had opened inside me, and it hurt, it hurt!

"You all right, son?"

"I . . . I don't know," I sniffed. "I thought I hated him, Gideon. But now I'm sitting here feeling so bad for him that I'm crying. I don't hardly understand . . . "

"It's who you are, Son."

"Who . . . I am?"

"That's right. You're the blood of Israel, boy. You know, a descendant of Abraham, Isaac, and Jacob, which Jacob's name was changed by the Lord to Israel. You're descended straight from them. And Jons, the Lord gave Israel the responsibility to love and bless mankind, and that 'love and bless' sort of blood flows in your veins. Being righteous, like you're trying to be, it'd be wrong to feel anything but sorrow for the man."

"But . . . but he took Steenie, and he had evil designs toward her."

Gideon grunted. "Maybe, but that don't make no difference in how you should feel toward him, especially once you get past the anger. Fact is, the more wicked he might have been, the more you had ought to sorrow for him. Unless the man's repented recently, which doesn't seem likely, then the poor misbegotten fool died in his sins. And that's tragic, Jons, terrible tragic! The whole world ought to sorrow after the death of a man like this."

Well, I could see what Gideon was saying, and of a sudden I began to understand a lot of other things. Like why the Lord was always sending out missionaries. Or why Gideon and Eph Hanks had turned so strongly against the shedding of blood. Or why Pa was always helping folks out, paying special attention to the ones who likely didn't deserve it. Or why Ma was always praying and exercising the bulk of her faith for her enemies. It was their heritage not to hate, but to love and lift and improve the lot of other people. I'd got that from them, being their son and a member of the Lord's earthly kingdom as well, and that was why I'd never been able to imagine, even wildly, the actual killing of Ben Crost.

"He . . . probably had lots of good points," I said quietly.

"Most of us do. It's nice to know that the Good Lord takes all them points into account, ain't it."

"It surely is. Poor fellow. Maybe if I'd got to know him better, I would have liked him. I surely did like his wife."

"Speaking of which," Gideon said, reining around, "where're the rest of the folks that had ought to be here?"

Helplessly I looked up. "Only . . . only the Lord would know that, Gideon."

Gideon looked hard at me. "Yeah, I reckon He would. The trick will be getting Him to tell us. Too bad friend Hanks is not nearby. He seemed to have a pretty good conduit into Heaven."

The old man was interrupted by Lazarus's growling, and we turned to see the dog on the uphill side of the post, facing a heavy clump of brush. With hurried step I ran up the slope and, pushing past the brush, came upon a sight such as I had never imagined, even in my worst nightmares. I was still staring, horrified, when Gideon pushed his little mustang through the brush and stopped beside me.

The man on the ground had been an Indian, of that there was no doubt. But when I say ' had been,' I mean that literally — for his body had been systematically destroyed until it was almost beyond comprehension. He had been a large man, large and very muscular. But someone had somehow overpowered him — and then had tied him, spread-eagled, between four deeply driven stakes, positioning him so that his lower back arched over a red ant hill.

"Whoever did that was good with a knife," Gideon said.

I nodded, but I didn't speak for fear of losing all I had eaten. Yet still I stared, and as I did I found myself wondering at the cruelty that had driven someone to do such as this to another. For there was not a place on the man's entire body that had not seen the slow and patient work of the murderer.

Of course, the Indian was dead, but he had not been dead while the cutting had been going on — and the expression of horror on what was left of his face mirrored that of my own.

"Friend Gideon," I whispered as I rubbed Lazarus's head

to calm him down, "what . . . what do you think happened here?"

The old man shook his head. "I haven't the least possible notion, except that this occurred no later than yesterday. Remember that, Son. Lot Smith and his boys not excepted, we couldn't have got here in time to do a thing about it.

"As for the rest, that wagon looks Indian burned, and this here is sure enough an Indian. But he's been kilt by other Indians, or by folks who want to make it look that way. Either direction doesn't make much sense to me. From the looks of the flat down yonder, Crost wasn't robbed of much. Indians are like that. They're also partial to taking captives of women and children and making them over into their own people. But if that's the case, who in tunket buried Crost, and where is the trader who runs this place? And last but not least, why did this poor soul get used up in such a sorry way?"

Well, old Gideon was only thinking out loud, not asking questions, so I remained silent. But I had no answers either, only that Ben Crost was dead and that Steenie was gone.

Again.

Slowly I turned away from the dead man, my mind whirling and my heart aching with sorrow and fear. Would I ever find Steenie now? Which way could she possibly have gone — or with whom?

Somehow this all seemed my fault, for if I had only been there a little earlier . . . But no, Gideon had said that the man had been dead for at least a day and maybe more. That being the case, I *couldn't* have helped! But if that was so, then why was I feeling so awfully guilty?

With head down, I made my way past the trading post, Lazarus and Perdy following closely behind. But I paid no attention to them, for my head was spinning and hurting so awfully that I couldn't even think. Finally, out of pure pain and anguish, I dropped to my knees and began at last to sob.

Later, when I was pretty well spent, I realized that I was praying. It hadn't been intentional, I don't think. Rather, I was praying because there was no one else I could turn to. Oh,

173

Gideon was there, but he didn't have any more answers than I did. But God had the answers, I knew that, and from what Ephraim Hanks had told me, if I wearied the Lord long enough, He would grant me what I asked. So now as I prayed, I realized that I was asking only one thing, and I was asking it over and over again. *Which way had my beloved Steenie gone?*

I prayed and prayed but still felt nothing. The shadow of evening started up from the bluff above the Green, and the warmth of the sun was suddenly gone. But still I stayed on my knees, pleading, praying . . .

"Jons, we had best get along."

Looking up, I stared at the old man.

"To where, Gideon? The foxes have holes, and the birds of the air have nests, but I don't hardly know where to go any-more — not now that Steenie has been taken from me again. Oh, lawsy, I just wish that — "

"Son, a wishbone ain't no substitute for a backbone."

"What?"

"You want that little gal, prove it! Stop feeling sorry for yourself. Get up off the ground and get after her."

"But I don't know which way she went."

Suddenly an idea hit me, and, lunging to my feet, I ran to the empty horse corral behind the post. On my knees again I examined the dirt near the gate.

Nothing!

No sign of the splayed hoofprint of Ben Crost's horse.

Jumping up, I sprinted down off the bluff and onto the flat below, and in just a moment or so I saw that the horse hadn't been in that corral, either. Running then to the burnt wagon, I soon found where the horse had been staked. Ranging out, I began walking slowly in a big circle, and in less than five minutes I had found the track heading south along the river, moving at a high lope.

"Gideon," I called, "does hurried trail of splayed hoof mean pursued or pursuer?"

"In this here instance," the old man said as he drew up his

Kettle horse and studied the trail I had found, "it means pursuer. See how the splayed print is over the other?"

"Then friend," I grinned thinly, "the Lord has given us the direction that somebody took my Steenie. I would think—"

But I never got to finish what it was I had been about to say, for Lazarus gave a warning growl, and Gideon and I turned to find ourselves facing the aimed rifles of three bearded men.

Chapter 19

"Which one of you is Yates?"

The men were obviously Mormons, so I did my best to smile.

"Neither of us, Sir."

"Then whatcha doing here?"

I looked closely at the man, wondering what was troubling him. I had been questioned by other Mormons, but never before had I felt such anger or bitterness from the questioner.

"Friend," Gideon said from behind me and off to my left a little, "the boy said neither of us was Yates. We ain't, and that concludes any right you might have had to hound us with questions. Keep pressing, and it'll be the last pressing you'll do."

The three looked at Gideon, saw Henrietta's solitary dark and unblinking eye, considered for a moment or two what they were looking into, and backed off. A little.

"Very well," the man said softly as he lowered his rifle a few inches, "*please* tell us who you are and why you are here at Yates's post."

"Be glad to," I answered. "The past few days we've been back and forth across the plains with Lot Smith and Ephraim Hanks, kinking the government's works — but today we left them and came here, seeking the one I love. Trouble is, the Indians got here first, and now we're trying to work out their trail."

The men consulted briefly, and then the lead fellow began

quizzing us again. "You say you know Lot Smith and Ephraim Hanks? Describe them for us."

Gideon shook his head. "Lawsy, Jons, there's no more pleasure in some folks's company than in a wet dog's. Makes me ashamed to be in the same church as these heathen idjuts."

I nodded, described Eph and Lot, and threw in Al Bagley's description to boot, but even that wasn't enough. I could feel these men's suspicion almost as though it were a blanket that had been thrown over me.

"Well, anybody could've met those fellers," the one man said. "But if you ain't Yates, do you know where he is?"

"We've never seen him in our lives," Gideon replied. "Now for the last time, who are ye?"

"Mormons," the man replied. "My name's Bill Finkman, and these are a couple of the boys assigned to fight this war with me. We have word that Yates has turned traitor on us, taking up with the Indians and selling gunpowder to the army. All along he's told us he would do otherwise, but now Mrs. Crost tells us —"

"Mrs. Crost?" I asked quickly, interrupting him. "You fellers have seen her?"

The man nodded. "We found her and the little ones hiding down river a piece and took her captive. Her husband had been killed by the Indians ol' Yates had taken up with, probably the same ones you mentioned, so we came up here and buried him. Since this morning, the boys and I have been waiting for Yates, for the man has turned traitor and must be dealt with."

"We heard that Yates was a fine man," Gideon declared then.

"Not hardly, not when he tampers with the Indians to turn them against our people, and when he helps arm the troops to come against us. Oh, I know folks such as Dan Jones and Eph Hanks swear by him, calling him liberal in his views and kind-hearted and other such rot. But the boys and I have the goods on him, and he won't be getting away."

I shuddered at Finkman's vehemence. More than anything else I wanted to get away from these men, as far away as I could. Something was wrong with them, something that didn't feel right. But I couldn't leave, not until I had learned from Ben's wife what had happened to Steenie.

"Do you know where Maria Crost is now?" I asked.

"She's at camp with a couple more of my men."

"Will you take us to her?"

The man grinned. "No problem with that, is there, boys? I don't hardly — "

"Say, what goes on here?"

Spinning, we all looked as a burly man started his horse down the bluff behind us, a string of mules following him. Unconcerned, he reached the level and rode forward — and if he noticed that the rifles of Finkman and the others had shifted and were pointed at him, he gave no note of it.

"Howdy, boys," he said as he drew rein, "you here for supplies?"

"You Yates?"

"As ever was."

Finkman grinned. "Then you're under arrest for a dirty, low-down traitor."

"Now wait just a confounded minute — "

"Take his guns, boys."

Without a word the two rode forward and relieved the trader of his rifle. A quick search revealed no hand gun, and so they roped his arms behind him. Then one of the men dismounted and tied Yates's feet under his horse's belly, the other slipped a riata over the horse's neck, and then they backed away.

"Just like that, huh?" the man said bitterly. "No trial or chance for explanation?"

Finkman shook his head. "We're not that hard. You'll have plenty of chance to defend yourself. Now come along — "

"Wait a minute," Yates said, suddenly pleading. "I've got some fine thoroughbred racing stock that needs caring for, out back. And there's a runaway Mormon family that I should tell."

"You have no stock left at all," Finkman averred. "Your Indian brothers took every horse and cow on the place. Likewise, they killed Ben Crost before they left."

178

"They *what?*"

"You heard me."

"Yeah, I reckon I did. And the girl?" the man asked, sounding anxious.

"Crost's wife's fine, though pretty upset by what those heathen friends of yours did. Traitors turning on traitors. The Lord's using the wicked to use up the wicked, I say. But you'll be seeing Crost's widow soon enough, and you can answer your guilt to her yourself. Now let's ride!"

We started out, and though I wanted with all my heart to talk with Yates, I couldn't do it. Finkman and his boys were still suspicious of Gideon and me, and it felt like we were riding under guard the entire short journey.

"This is awful," I muttered to Gideon as we rode.

"Amen, Son. But when things don't please you, the best medicine is to swallow a little tincture of time. Our chance'll come."

"You actually think this is going to help me find Steenie?" I asked, surprised.

"You were given your pa's blessing, weren't you? And Eph Hanks told you that you would find the gal. Was I you, I'd start believing. That's called having faith, Son."

"Yeah, I suppose it is. But Gideon, these are mean folks we're amongst."

"True enough. Most folks feel just about how they've made up their minds to feel, and these pilgrims have simply concluded to be miserable. That's their problem, not ours. As for being meaner'n hydrophoby skunks, Son, just you remember that hard-boiled eggs tend to be yellow inside."

I snickered through my emotional pain and was told to knock off the chit-chat. In less than two miles more of silent riding, we came upon Finkman's camp. It was located on a small spring in the bluffs along the river, and it was a nice spot, I had to admit.

It was almost dark when we rode up, and the light from their small fire hardly helped. But finally I saw Maria Crost, and seconds later, after I had dismounted, she recognized me.

With a squeal she ran to me and threw her arms about my neck, and that did a lot to help me feel better.

"Jons—oh, Jons . . ."

"Sister Crost," I said, trying not to cry again, "I . . . I'm right sorry about your husband."

"I . . . Oh, Jons, he never had a chance."

"Ma'am," Yates exclaimed from behind me, "what in thunder happened?"

"That's enough out of you," one of the men who had ridden with Finkman ordered, and for the moment Yates grew silent.

"So you know each other," Bill Finkman said to Maria Crost and me as he dismounted and came toward us. "That must mean you're *all* runaway Mormons. Such doings need to be dealt with."

The man's animosity was amazing to me. It was a thing that could be felt, and I hardly knew what to do about it. The thing was, I didn't want to turn my back upon him, no matter what the occasion. I know Gideon felt it, too, for he never stopped glaring at Finkman and the group of men who were with him. And, too, old Henrietta was always on the ready. The whole situation made me wish, for the first time since I had left home, that I carried a gun of my own, no matter what Eph Hanks had told me.

"Sister Crost," I said, "do you know what happened to Steenie?"

"Only that I know who took her, Jons. It was during the night, and something awoke me. I don't know what it was, but I lay in my blankets for some time before I became aware that the wagon under which we slept was on fire and that I was seeing movement out in the dark. I crawled from under the wagon, and there was just enough light from the growing fire for me to see Christena being pushed onto the back of one of Yates's big Thoroughbred horses. She . . . she looked dead . . ."

"No," I cried, "she can't be . . ."

"Son," Gideon said softly, "remember the prophecies and blessings. Besides, it don't make no sense for some fool to haul

off a dead body. More'n likely the little gal was only unconscious."

Bleakly, I nodded. "What else?" I asked the Widow Crost.

"I . . . I suppose I gasped with fear and surprise. That was
when the Indian, for so he proved to be, stopped tying her and
leaped upon the other Thoroughbred, and in a second the two
were gone. It was only after I could no longer see them that I
started to scream."

"Which Indian, Ma'am?" Yates asked, ignoring the threat
of the man who guarded him.

"Yates, so help me—"

"I'll help you!" the bound trader thundered, glowering at
the surprised guard. "I'll help your black soul on its way to
hades if you don't back down.

"Now Mrs. Crost," he said gently, turning back to her, "you
go ahead and answer me. Which Indian was it took the girl?"

"The . . . the little one. I never saw the other one at all,
except for just a minute, up by the post. But . . . but I shouldn't
have . . . have screamed! Oh, if only I hadn't carried on so when
I saw Christena taken."

"Why the dickens not?" I asked, not understanding. "Surely
the voice of warning had to be raised."

Maria Crost wiped at her eyes. "P . . . perhaps. But the cry
did not bring Christena back. Instead it hastened . . . oh, why
did I cry out as I did?"

Maria Crost dissolved into deep, wracking sobs, and it was
only gradually that I learned from her how Ben had leaped to
his feet at her screams and had pulled the groggy children from
under the burning wagon. Then he had grabbed up the rope of
his splayed-hoofed horse to give chase after Christena. He had
only just gotten it saddled and climbed aboard when out of the
darkness came running the dirty, buckskinned white man who
had ridden in with the two Indians.

In disbelief that had turned quickly to rage, the man listened
to Maria Crost's terrified account of Steenie's abduction. And
then, with no more thought than if he had been shutting a door,

181

the man had lifted his gun and had shot Ben Crost from the saddle, killing him instantly.

Stepping to the frightened horse, the man had yanked the reins to settle it down, jerked Ben's boot from the stirrup where it had caught, and then had vaulted into the saddle.

"Limpy!" he had shouted loudly, yelling into the darkness in the direction of the post. "Limpy, you listening to me?"

There was no answer, and so with a string of curses and Ute words that she didn't know the meaning of, the man had spurred Ben Crost's horse viciously and had ridden the squealing animal into the darkness, following after the little Indian and Steenie.

"That was José Vasquez," Yates said quietly. "He's a mean one, all right. I'm sorry it had to be your husband that got in his way. And it was the crazy Ute called Knife that took the girl."

For a moment Yates stared ahead, deep in thought. "So old Knife split the blankets with them, did he? He must have taken a shine to the girl when she walked into the post yesterday. That's good, in a way, because he won't hurt her, at least deadly hurt. He just wants her for his squaw."

"His *what?*" I asked, horrified.

"Squaw. But like I say, that ain't the real problem. The fact that Vasquez went after him tells me something else. It tells me ol' José had his eye on the girl, too, though probably not as his squaw. Vasquez is a slave trader, Son, and that little filly is likely to be worth several hundred American dollars, even from the Spanish. From the Utes she might bring a good deal more. And that, as I see it, is the real problem."

Well, poor Maria Crost was fit to be tied, and I was even worse off than that. Steenie, my Christena Bergman, being sold into slavery? I could hardly comprehend the thought. And worse, I had no idea what to do about it.

"Two things," Yates went on, thinking out loud. "If the girl and Knife are on my two racers, which looks likely, there's little hope that Vasquez will catch them. Lightning is a Thoroughbred and Hambletonian cross, and Dancer is a Morgan and Standard cross. Both of them are bred for distance racing, and they're both good at it. So far as I know, there's nothing alive that will beat my racers."

Gideon, seated beside me, snorted in disgust. I didn't know what had upset him, of course, but I didn't think that then was the time to find out.

"You said that *two* things bothered you?" I asked.

"Aye, that I did. The second is that big Indian Vasquez called Limpy. He could be anywhere, and wherever he is, the man is trouble."

"Not anymore he ain't," Gideon squeaked softly. "Leastwise, I reckon it's him that won't be bothering folks no more. In the brush upslope from your post, staked over an antbed and cut up something fierce, lies the mortal remains of a tolerable big Indian. His moccasins were there, tossed into the brush, and they had a peculiar sort of bell design beaded onto them. I've never seen the like."

Yates looked startled. "That's Limpy, all right. And you say he's dead?"

"For at least all of today. The magpies have been at him, and maybe the crows, too. But all that was after his killer had got through cutting. So yes, friend, he was real dead."

"If he was cut up," Yates said then, thinking further, "that has to have been Knife's work. Torturing with a blade is what he likes to do. There must have been bad blood between them for a long time for this to happen, but with an Indian it's hard to tell."

"Do you know the direction the Indian might have gone?" I asked then.

Yates considered. "Maybe. I know they rode south. Last I heard, Vasquez had a camp way south of here, down on the confluence of the Dolores and Grand Rivers, near the Santa Fe Trail. So, far as it is, maybe he's going there. Fact is, now that I think on it, Knife used to be a southern Ute, from down off thataway. The story is that his people cast him out years ago for killing his mother, but you never know. Taking up a squaw like he's done, he might be figuring on going back."

"He won't make it," I said, "not if I can help it. I'll get Steenie back if it's the last thing I ever do."

"Hold on, Son," Yates said, sudden alarm in his voice. "There's three, four hundred miles betwixt here and that camp, hard miles of mountains and desert, most of it filled with angry Indians and meaner whites. Besides, Knife is on my racer. You'll never catch him, Boy, but you'll likely die trying."

"You'll die trying to leave here, too," Bill Finkman said quietly. "You'll all be going back to the Valley as my prisoners. The Saints don't hold with spies running out here and spilling their guts to the government ninnies about what they saw in the Valley."

"Friend," I said, anger making my voice tremble, "you're sure enough mistaken. We aren't spies, unless it was Ben Crost, who has passed beyond the veil and is of no further threat to anybody. But for us, there is no guilt.

"Now Gideon and I will be going, and you'll be giving me your word that Sister Crost and her children, as well as Mister Yates, will be escorted to the Valley in safety."

"Not hardly, I won't," Finkman snarled, lifting his rifle as he spoke until it was pointed roughly at me. "I said you were my prisoner. You ain't a'going—"

But Bill Finkman's orders were cut short in a terrified scream as a scraggly dog came hurtling out of the darkness to clamp vice-like teeth upon his arm. The rifle exploded harmlessly, and both dog and man slammed back to tussle with each other on the ground. Finkman continued to scream, and Lazarus continued his silent attack, intending, no doubt, to use the man up. But finally I called him off, and with raised hackles and stiff walk the dog backed away.

"You can educate a fool," Gideon said with disgust as he looked at the injured man who was scrunched on the ground. "You can educate him, all right, but you sure can't make him think."

"Brother Finkman," I said as I climbed aboard my Perdy mare and backed her toward where Gideon sat with rifle ready, "swear that the Crost family and Mister Yates will get to the Valley safely."

"I won't swear nothing," the man growled as he nursed his dog-bit arm. "I told you they were traitors and warmongers. Now get them, boys!"

"Anybody raises a rifle will never raise another one."

The voice from the darkness was soft, but it had an electrifying effect upon the men who stood around the fire. As one they lowered weapons and backed up a step or two, and then we all stared in surprise as Lot Smith and several of his men stopped into the light.

"Lawsy," Gideon breathed beside me. "I never thought I'd be glad to see that feller again."

"You boys all right?" Lot asked.

"We are, but ... "

Lot Smith grinned through his long beard. "We heard it all. I told you we might be of some use to you, and by the time some of the boys get Sister Crost and her children safely back to the Valley, my word should have been pretty well fulfilled. Maybe I'll become as much a prophet as ol' Eph Hanks."

"Smith," Bill Finkman growled, "these people are my prisoners, and I won't have you interfering."

"I am *Major* Smith to you, Finkman," Lot Smith said sternly, cutting the man off, "and I direct you to remember that.

"As regards your charges, you may have a case against Mister Yates, and a fair trail down in the Valley will determine that. Therefore I order you to escort him there immediately. As for the Crost family, I shall take charge of them personally.

"Now, Brother Soderberg and Captain Monson," he said as he turned his attention to us, "you said something, I believe, about taking a ride to the south."

"Yes, Sir, we did."

"You'll be needing fresh horses, I suppose? And weapons?"

"Fresh horses," Gideon grunted, "wouldn't make it. Kettlebelly here will do just fine for me, thank you."

"Do you think I should do the same?" I asked Gideon quietly. "Keep my Perdy mare?"

"Up to you, Son, but my feeling is that one ought to dance with them that brought him."

Well, I looked down at the dingy gray mare who stood motionless beneath me, and I wondered. We had covered several hundred miles in less than a week, she and I—and I knew she had done her best for me. Now I looked again at her stringy mane, her big head and short neck that were joined like the two parts of a hammer, and at her flanks that were hollowed with use and hunger. Perdy was smallish and stunted, and there wasn't much about her that would catch the eye at a first glance. But if a man looked again, which I had had occasion to do quite often in the past five days, he might note the depth of chest and the strength of bone beneath the dirty hide. Or he might notice the trim neatness of legs dropping down to rock-hard hoofs that had no need of being shod. Scrubby, yes, but scrubby proud, as shown by the swelling of that short neck holding that almost-too-big head. Perdy, in spite of the name I had given her, was not pretty, nothing splendid or noble looking. But she was filled with power and endurance in her compact solidity, and the look of eagles showed occasionally in her eyes. I felt certain she would stay.

Besides, beneath the mare's nose squatted Lazarus, his tongue hanging out, his eyes resting upon her. And I knew that he would never forgive me if I gave over the horse he had personally trained for my use.

"Brother Smith," I said, "good ol' Lazarus seems to have spoken, and the mare it is who will carry me, as Eph Hanks might say, into the camp of the Philistines."

"Is that the southern tribe we'll be visiting?" Gideon asked by way of a joke—and to the ring of Lot Smith's laughter, the boys packed a mule with supplies, and we started south into the darkness.

Chapter 20

For Christena Bergman, regaining consciousness was not much of a blessing. She had never been in such pain, and every jolt of the big horse made her wish that she could once again drop into dark oblivion. She was draped over the saddle like a sack of grain, and her hands were secured to her feet under the horse's belly. A coiled bullwhip tied to the pigin strings on the saddle kept knocking her in the head—which was throbbing anyway—and she knew from the taste in her mouth that she had been sick. Worst of all, though, was the fact that she couldn't get enough air. Each jolt of the horse smashed into her abdomen, and gasp and struggle as she would, she could not adequately fill her lungs.

"Help," she cried into the darkness that was just turning gray with morning, "help me please . . ."

Nothing happened—so she drew air, held it, drew in more, and finally let it all loose in a scream of which she felt justifiably proud. There, she thought, that ought to bring that evil and unsympathetic Vasquez back to help her. And Christena knew that the man who had taken her, who had somehow knocked her out and tied her to this horse and abducted her, was the man Mister Yates had called Vasquez.

Again she held her breath and screamed, again and again, until finally she felt the horse dragged to a quivering stop.

Seconds later rough hands reached under and freed the

ropes from her ankles, and then unceremoniously she was pulled forward off the saddle and dumped onto the ground.

"Now you listen here—" Christena started to complain, when a moccasined foot kicked her in the ribs, sending her reeling. Gasping with the new pain, she struggled to her knees and looked at the dim form of the man who had kicked her. She had barely come to the realization that it was not the filthy Vasquez, when his hand slapped her in the mouth, sending her stumbling once again to the earth.

"Squaw no talk," the man stated with guttural emphasis. "Squaw listen to *towats*, to man, and obey. More *at-am-bar*, more talk, and this!"

He slapped her again, hard—and with a sob Christena rolled over on the ground, the salty taste of blood filling her mouth.

Instantly, the Indian grabbed hold of her hair and pulled her to her feet. Then, roughly, he squeezed her arm.

"Good! *Tshar nan-zitch*, white girl, learn fast. You make okay squaw for Knife, maybeso you do what I say. *O-net-shpee*, conceive many sons. But for now you ride. Get back on *kuvah-u*, horse."

Sobbing, wide-eyed, and frightened, Christena struggled to mount the huge horse. She was not fast enough to satisfy the Indian, however, for he slapped her again. He then boosted her into the saddle and quickly tied her feet under the horse's belly—causing terrible cramps in her legs.

Laughing at her cry of pain, the Indian leaped aboard his own horse and kicked it viciously, and the two were once again flying up the gradually lightening trail.

For a time Christena tried to shut out all thought, to force her mind into oblivion. But gradually an awareness of the strength of the beautiful horse she was riding stole upon her. She had truly never been upon such an animal—and after a time she found herself no longer reveling in self-pity but marveling instead at the flow of muscle and sinew beneath her. The horse, a sorrel, was incredibly pretty, and as morning rays crept across the peaks to the east, its beauty became more and more evident.

Christena had seen the horse before, back at the post. She had even admired and petted both it and the one the Indian was riding. So she knew that both animals had been stolen. Yet with strength and courage, the stolen animals galloped along the trail. The girl marveled at that and gradually began to take from the horses a little peace of her own.

The Indian was abusing his mount terribly — kicking it, flaying it with a quirt, and not giving it adequate rest. Christena's own mount, the sorrel, was heavily lathered, and she knew it would be only a matter of time before the horses could run no farther. For her that would be good, and so she pushed thoughts of the horse's pain from her mind and concentrated instead on the animal's courage and her own hoped-for rescue.

The country they rode through was higher, now, and dotted with juniper — more commonly called cedars. They followed a deep canyon, riding high on the rim, and she could see that a dim trail led ahead of them toward the snow-covered peaks. Also ahead were slopes covered with thick stands of timber — pine and fir — and she realized that the Indian was taking her high into the mountains she had heard called the Uintahs.

For a moment she felt panic, wondering how Jons would ever find her there. But then the confidence of the stolen horses struck her again, and instantly she began to feel better. If animals could go forward courageously, then so could she.

"Heavenly Father," she pleaded in a quiet whisper, "I know that thou knowest where I am. Wilt thou please tell Jons and give him the power to find me? And Father, please give me the strength to do what I must do until Jons comes for me . . ."

The sun was an hour high when the Indian pulled off the trail and into a clump of trees. There was a seep there, enough water for the horses and themselves. And so without a word the man dismounted, untied Christena's feet, and ordered her to dismount and build a fire.

Slowly she complied, wondering as she slid down what she would use to accomplish her task. Then, almost in answer to her silent question, the Indian threw a bag onto the ground before her — and within it she found some coffee and some other foodstuffs.

"You fix food," the Indian declared. "Me eat. Then we *ah-be-quy*, then we lie down — together. Later we *ep-weh*, we sleep."

With numbness and horror, Christena worked at building a fire and then fixing a meal from the bare necessities she found within the sack. She wanted to run but could think of nowhere to go. She thought of stealing a horse, but she knew that, after having removed the saddles, the Indian had staked the animals firmly. There would no be time.

Over and over she prayed, pleading that Jons would come quickly and save her. But he did not come, nor did anyone else. She was alone on the mountain with the scrawny Indian who called himself Knife, and she knew that if anything was to be done about her situation, she was going to have to do it herself.

But she could think of nothing.

As the coffee boiled and as the food cooked, Christena sought desperately for escape — and finally she found a little relief, of sorts, in her imagination. In that mental citadel she saw herself in a snug cabin, somewhere back in the Valley with the Saints, happily married to the handsome Jons Soderberg.

Of course he was away somewhere, taking care of a Church calling — so she was lonely for his presence. But the children, four of them, were in bed, and now she was standing outside, the wind in her hair, the glittering stars giving her comfort. Off in the hills a coyote cried, and she smiled at the sound, liking it. Behind her, the windows of the cabin reflected the glow from the fire, and from down in the corral there was a faint stirring among the horses.

Goodness, she would be glad when Jons returned. She needed love, she needed tenderness, and Jons had given her both. Now he was gone, but soon he would be back, and the joyousness of their lives would continue.

Stepping back inside the cabin and closing the door, she looked around the shadowed room, lit only by the lantern and the faint flickering of the fire.

A loft above was for the children, and down below for her

and Jons there was a double bed, a table, some benches, a chair — pots and pans shining upon the wall or near the fireplace, the hard-packed earthen floor — would she ever have a plank floor, she wondered? There was an aroma of cooking food in the air that lingered from their supper, almost as if it was burning —

Slap!

Reeling from the unexpected blow, Christena looked up in shock. The Indian was standing before her, his face dark with anger. At his feet rested the pan of cooking gruel — on its side in the grass where he had kicked it — smoking with a deep scorching. Raising his hand, the man slapped her again, sending her rolling and tasting more blood, and then he strode over to stand above her.

"*Katz-te-suah nan-zitch!* Foolish girl! *Pe-nun-ko*, in the future you will pay attention to what you do, or I shall beat you until you have no face left. Now *wo-tun*, kneel down before your man!"

Stifling her sobs, Christena dragged herself to her knees, and when the kick came she rolled with it and hardly felt the blow. Nevertheless, it stung, and she wanted to cry out with the waves of pain she was experiencing. But she didn't cry out — and when she realized that, she suddenly took perverse pride in her silence. She wouldn't cry out — she wouldn't give the mad Indian the satisfaction! She would be like the two thoroughbred horses — silent, strong, enduring, waiting for Jons to arrive —

She had heard that Indians often beat their wives, but she could not believe that such brutality or cruelty actually existed. Only now the ringing in her head, the salty taste in her mouth, as well as the pain in her side, gave terrifying evidence of what she had heard.

"Father in Heaven," she again pleaded as she lay on the dry grass next to the two saddles, "help me . . ."

"Come," the man growled, still standing by the fire, "spread the blankets. There will be time enough to *tick*, to eat, later."

Staring blankly at him, Christena closed her eyes, willing herself to be somewhere else. Nothing changed, however — and

191

so, steeling her mind against whatever might be coming, she rolled to her knees to stand up.

And saw before her, still tied to the stolen saddle, Mister Yates's well-used bullwhip.

Having mastered the use of the whip while crossing the plains the year before, Christena stared at the whip, realizing that the Lord was answering her prayers — and suddenly she knew what she was going to do.

"Squaw hurry!" the man growled from behind her — and with a low cry, Christena determined to do just that. Quickly, before she could convince herself that the idea was a bad one, she moved. In an instant the whip was in her hand, and in another she was on her feet, facing the man called Knife.

The whip had a foot-long swivel stock and a ten-foot braided lash, and as the Ute watched with surprised fascination, it became instantly obvious that the young woman he had selected to be his squaw knew how to use the weapon in her hand.

She struck swiftly, then, and surely. The whip cracked like the report of a pistol, and the buckskin popper on the end of the lash lifted flesh from Knife's neck. With a cry of pain and startled anger, he stepped back, and the second blow of the lash took him over the shoulders, the third on his leg.

With a growl, the Indian lunged toward her, but Christena stepped quickly aside and struck again. Turning from his misdirected lunge, the man ran away from her in a stumbling run, the popper ripping his buckskin shirt with one last blow.

At that, Knife stumbled and fell. In the same instant, Christena gathered the whip and was fleeing to where her horse was tethered. Anxiously, desperately, she tugged at the rope, finally pulling it loose from the stake. Spinning, she ran for the horse. Then, dropping the whip and grasping the animal's mane, she struggled to drag herself onto its high back.

Anxiously she pulled herself up, throwing her leg as high as she could throw, pulling, straining —

"Woman!"

With a chill of fear, Christena stopped struggling, and slowly her feet dropped and came back to the earth.

"Woman, hear my words."

Numbly the girl turned and faced the gaunt Indian, who was standing with the rope to her horse grasped in his hand. Blood trickled down his neck, and there was a livid streak across his shoulder and down his back. Yet he stood calmly, and she could hear no trace of anger or disdain in his voice.

"Woman," Knife said, his head high and his eyes steady, "I see that I have chosen well. You are *te-a-now-er*, an equal, a warrior fit for mothering many strong sons. I too am fit for fathering many strong sons. This is good.

"You have also brought to my thinking that I must not *tur-reb-by*. I must not throw away the path of honor, the true way of my people. I am not white, and I must forget the ways of the man Vasquez, the white ways of evil."

The Ute stood straight, breathing deeply, and his knowledge of English startled Christena. "The two of us will be one," he continued, "but it will be as it has always been, as such a joining always must be. It will be after the manner of purification and feasting in the wickiups of my people. Until then there will be no fear, and there will be no fleeing. I shall tie you, and if escape is attempted, you shall die. If it is not, then we shall go together, and we shall go in peace.

"Woman, the warrior called Knife salutes you."

Stepping forward, Knife picked up the whip Christena had used against him and solemnly tied the lash end of it around her neck. Then, turning away, he led both her and the horse to where the packs had been tossed to the ground. Taking one of the blankets, he walked to the other horse, pulled the rope from the stake, and led the two animals, with Christena stumbling before them, to a place of shade on the far side of the clearing. Tying the two ropes to his arm and cradling the stock of the whip against his chest, he lay down, rolled up in the blanket, and, so far as Christena could tell, went instantly to sleep.

She didn't move but for a long time stood and sobbed quietly, devastated by the fact that she had come so close to escape and yet had failed. Why, oh why?

Moments later, as her tears gradually dried, Christena took

the blanket the Indian had left for her and spread it as far from her sleeping captor as the whip would stretch.

Then, sitting down and watching him, Christena finally marveled. She knew that it was no longer practical to attempt escape, at least not yet. But she knew, just as well, that the Lord had protected her, and that such divine protection would continue until her beloved Jons would come for her.

"Please hurry, my darling," she whispered as she stretched back on the blanket and finally closed her eyes, "please, please hurry . . ."

Chapter 21

A dust devil whirled across the trail before us, slapping a few tiny pebbles against my face. I winced, but I noticed that neither of the horses were troubled, and that old Gideon simply stared ahead. He was a tough old man, tougher maybe than anyone else I had ever known — old, crippled, in constant pain, but never quitting, never saying die. He was truly amazing, and of a sudden I once again felt glad he was riding with me.

We were still ramming southward, right then following a trail that was probably Indian — and the land stretched empty and endless before us. It was the morning of our fifth day since leaving the camp of Bill Finkman, and the pace old Gideon had insisted on setting had burned itself into my brain until I no longer even thought of it. We moved steadily — not fast, not slow — but at a jogging foxtrot that gnawed away at the miles.

"No long-distance race is ever won by speed at the start," Gideon had said that first morning as we had started into the Uintah Mountains. "Too much reserve energy is burned up in the speed. No, what we'll do, Son, is play to their weakness, their hurry. We'll do an easy trot for an hour, then an easier flat-footed walk for the next hour — and then trot again, and so on. We'll be out of blanket at daybreak every morning, then walk-trot-walk until the sun is overhead. We'll stop for water if we can find it, strip the horses, water them and rub them down, let them eat a little while we do the same, and then we'll rest for two or three hours. In the afternoon, we'll follow the same trot-walk-trot, and we won't stop until dusk. Then an hour's feed, rubdown, and rest for us and the horse, and more walk-trot-walk until midnight or thereabouts. Then we'll camp in the best grass we can find, give the horses a full length of rope, and sleep until dawn. Then we'll start it all over again. If we do that, we'll catch up with 'em sure."

"And what about the trail?" I had asked. "How in the dickens will we follow those fleeing heathen in the dark of night?"

"The dog," Gideon said, nodding at Lazarus. "I've been watching, and he's already got the scent of the trail. Betwixt his nose and the print of that splayed-hoofed horse, we'll not lose 'em."

Well, I knew that old Gideon was certain he was right, both about Lazarus and our mustangs. But still I was worried. Maybe that was because Yates had been so positive that we had been playing the fools when we had declined fresh mounts. And maybe, too, it was because Gideon and I had talked so big about our horses. The look on Yates's face, and on some of the other men's faces as well, had said it all.

"What?" their expression had said as we had ridden out, carrying Yates's crude map and leading a long-legged mule lightly loaded with food and what else they had tossed in, "You're keeping those scrubby, misfit pieces of wolf-bait that must already be worn out from five hundred miles of trailing the army of the United States all the way from Echo to the Little Sandy and back? And you expect to catch the big, strong half-bred and thoroughbred horses that have been hand-picked for their speed and distance? Why, two scrawny little half-dead mustangs like those won't even be in the running against those big horses, bred right and fed right, that have almost, as it were, lived their entire lives in preparation for this race."

Oh, I could hear the men saying that, all right. Trouble was, mostly I believed they were right. Mostly, that is, until I looked down and saw Lazarus ranging ahead of us and pausing frequently to look back and give a soft whine to the mare. Invariably she flicked her ears at the dog, and I could almost hear her say,

"Don't worry, friend Lazarus. I'm getting on just fine—and as long as you set the trail, I'll be behind you."

Lazarus believed in our horses, I knew that—and I also knew that if he had been able to bet, he would have given odds, for that coyote dog knew a thing or two of his own. He had tamed and calmed that Perdy mare to a faretheewell in the corral on the Weber, had seen her take to him and to me almost instantly, and had seen her go all the way to the Little Sandy and back, plus all over the landscape in between, without ever turning a hair. Somehow old Lazarus knew that when Perdy appeared to be done, worn out, finished, the little gray southwestern mustang had only just begun to fight.

There was something else, too—the prophecy Ephraim Hanks had made. I believed that, and I believed just as strongly in the blessing my father had given me before I had left home. From those two sources, I knew that as long as I did my best to do what was right, I would be successful in finding and rescuing Steenie Bergman. And that was the rest of what kept me going.

Every time I thought of Ephraim Hanks, I shook my head. How had the man done it, I wondered? How had he ever learned to be so close to the Spirit of the Lord? He had told me one night that spiritual abilities were like any other muscles—the more they were worked, the stronger they became. When I had asked how to work them, his reply had been simple: "Pray regularly and sincerely without just mumbling memorized words, Son. The Lord truly wants us to talk to Him. Then read some from the scriptures every day, just to get in tune with how the Lord speaks. If we aren't familiar with the sound of his words, how will we ever recognize the message we ask him to send us?

"Finally, you need to keep the commandments, every one of them, and feel bad enough to want to repent every time a slip occurs. Jons, most Mormon folks I know are fairly righteous. They are active in the kingdom and follow the Lord and His leaders. But hardly a one of them but doesn't complain that the heavens seem closed to them, except for an occasional dream or flash of inspiration or instance of divine protection.

"The reason for their lack of ability to get answers from the Lord, I believe, is because in spite of their predominant righteousness, those poor souls still grasp tightly to a few of their favorite, howbeit small, sins.

"But Son, they can't do that, not and grow closer to the Spirit. The Lord is a God of law, and He won't look upon sin with the least degree of allowance. Nor can He respond with great power to a person who is too lazy or selfish to become really pure. That's why He told Brother Joseph that all blessings were predicated upon obedience to law. The more laws we obey, the more blessings we obtain — or in other words, the closer to the Spirit we get.

"I'll tell you, Boy, the trick is to reach a point where you never, on purpose, commit a sin. And when you slip and do something wrong accidental-like, you get rid of it and cry unto the Lord to forgive you just as fast as you possibly can. According to Alma and King Benjamin, Saints who really feel this way have experienced what is called 'the mighty change.' They are adopted as sons and daughters of Christ, and they abhor sin because they have come to understand the pain that their own sins caused the Lord. They can't bear to inflict any more of that selfishness-caused pain upon Him. You see, it has finally become clear to such souls that it is they themselves who drove the nails into the great Being who has loved and redeemed them. Do you understand what I am saying?"

"I . . . I believe so," I told him.

"Good. But remember, all this is just the beginning. Shun sin for long enough, and you will become purified. Become purified, Jons, and the Lord will give you knowledge whenever you call upon Him. That is called receiving personal revelation, and it is what Brother Joseph said we should all strive daily to achieve.

"If you continue to progress, you will receive all the higher blessings that will be promised you when you receive your endowment. After that, as Peter says in the New Testament, you will be given the power and knowledge, by the Spirit of God, to open the heavens and commune with the righteous hosts who dwell therein. That is one of the fruits of paying the price to be close to God's Spirit.

"But for you, young man," Eph had said, grinning, "a more important fruit of diligently seeking righteousness would be that you will be given power to take that sweet little Christena to God's holy altar, to be sealed to her for eternity, and then to go forward in righteousness until you can claim her as yours beyond the grave. Unless you love her enough to do that, all this sashaying around the country makes very little sense at all.

"From my own experience, Son," Ephraim Hanks had concluded, "I have found that paying the price to be righteous is a peaceful thing. I don't have much fear about things anymore, and, as the Lord promised, my confidence is waxing strong in His presence. In other words, I have great faith in the impressions He gives me. If you want such faith and confidence, and if you want the eternal rewards of Christena's companionship, why, I'd recommend that you pursue the course I have shown you."

So for days I had been riding, thinking over and over about what Ephraim Hanks had told me. And the more I thought of it, the more sense it made. For some reason, though, it frightened me, thinking of putting every fault aside. I knew myself pretty well and was mortally afraid of backsliding. Yet I wanted to be in tune with the Sprit of God, and so as I rode I was praying almost constantly. And in spite of my self-doubts, I was doing my best to dredge up those favorite sins, make commitments to the Lord concerning them, and finally cast them off my shoulders by giving them up to Christ.

That was embarrassing, asking Jesus to lift burdens from me that I had committed apurpose. But mile by mile I was feeling better about things, and I had no doubt that the Lord would direct me until I had not only found Steenie but had achieved my spiritual goal as well.

"Time to walk 'em," Gideon said as he reined his Kettle down.

I followed suit, and the horses moved slowly forward into the day, walking that flat-footed walk that Gideon said was a resting for the mustangs. But I hated that slow walk, for with each passing minute I seemed to see Steenie and her abductor drawing farther away.

"At this pace, it seems like they're going to get away," I finally said.

"It does seem slow," agreed Gideon.

"Then why the dickens do you think we are going to catch the evil souls?"

"Because they're starting to go slower than we are."

"What?"

"Apparently you ain't noticed the tracks, friend Jons. The two 'breds are walking quite a bit now, and back there apiece I saw where the splayed-hoofed horse had stumbled. And it wasn't from a rock or a hole, neither. You see any sweat streaks on your Perdy mare?"

Silently I shook my head, for there were none. Reaching out, I rubbed my hand along Perdy's neck, and then I felt back along her flanks. No moisture — only an even warmth. My Perdy mare could do what she was doing all day without working up a real sweat.

"She's dry," Gideon affirmed. "But if we were to ride up to the splayed-hoofed horse, or to the 'breds, we'd see plenty of sweat, as well as flecks of foam at their mouths and plenty of energy-wasting head-shaking. By now, you can bet that all three horses are getting mighty jaded. Besides, the two 'breds, at least, have been fed on rich feed and consequently are overweight with hot flesh. Not so with Kettle and your mare. That gives our horses more pure endurance, you can bet on it.

"Another thing. When a man's being chased, or sometimes even when he just thinks he is, he doesn't cogitate right. That's what guilt does, for guilty men run even when no one's behind them. A guilty man rides his horse too hard and has to stop too often to breathe him. Doing that, he takes too much out of his horse too early.

"The way we ride may be slower, but it is also steadier and

goes on for longer hours. Those fellers started a good twenty hours ahead of us — but Son, these tracks in the trail today are fresh, and I'd say we're less than six hours behind them now.

Gideon paused for a long moment and then concluded. "All the same," he muttered, "those horses'll be something to beat. Both 'breds. Never know just what they've got left when the finish line's in sight."

Sometime later, with me still worrying over Gideon's last unencouraging statement, the time clock in his mind had given its silent signal, and he relayed the message along the reins. Kettle-belly had picked up to a mile-eating fox-trot, and without thought I had urged my Perdy mare to the same gait.

We had followed the Green River south until it had drifted off to the east, and then we left the river and made our way over the Uintah Mountains. That was cold country — cold but beautiful — and I marveled at the hidden lakes and vast stands of timber. There was a little snow up high, but nothing fresh, and it served only to highlight the tracks we were following.

Our only high-up camp was at Iron Springs, and it had been a cold one, all right. I had fussed a little about it, and Gideon had scornfully tossed another log onto our fire.

"Shallow rivers and shallow minds freeze first," he had growled, and I had said no more about the cold.

From Iron Springs the trail had led down Hole-in-the-Rock Canyon and out into the vast and barren country to the south. Actually, it wasn't really barren, for the country was much like that in Wyoming — sage-covered valleys, flat tablelands, and innumerable draws and washes. It was also a dry country, but the season was a good one for traveling — and water, at least during the early part of the day, lay in many of the usually empty arroyos. There were also seeps and freshwater streams, and the trader Yates had marked the best of these on his map. But the men we followed had known of these as well, so Gideon and I had only to keep to the trail they had laid out for us, and we had no trouble.

It was nearly noon when my Perdy mare raised her head

higher and quickened her pace. Gideon was behind me, but as usual Lazarus was out ahead, and so Perdy had no fear.

"She smells water," Gideon informed me.

"Good. I'll bet it's been twenty miles or more."

"At least," Gideon agreed. "When folks say this country gets a six-inch rain, I reckon they mean one drop every six inches."

I chuckled over that, and ten minutes later we topped a low hill and saw what had to be the Green River again, a quarter mile ahead. It was a wide expanse of sandbars and shallow water and deeper-cut channels, but it did look inviting.

I rode to the bank and stopped, and Gideon and the mule soon reached my side.

"It seems high," I said.

"Been raining up-country, I reckon. Yates said to watch for quicksand."

"Do you know the look of it?"

Gideon shook his head. "Never seen any. But I reckon the horses have, or maybe their ancestors. Whichever, the fear of it will be bred into them, so we'll let them pick their way. Put the blankets around your neck, and this bag of food. I'll pack the rest of this."

Undoing the blanket from behind the cantle and draping it over my shoulders — along with our bag of grub — I tickled Perdy with my spurs, and she stepped into the shallow water, splashing some and seeming to enjoy it. For a minute she snorted and bucked at Lazarus's antics, but then she sobered to the serious business of feeling forward for footholds in the gravel, mud, and sand of the bottom.

We came to the first of the deeper channels, and Perdy surged into it, swimming strongly and steadily — and then scrambled out on a sandbar beyond, Lazarus directly ahead of her. That partial crossing had not been bad at all, and with greater confidence Perdy launched into the main current, swimming evenly, following Lazarus. I urged her forward, turned and saw that Gideon and the pack mule were directly behind, and then gave my attention to the crossing.

We drifted downstream some, but at last we reached a sand-bar on the far side of the river, and Lazarus scrambled up onto it. Perdy started to follow, then snorted with fear and, before I hardly knew what was happening, had reared and plunged back into the water.

Lazarus leaped as well, or tried to. But the sticky substance of the sandbar mired him, and he could gain no footing.

"Lazarus," I shouted, "come here! That's *quicksand!*"

The dog tried, and Perdy fought the current, the entire time watching the struggling coyote-dog.

"Jons," Gideon shouted as he threw the mule's lead rope to me, "take the mule! Head upstream and hit the bank where those other fellers came out. Now git!"

"But Lazarus—"

"I'll get him. Now go on!"

In anguish I urged Perdy forward, but she fought me and tried to go back. I yanked her head with the reins, yelling and trying not to think of my dog. And the next thing I knew, we were on dry ground and Gideon was splashing out behind me, a poor, bedraggled Lazarus on the end of the rope behind him.

Lazarus shook himself, and to my surprise, Perdy did the same, almost unsettling me. But the water flew, and with that she seemed ready to be on her way.

"Good a place as any for a nooning," Gideon said, not commenting at all on his rescue of Lazarus—and he rode to a small clump of cottonwoods and swung down. Following him, I dismounted, and we spread-eagled our saddles on the ground so they would dry. Hanging our saddle blankets over a low tree limb, we unpacked our mule, unrolled the blankets, and dumped our meager gear out into the sun.

"Don't leave your boots off," Gideon warned as I pulled them off my feet and dumped the water from them. "They'll dry stiff and shrunken, and you'll never get them back on again."

So I struggled, hopping about on one foot and then the other, getting my wet boots back on my feet again. Then I sat down with my back against one of the trees and stared at a hunk of dried beef that I knew I needed to eat. Only somehow I just couldn't.

"Brother Gideon," I said, suddenly having a hard time of it, "you saved . . . my dog. I . . . I thank you."

Gideon chewed for a moment longer, than swallowed. "Glad I was there with the rope, Son. Seeing that over yonder makes whatever I done seem worth it."

Following his gaze, I looked toward the bluff we had yet to climb. And only then did I notice the horses and mule where Gideon had staked them to feed.

Kettle-belly and the mule were cropping grass at the end of their picket lines, but Perdy wasn't eating at all. She was standing still, all atremble, her nose down — and Lazarus was squatted before her, his face lifted against hers.

The poor coyote-dog had nearly lost it back there in the quicksand. But, bless his heart, there he was — giving comfort to a frightened little gray mare who could not abide the thought of losing her best friend.

"And it came to pass that she fell to her knees," Gideon said as tears started from my eyes, "giving Him thanks. Son, we'd better do the same."

And then and there, we did.

Chapter 22

In the hush of dusk dropping toward dark, I sat on a flat-topped rock in a low swale, enjoying the small fire and wolfing down Gideon Monson's recent and only cooked specialty, singed beef and refried beans. Off to the side lay Lazarus, apparently asleep, while next to him the skimpy pack of supplies sat squatly in the dimness. Forty feet beyond, Perdy and Gideon's horse cropped grass in companionable competition with the long-legged mule.

"That mule," Gideon said softly, "he's almighty tired."

I grunted, being too busy eating to say much else.

"We've come three hundred, three hundred and fifty miles by now," Gideon declared. "I don't hardly know if that mule will hold up much longer."

"Perhaps there will be no need," I said then. "The pack's got next to nothing in it."

"Yeah, there is that," Gideon agreed. "Boy, we've got to catch up to them pilgrims pretty soon. Not to mention being plumb tuckered out, we're next to flat out of grub."

The darkness deepened, and I thought about what Gideon was saying. He wasn't the sort to holler out when there was no need, so I knew that he was justifiably worried. It followed, then, that I had better be worried myself.

Lazarus lifted his head and thumped his plumed tail as he looked at me, and I grinned. Somehow I still had all my hope, and I couldn't seem to feel the gloom that had apparently settled upon Gideon. Perdy and Kettle were running strong, the tracks in the sandy trail we followed were deeper and fresher than ever, and I just knew that we were getting close. It was only going to be a matter of hours now, another day at the most, and Gideon and I would confront those heathens and I would have my Steenie back again.

"You positive sure you want to go on?" Gideon suddenly asked.

"Excuse me?" I said, not certain I had heard.

Gideon coughed nervously. "I said, you positive certain you want to keep going?"

"Why do you hesitate now?"

"Son, its . . . uh . . . been five full days since we left Lot Smith, and six since the girl was taken. I . . . uh . . . well, Indians do things to purty young girls . . . "

"Not Steenie," I said flatly.

"But you don't know that!" Gideon argued. "I do. I've seen it afore, way too often. I thought we'd catch up with 'em sooner, and there would be a chance. But it's been too long . . . "

"Would you want me to just walk away?"

The old man poked at the fire. "I know it seems harsh, Boy, but the girl's likely dead now, or worse. If she ain't dead, likely she's been used so she won't *want* to be found. Not especially by the young feller she loves more than she loves life itself. The way I'm thinking, Son, time is the best doctor there is—and distant memories of the good things are a whole lot better than fresh realities of the bad, for both of you."

I noticed that one of my fingernails was cracked and needed attention, so I took out the knife Pa had given me and went to work on it, thinking hard and fast. It was true that Steenie had been gone an overly long time, and the things Gideon had said certainly made sense. I didn't want to see Steenie dead.

And worse, I didn't want to see her used and humiliated. And she would be, I knew that, if her abductor had had his way with her.

There were also the animals to consider. As Gideon had pointed out, the mule was about on its last legs. The same was probably true of his horse Kettle-belly and my Perdy, though neither of them was showing as much strain as the mule.

Besides that, I was tired — bone weary — and so sore it took all the power of my will just to mount up each time we stopped. That being the case, I could hardly imagine the pain that poor old Gideon must have been enduring. For all I knew, the chase was killing him, putting him to death just as certain sure as the Indian called Knife, or his companion Vasquez, would do it. Maybe with his subtle questions he was even trying to tell me that. But whether he was or not, if Gideon died, I would always carry the burden of it on my soul.

Yet he wouldn't stop, not unless I stopped beside him, and I could hardly carry the load of that knowledge, either.

Staring down at my nail, I tried to balance my love for old Gideon against my love for Steenie. She had faith in me that I would come, I knew that, and the old man had faith in me that I would have the sense to know when to give it up.

Truthfully, I did not have the least possible notion of what I should do. The horses were tired, the mule was about to give out, Gideon was caving in of exhaustion and old age, we were about out of supplies, and I was nearly dead myself . . .

"Father in Heaven," I pleaded silently, "what wilt thou have thy servant do?"

Perdy snorted softly, and as I looked up I saw Lazarus trotting over to her. They stood together then, a smallish horse and a scraggly, tawny brown coyote-dog — and in the almost darkness I suddenly realized something. Those two creatures had never asked odds of anything life had ever thrown at them. I had talked big, but ol' Lazarus and my Perdy mare were ready to give it the last ounce of stubborn endurance, just to back up my talk. This was Lazarus's and Perdy's race, too, and it was just as important to them that we get to Steenie, as it was to me.

"Friend Gideon," I said softly, "I can't hardly quit now, not with what you, Kettle, Perdy, and ol' Lazarus have done for me. No sir, with the help of the Lord, I'm convinced that Steenie will be delivered, unharmed, into our hands."

Slowly Gideon shook his head. "Son, as the Bible says, we are troubled on every side, yet not distressed; we are perplexed, but not in despair. Second Corinthians four. And why ain't we? Mostly, Jons, because of you. They say that no man in the wrong can stand up against a feller who's in the right and keeps coming. Those fellers in front of us had best be getting worried, for they've no idea the kind of man behind 'em. I'm only just starting to understand you myownself. If you've got the sort of faith to keep going, then I've about got to go along just to watch those sorry brethren learn their lesson."

"So you think I'm doing the right thing?"

"I didn't say that, but I reckon you are. Further," Gideon declared grinning, "if you always do what's right, you'll please the most important folks, and you'll keep the rest of 'em up nights awondering what you're up to."

I chuckled. "It would be better," I then said carefully, "if you came after me, more slowly . . . "

Gideon snorted. "Not on your life! I ain't that old — not yet, at least. Now, let's hit the hay — or in this case, the sagebrush and gravel. Otherwise, you'll be too tired to travel when I roust you out about an hour from now."

Sounds of hurried doings tapped at my eardrums, penetrating at last to awareness. I came out of my sleep still tired and with a stiffness in my backbone that was getting worse by the hour. The darkness of sky overhead had shifted to a dull gray, and a few stars still fought against the seeping glimmer of the false dawn.

Rising on one elbow, I looked around and saw old Gideon slapping the pack on the long-legged mule. I pushed up, stretched, and took the bucket half full of water that Gideon had placed near me and walked a short distance away for a quick and cold wash-up. And it was while washing my face that I first realized something was wrong.

It wasn't anything definite, just a gloomy feeling, a sense of foreboding. Yet as I thought of it, the feeling seemed to grow, and it wasn't long before it was all I could do to keep from bawling.

Five minutes later, standing by the dead campfire, I watched Gideon hurrying toward me with a tin cup in one hand and some cold beef in the other.

"Gobble these," he growled. "Fast. And kick me when you're through. Hard."

"Something feels mighty wrong," I said.

"Don't I know it! I overslept, and it's near morning."

"I know, friend Gideon," I said, trying to chew dried beef while I talked. "But there's more, lots more. I feel a sense of doom that almost brings chills—"

"Being late's enough, Jons. Those fellers could have fifteen, twenty miles more on us by now, and it's all my fault. I'd of saddled Perdy, but you know how she fights anyone but you."

Gideon grabbed the bucket, emptied it, and shuffle-hurried to the mule, where he stuffed it into the pack. Then he grabbed the lead rope and limped rapidly toward where his horse was standing ground-hitched.

"Well," he snarled back at me, "get the lead out, boy! Like you say, daylight's a'burning."

"But there *is* something wrong, Gideon . . . "

His sour look stopped me from saying more, but that bad feeling was getting worse by the minute. Still, Gideon hadn't felt anything, so what was I worried about?

I swallowed the bite of beef I had been working over, took a long drink of water, and stuffed the rest of the beef into my shirtfront. Then, grabbing up the blanket and my saddle, I ran toward my Perdy mare.

I was tugging at the cinch when I realized that Perdy's head was up and her ears forward, staring off into the darkness. Then I heard, off toward the trail, the sound of Lazarus snarling. But before I had a chance to shout a warning to Gideon, I heard a series of fierce shrieks that sent shivers down my spine and all the way to my toes.

I hesitated briefly, unable to move, and then the shrieks were interrupted by the heavy boom of Gideon's Henrietta rifle.

The shrieks stopped abruptly, there was the faint sound of diminishing hoofbeats, and I could hear nothing more.

Swiftly I finished saddling and swung up on Perdy, and obstinately she rose into the air, head down and back arched, bucking once, twice, three times in her nervousness. Then she leveled into a fast lope toward the trail.

Gideon was standing on a little rise, just finishing reloading his rifle, when I slid Perdy to a stop. Lazarus was walking stiff-legged back and forth in front of my companion, the mule was standing motionless, and there was no sign at all of Kettle-belly, Gideon's faithful little mustang.

"Confound it," he growled as he rammed the rod down the long barrel. "When am I ever going to learn? Brains in the head sure saves blisters on the feet!"

"Gideon, are you hurt?"

"Not hardly. But I got to learn to listen to you fellers who can hearken to the Spirit — especially when you tell me to listen. I don't hear them things much, so I tend to doubt. But every single solitary time I ignore Eph Hanks or you, I end up looking the sorry fool. Now I got *two* kicks coming."

"What? You're making no more sense — "

"Yeah, I am," the old man snarled. "You told me there was something wrong. But oh, no, I wouldn't listen. I'm so confounded used to thinking that when a hen cackles she's either lying or laying, that I forget she might be giving me warning. Now I've gone and lost my horse."

"Kettle-belly is — "

"Away and gone!"

"Somebody stole him?"

"No, he just spooked when that Ute kid jumped out of the brush when I nearly ran over him. The poor kid was scarder'n me and Kettle. I shot old Henrietta into the air I was so startled, my horse pitched me on my noggin, and then the fool animal took off."

"What you going to do?"

"Do?" Gideon growled. "Why, get even with the ornery

critter, of course. I'll make that fool horse walk all the way back to me, all by his lonesome. That'll teach him."

"Gideon . . ."

The old man grinned wryly. "He'll be back, Son. He always ends up tracking me down, given time. But confound it, that's just what we ain't got—time. But don't you worry none about me. I'll ride the mule till Kettle makes it back, then I'll ride like the dickens and catch up with you later today."

I looked forward along the trail that stretched to the far horizon, where the first faint blush of color was creeping up the sky. Lazarus was no longer walking stiff-legged back and forth, so I knew that the Indian boy had to be gone. But out there somewhere were likely to be other of the Utes, perhaps waiting for the boy, though perhaps not. But each would be anxious to obtain a new horse, and maybe even to lift a white scalp.

Trouble was, also out there, knocking off more miles, were the Ute named Knife and the white man Vasquez, and with one or the other of them, or maybe both by now, was my Steenie Bergman. I could not afford to wait.

"Take your time," I said to the disgruntled Gideon. "There'll be no catching up, not the way Perdy, Lazarus, and I will be riding. But fear not, old friend. The three of us, and Steenie, will meet you on our return."

"Now hold on, Son. You can't do this alone! Getting your little gal away from those two heathen will be trickier'n braiding a mule's tail."

With a heavy heart but brave smile I bid my friend farewell, and even while he was protesting I rode away down the trail.

"Consarn it," he shouted after me, "that's the best thing about talking to my horse! He don't talk back, and he don't ignore me . . ."

Gideon was right, and I knew it. I could never do what had to be done, alone. But still—

"Remember, Jons Soderberg," Gideon shouted from behind me, "every fool on this earth is afraid of something. You find what those heathen are afraid of, and you'll beat 'em sure."

With a last wave to my friend and a glance into the brightening sky, I knew suddenly I wasn't alone at all. After all, no less an authority than Gideon himself had declared that I was as in tune with the Spirit as Eph Hanks. I knew that wasn't so, of course, but I *had* felt something back there, a warning that I knew full well had come from above. That being the case, the Good Lord would surely be willing to direct me from where I now was. All I had to do was ask.

And I *was* asking—believe me, I was asking.

Chapter 23

An hour later I found two more bodies, and I didn't know whether to feel relieved or terrified. The first, the splayed-hoofed horse that had belonged to Ben Crost, was lying in the trail where it had fallen, literally having died on its feet. I had noticed the tracks for some time, and though I was no expert at reading sign, I could tell that Vasquez, or whoever had been riding it, had ridden the horse especially hard for the past mile or so. The tracks were spaced wide and deep, and more and more often it had stumbled, so it was no real surprise for me to come upon the horse's dead body.

I was still looking at that and the deep boot tracks leading forward from it when I heard Lazarus's deep growl from maybe fifty feet ahead. Riding forward, I came shortly to the second body. Instantly I knew that I was looking at the man known as Knife — and just as instantly I felt a deep sense of pity for him. He had been shot and dumped aside as if he were no more important than a used blanket, and I had the feeling that maybe he had deserved more. Still, I was glad to know he now had no more power over Steenie.

Gulping and taking a deep breath, I rode around him — and within a few yards I came to the remnants of a camp. It had not been a permanent camp at all but was more like the ones Gideon and I had left behind us each morning. The difference was that in this camp were the tracks of three people — the moccassined Ute, the booted Vasquez, and the smaller tracks of a woman's shoes that had to have been made by Steenie Bergman.

With heart racing, I searched for any sign left by her, any indication that she was still hoping for my arrival. I found nothing but scuff marks indicating that she had fought her abductor, and off in the brush a ten-foot leather bullwhip. I also discovered that the coals from the fire were still warm, and that renewed my excitement. I was close, so close that I could feel it. Now all I had to do was catch up to them and somehow take Steenie away from José Vasquez.

For the first time I wished for a gun, feeling bad that I had taken Eph's word that I hadn't needed one. He had not seen the cold-blooded murders that the man I was following had committed. But I didn't have one, and so I would need to rely on the Lord and my wits, something I had to admit I had watched Ephraim Hanks and Lot Smith do to near perfection.

Perdy moved strong and steady under me as I followed the flowing shoeprints of the two long-legged 'breds. Lope-trot-lope. Lope for half an hour in the smooth undulating stride familiar to anyone who had ever seen a herd of wild mustangs flowing over the land, their backs rising and falling as easy and regularly as water waves. Trot for the next half hour in that swinging double-beat stride that Gideon had told me mustangs themselves favored for making maximum distance with minimum effort.

It was hard, not knowing what was happening ahead, to hold down, to keep from spurring Perdy into full gallop. But the tracks those 'breds left behind looked smooth and steady, and if it turned into a 'long' race, as Gideon had called it, I wanted Perdy to be able to make it. Lazarus, too, appreciated the pace, and though I could never tell if he was tired or not, I knew that he had to be. No animal can cover four or five hundred miles and not be worn by it. And I knew that Lazarus was worn. He no longer ranged far ahead or to the side of us but always ran just uptrail, never more than fifteen feet ahead, no matter whether Perdy was loping or trotting.

When I ran into my first living human of the journey, the

sun was standing at an hour or a little more before noon. He was an old mountaineer, a trapper and prospector, riding a little burrow and leading three others—and he looked like he was heading back into the Uintahs to do his winter trapping. Quick as a flash he had a bead on Lazarus, but at a warning shout from me, he dropped his old weapon.

"Friend," I said as he quizzically regarded me, "have you seen a man and a girl, him of vicious countenance and her filled with fright?"

"You train the wolf?" he asked.

"He isn't trained but follows or leads as he chooses. Have you seen the pair?"

"A trained wolf. Who'd have thought it? You're talking about José Vasquez," the man replied evenly. "I'd make it a shade under two hours ago they passed me. But was I you, I'd turn around while I could still breathe. That's a mean man, Boy. *Mighty* mean."

"It won't matter. I'm still going after him."

The old man shook his head. "Then you'd best start praying, boy. There ain't a man I know who ain't afeared of him, Injuns included."

"Have you a weapon to spare?"

"Against Vasquez?" he chuckled. "Not on your life. He'd kill you and see that your weapon was mine. Then I'd be a dead man myself. And me, I've got some gold to get out of those mountains come spring."

"There's gold up there?"

"Son," he said, sending a squirt of dark tobacco juice shooting over the head of his burro, and then wiping his stained beard with the back of his dirty hand, "out here every prairie dog hole is a gold mine, every hill is a mountain, every creek a river, and every prospector you'll meet is a forked-tongued liar. I tell you there's gold in them there hills, and you'd best know better. Let me be the fool, not you.

"And I'm right sorry about not giving you my extra gun. If you're still crazy enough to go after Vasquez, you'll have to do it with the weapons you brung with you."

215

At noon I gave half of the meager contents of the feed bag to Perdy, and Lazarus and I chewed down half of what I had left of the dried beef. But there was no water—nowhere along the last miles had we come on a stream or a wash with any leftover moisture in it. Nothing but barren, friendless, sandy country.

"Doesn't seem much like manna," I said to the two animals, "and I don't hardly have no rod with which to strike rock for a drink. But the Lord knows of our plight, and if He's really watching over us . . . "

I could see it far ahead, two adobe and two weathered and burned board buildings that comprised what I thought Yates had said was Fort Rubidoux, an abandoned fur trader's outpost. But Yates had also said there was a flowing well there—water.

And he was right, I discovered as we drew closer—for there was not only a well, but a log that had been hollowed into a small watering trough.

Holding Perdy to a trot and then a walk, I moved cautiously forward. The tracks of the two 'breds led to the trough and then away, but I was still suspicious. Pulling up twenty feet away from the trough, I waited.

Nothing.

Dismounting, I left the mare and walked slowly forward, Lazarus gliding silently at my side. Again I looked around. There was no sign of life anywhere, and that made me nervous. Above me, the tired, seasonal remnants of the cottonwood leaves rustled, and I could hear the slight trickle of water spilling from the well spigot, as it had been somehow diverted past the trough onto the ground.

"You see any trouble?" I asked the dog quietly.

Leaning over the shallow trough, I scooped water into my hands and drank, intending in a moment to go back and lead Perdy forward. One scoop I drank, then another, and I was just starting in on the third when the dog, who had placed muzzle to water just below me, snarled and leaped away.

"Lazarus," I called, "what the dickens is wrong? See, I'm drinking . . . "

With another snarl Lazarus leaped at me—and as I staggered backward I saw, out of the corner of my eye, an Indian woman dart forward from one of the empty buildings and grab Perdy's bridle. She then held something out under the mare's nose, her palm flat, and I jerked around.

"Say!" I shouted. "You get away from that mare—"

The rest of my breath was jolted from me as another squaw leaped onto my back from behind. I struggled to free myself, but the woman, wide and heavy and stronger than I could have imagined, clamped her arms around me. I tried to call Perdy, but only a small sound came forth, not nearly enough—

But Lazarus heard, and his snarl was more than enough to activate Perdy. The mare reared back, jerking her reins. Still the Indian woman hung tenaciously to them. Perdy reared again, and this time the little mustang plunged forward with forehoofs striking. The woman shrieked and went down, and then Perdy was swinging in a fast circle, head high, coming right for me.

"Blow the horns over Jericho," I grunted—and between my stomping on the woman's foot and Lazarus's chewing on her leg, I finally broke free. "Now let the walls of the city come tumbling down!" I shouted as I grabbed the horn and pulled myself into the saddle. And with that, my Perdy mare surged ahead, picking up speed, getting us away from the abandoned fort.

Out in the trail and moving away I looked back, but no one was following. If the Indian women had horses, they were still hidden. The one woman was on her feet—but the other, the one who had been kicked by Perdy, was still flat on her back, which I thought served her good and right.

"You did good," I said as I patted the mare on the side of her neck. "And like friend Gideon, I've sure got a kick coming."

The wind of motion was tugging at me, and gradually I became aware that Perdy was pounding in full gallop, while Lazarus was running effortlessly at our side.

"Easy," I said as I tugged the reins. "Easy, girl. There's no need of such hurry, not yet . . . "

And then I became aware of a nagging ache inside me, under

my ribs — growing, increasing. That was followed by a wave of nausea that swept over me, blurring my vision and constricting my breathing in sudden, dry retching.

I pulled on the reins and Perdy stopped. Then I all but fell from the saddle — and was immediately on my knees by the trail, bent over, while both Lazarus and Perdy stood silently, watching.

"Now I've . . . got *two* kicks coming," I breathed, and that was about all that I could say.

It was the water, I knew. Sensing that I was following him, or maybe even having seen me, Vasquez had poisoned the water and instructed those two women to stay and make sure I was put out of my misery. But the knowledge of his deeds gave me little consolation, for I was more sick than I had ever been in my life.

Pushing two fingers down in my throat, I felt my shoulders shake as my throat muscles reacted in spasmodic constrictions, and then the foul stuff gushed forth. The taste in my mouth was loathsome, and the smell of the mess before me was more so — and all I wanted to do was just fall away from it and stretch out in the trail and die. But not far ahead my Steenie girl was praying for me to come, so I staggered to my feet and to Perdy and then pulled myself into the saddle.

Fingers fumbling, I tied the reins around the horn, and then grabbing Perdy's mane I fell forward. "Get going, good and faithful friends," I mumbled to the animals. "I'll hang on somehow."

Lazarus ran to the front and looked back, Perdy started moving, and the three of us were on our way again.

Time passed, though I had no knowledge of it. Hunched forward, head hanging down, fingers wrapped in Perdy's stringy mane, I rode in a sort of trance, aware of nothing, not even the insistent joggle of Perdy's swinging trot or of the already habitual response of my own muscles that held me in the saddle.

But gradually awareness returned, and I knew both who and where I was. I was on my Perdy mare, Lazarus was out before us, and ahead of us somewhere was a young woman named

Christena Bergman, who was surely waiting for me to save her. And I was letting all of them down. Without a doubt, I was the stupidest fool in the whole world, and I was letting down the best friends I had on God's green earth.

I tried to straighten in the saddle, be less of a spineless blob of dead weight on Perdy's back—and I managed to do so, somewhat.

But Perdy was moving strong and steady beneath me, not even letting down a little—and Lazarus, who had tried to warn me of the poisoned water and had even pushed me away from drinking more of it, was running free ahead.

Suddenly all I wanted to do was cry, to blubber like a little child. For I knew, somehow, that these two friends of mine, the ugly little gray mustang and the scraggly coyote-dog, were saying something to me—saying it in the ceaseless steadiness of stride, in the flex and flow of muscle under dusty gray or tawny brown hide, in the tireless thudding of hoofs or the endless padding of almost silent paws.

"Stop your worrying," they were saying to me. "The Lord has raised us up to do this thing for you, and we are doing it well. Of course you're a fool, but all men are fools, and we hold that not against you. Besides, you're good for some things, such as combing the burrs from our tails, and we rejoice in that. But, Jons Soderberg, you could never do what we do now. So cease your fretting, look to yourself, and let us do this little thing that we have been raised up to do."

So time passed, and slowly I began to feel better. I may have been all sorts of a fool, but I was young and strong, and finally I was straight in the saddle again, doing my best as a balanced rider to help Perdy and my Lazarus dog bring me to my frightened but waiting love.

Chapter 24

In the darkness of the night, back away from the trail and well screened by high bushes, I gave Perdy the last grains of the meager feed bag Gideon had given me. While she ate that, Lazarus and I chewed down what was left of the dried beef.

"And he would fain have filled his belly with the husks that the swine did eat," I said to my two silent companions. "Luke fifteen, the story of the prodigal son. Ma taught it to me. Good friends, are you as confounded hungry as I am?"

Neither of the animals answered, and I swallowed the last tiny bits of the beef. Then I took the end of the rope trailing from Perdy's neck and tied it to my arm.

"Half an hour, no more. Take longer and I'll be gone in sleep, certain."

Leaning back on my saddle, I closed my eyes—but thoughts of Perdy and Lazarus and two long-legged 'breds speeding Steenie away from me chased themselves through my mind, and I could not seem to relax.

"Father," I prayed silently, "thy servant knows he is close to Christena, and tomorrow I'll likely come to her and the heathen Vasquez. I don't know what I'll do then, but thou knowest all things, and I pray that thou wilt open a way ..."

A few feet away, Lazarus lay with head down on paws, absolutely still. Beyond him Perdy stood, motionless, head low. Both animals were gaunt along the ribs and sunk in some at the flanks. They were dirtied, clumsy-looking caricatures of their former selves that seemed to have died, one on the ground and the other on her feet. They looked finished, done for, ready to collapse into heaps of bone and hide.

But they were not, neither one of them, and I knew it. Each of those wonderful animals was resting. They were relaxed all over, dropped, stretched out, sagged into absolute limpness. That was because, somehow, they knew. The gray mustang mare and the tawny brown coyote-dog that called me his were wasting no extra energy in twitchings or stompings or tail switchings or thumpings or other movings about. They were making the most of a very brief rest. And they were both just about ready to begin to fight.

And by gum, I thought as I looked at them, so was I!

Struggling out of a doze a little later, I dragged myself to my feet. "Let Gabriel blow the trumpet," I mumbled, for some reason thinking more and more of words from the scriptures that Ma had read me. "We are on to find my Steenie . . ."

There was only the dark of night and the trace of trail like a ribbon under faint, cold starlight and the wind of our own motion as we moved at a fast lope into the lonely miles. Off and on I thought of old Gideon and hoped that he had found his horse, and I wondered where he would be right now. At other times I thought of Eph Hanks and Lot Smith and tried to picture in my mind a way that I could trick José Vasquez into releasing Steenie into my hands, the way they might do it if they were with me.

I could not come up with an idea, however, and so I tried during the rest of the time to think of nothing, but just to hurry so that I would be in time. Urgency, therefore, talked along Perdy's reins — and stretching her neck, she responded.

Tiredness was an ache that covered my whole body, and hunger a hollowness that gnawed in my belly. Dizziness took me now and again, and at those times I knew I would never remember the night clearly. But it didn't matter, not anymore. All that mattered was that I find Steenie, and that I find her in time.

Lazarus loped ahead of us, never hesitating, and at times I

221

watched the dim rise and fall of his paws in amazement, wondering that such poetry could exist. Yet I knew that it did, for the drumming of Perdy's hoofs beneath me pounded to the same primal rhythm. I knew as well that Lazarus's nose was leading him, and not for a minute did I worry that we might pass Steenie in the dark.

And it was dark—though after an endless time, I realized that rocks and bushes along the trail were sharper, more distinct. We kept moving, and sometime later the songs of birds penetrated my thoughts, making me even more aware of the coming of dawn.

Suddenly I felt good and sat straighter in the saddle, as a man should sit. I no longer felt quite so tired, and much later, when the first rays of the sun hit me, I even managed a smile.

"Well done, thou good and faithful servant," I said as I reached down and patted Perdy on the neck. "Now keep those hoofs a'moving . . . "

And Perdy, warmed through to the very marrow of her bones, fully into our race to find Steenie though it should last for all eternity, leaned forward again into a fast, long-reaching lope. Lazarus responded in kind, and we were all eating the wind, gobbling the miles and feeling good as we flew into the morning.

And then I heard hoofbeats behind me. Twisting to look back, I was startled to see an Indian coming up, and coming up fast. For a moment I felt fear, and then I realized that the man was well within range of any weapon he might have wanted to use, and yet he had used none.

Well, I decided, he didn't want to kill me or to stop me, at least not yet. But if not that, then what?

The man pulled his horse alongside, five or six feet away from me. Then he slowed to Perdy's pace, and, yipping shrilly but not looking at me at all, he continued to ride.

And so did I.

Before I knew it, another Indian was on my other side, also riding at Perdy's pace, also shouting his war cry but ignoring me otherwise—and I could feel little shivers of fear going up and down my back. I was surely confused by what the two were doing, but as no harm seemed to be coming from them, I decided that three could play the ignoring game. So I kept my eyes as straight ahead as they did, and I kept Perdy pounding forward. And the funny thing was that Lazarus ignored my Lamanite brethren just as thoroughly as I was ignoring them, and so did my little gray mare. She was intent upon her work, strong and steady, never pausing, and Lazarus was intent only upon leading the way.

There were more Indians now, Utes I assumed, quite a crowd of them, and we all rode together, them shrieking, me riding silently, all of us ignoring each other. It was a strange experience, and I don't expect to ever again see the like. I wondered what old Gideon would do about such an escort and was glad he wasn't along. Then I thought of Ephraim Hanks. He would handle it coolly, I knew that, and I could almost see him in my mind, riding with these folks, paying no attention to them, beating them at their own game.

But I didn't know the rules.

We pounded across a long, brush-covered bench, the dust churning up behind us in clouds, and I was almost starting to relax about the Indians when I felt a sharp jab of pain in my shoulder.

Spinning, I was startled to see the first Ute riding with his lance outstretched, and his cries rang out louder than ever. He obviously thought that by poking me, he had just done something wonderful, but I didn't agree. My shoulder hurt like blue blazes, and I was still trying to puzzle it out when I was jabbed in the other side from another direction.

"Say!" I shouted as I glared back at the second man, "who do you think you are? Now back off."

The whole bunch was clamoring now, trying to get around each other to get at me with their lances and other such implements of war, not to kill, apparently, so much as to touch. And finally it came to me what they were doing. Eph Hanks and Al Bagley had talked one night about Indians "counting coup," being brave enough to touch a living enemy, pull away, and then come back in for the kill. Well, I was their enemy, they could touch me about as they chose, and I knew without a doubt that unless I did something very soon, we wouldn't be traveling much longer under such amiable conditions. The whole tribe would be swooping in for the kill.

Another lance probed my thigh. I yelled out in pain, then somebody else whacked me on the back of the neck, and suddenly another of Al Bagley's stories about Brother Hanks came to my mind.

With a sudden scream of my own, I threw my right arm high above my head. Then, pulling a hideous face, I twirled my arm in a rapid circle beside me. Then I began to bark, at the same time unbuttoning my shirt, pulling it over my head, and wrapping it around my neck.

A quick glance and I felt hope, for as one the Indians were staring at me as we rode, and no one had his lance out and poking at me anymore, either.

"Oh, the lady she died and went away . . . " I suddenly sang out at the top of my lungs, and then with another grimace that exhibited my front teeth in such a way that *anybody* looking on would wonder, I took my feet from the stirrups.

With a quick twist I spun about on the saddle so that I was riding backward, and I felt thankful that Lazarus was leading Perdy, and that she was paying more attention to the dog than she was to me. So far as I could tell, my ridiculous actions didn't even slow her down.

Now the Utes were truly staring, so at the top of my lungs I began orating to them in Swedish, pulling faces, swinging my arms, leaning forward and backward, and doing anything and everything I could think of to look crazy. For that had been the story I had remembered about Eph Hanks. Knowing that Indians feared crazy people, he had acted crazy once in a tight place, and it had frightened some truly hostile Lamanites away from him. My only hope was that the same ruse would now work for me.

And to my dumbfounded wonder, it did.

"*Pe-up,*" one of the Utes shouted as he pulled back until

they were riding twenty or thirty feet from me. They were still with me, of course, but I felt a whole lot better having them with me at that distance than I had felt at the skin-piercing distance we had previously shared.

Still singing and making faces, I righted myself in the saddle, patted Perdy's neck, and breathed a sigh of relief. I was going to make it, and I knew it. The Lord was protecting me, and my friends, even when they were far away, were still managing to save my obviously charmed life.

Crossing the bench, we swooped down through the wash, me way out in front of the Utes — and on the other side Lazarus suddenly swerved and then almost instantly veered back and was on trail again. Looking to the side where he had swerved, I was shocked to see a big black Standard and Morgan cross, gaunt, sweat-streaked, bedraggled, head-hanging, saddle empty, looking ready and more than ready to fall.

One down.

And that meant that the other 'bred was carrying double — that is, unless Vasquez had picked up a second horse from the Utes. But no, there was only one set of tracks stretching before us, one set of big hoofprints upon which the valiant Lazarus had fixed his mind.

Perdy suddenly shifted her lead from right forefoot to left — a sure sign, Gideon had told me, that she was feeling the strain. Her eyes were beginning to show red-rimmed, her chest was heaving, and sweaty lather dampened her flanks and stretched-out neck. But still that reassuring refrain came up from her pounding, rock-hard hooves, and I could hear her saying to me, "Fret not, good friend Jons. You've asked that this be done, and the dog and I are doing it well. Now stop fretting and prepare yourself for what you, alone, must do."

A dark shape appeared in the trail ahead of us, far in the distance, and I wondered. Lazarus and Perdy continued to run smoothly, and as we drew closer I saw that it was a big sorrel, carrying double. Beating down the excitement that surged through my body, I watched the man on the sorrel turn back to look at us.

Instantly he exploded into frantic action, slapping with his rein ends, raking with his spurs. His sorrel mount rallied some, trying, trying—and then broke into a jerky gallop.

I was debating whether to urge my mare forward or to hold my pace, when Perdy suddenly took charge, and I knew that it was no longer my decision to make. She shifted to right forefoot lead again and surged into full gallop, belly low, striving for distance in lengthening stride—the message of urgency suddenly reversed and coming back through the reins from the mare's hammering hammerhead.

"Go," I whispered, forgetting altogether the group of Ute braves who hung back but were yet following. "Go, you gorgeous, wonderful, lovely little mustang . . . "

There was no break in Perdy's long-reaching lope—but I could sense the laboring in it, and I feared. I could feel the extra jolting as the hoofs hit, and the straining muscles no longer cushioned the shocks in instant energy response. Perdy's breath was coming in long, sobbing gasps. Sweat drenched her gray hide, and a dingy froth whipped away from the sidebars of the bit in her mouth. But there was no break, no falter in that steady stride, and I loved her for what she was giving me.

And then I was alone, strangely, and I sensed without looking that the Utes had all dropped back, way back, and were following behind for a different reason altogether now, watching.

Ahead of me, the big sorrel Hambletonian and Thoroughbred cross pounded forward. José Vasquez was lashing with his quirt, jabbing with his spurs. And frenzied, foam-spattering, head high and tossing, wild-eyed, running on nerve and breeding alone, dragging the last burst of power and speed from the great Thoroughbred heart in him, the sorrel began pulling away.

But Lazarus saw, Lazarus with his tongue hanging a mile out of his mouth and his tail dragging deep in the dust behind, saw the burst of speed. With a low whine, that triumphant look of eagles appeared in his eyes, and he stretched out, encouraging the mare, encouraging . . .

And my lovely Perdy heard. With a flash of diving, taloned

raptor in her own red-rimmed eyes, she stretched out to follow her friend. And out of the long past of her kind in the wide and barren land of the far southwest, out of the stubborn endurance bred into her small but powerful body through untold generations, came the greater surge of strength in lean, hard flanks and hammering hoofs, the surge that could not possibly have been there, but was.

Gideon had been right, all along old Captain Gideon Peabody Monson had been right! There was not a finer horse in the whole wide world than the scrubby little gray mare who surged forward beneath me, carrying me after my beloved Steenie.

The sorrel, longer-legged but carrying double, covering more ground with each frantic leap, inched ahead. I watched as bloody froth flew from the horse's mouth. I heard as breath rattled and whistled in his throat. And suddenly I was angry, angry that men would do this awful thing to fellow creatures so wonderful as the horses we rode. But then I noticed that Perdy was creeping up on the sorrel again, inch by inch, and I forgot my anger in the glory of knowing that somehow, someway, because of Perdy and Lazarus and Gideon and so many other little miracles lying in the miles behind me that I could hardly count them, Steenie would soon be mine.

Then the big sorrel stumbled, caught himself, went on, and then stumbled again, badly. And as I swept past in my slowing and reining down of the mare, I saw Vasquez's face, pinched and angry, his teeth bared in a grimace that showed more hatred than ever I thought could exist in another human being. But I also saw my Steenie, her eyes wide with hope and joy of being freed, and of being freed by the man she loved. And if I live to be a hundred, I'll never forget that expression of incredible wonder, frozen into place in my mind as I hurtled past and as she and José Vasquez were in that exact instant being thrown by the falling horse, tumbling to the ground in a hopeless heap.

"Jons!" Steenie screamed from behind me as she scrambled to her feet. "Oh, my darling Jons, you came!"

And then, finally, with Steenie's frantic, hopeful voice ringing in my ears—and with the hope in her eyes glowing like the sun, I pulled Perdy to a turnaround halt and stared back.

Chapter 25

For the number of people who sat astride horses or stood watching, it was amazingly quiet. The slave trader José Vasquez was on his feet, a handgun in one hand and Steenie gripped tightly by the other. Around him, ringing themselves into a half-circle as they rode up, apparently so they could face me, were at least twenty Ute braves. All were heavily armed, and all but two sat on their horses, guns or bows at the ready. The two on the ground, the first to ride up beside me earlier, now stood on either side of Vasquez, and it was obvious that they were prepared to back him in any play he might happen to make.

"Jons," Steenie cried, "he's a killer. I . . . ouch!" Vasquez was twisting her arm though never taking his eyes off me, and his hurting Steenie was making me angry to the core.

"That's good, Vasquez," I snarled. "Using women and children for protection. Now I know why you used those squaws to do your dirty work. You were too afraid to do it yourself. Seeing how you operate, I imagine you shot Knife in the back too. It's easy to see you're sure no ordinary coward."

Vasquez gave me a toothy grin. Lazarus growled low, and with a nudge I urged Perdy forward. We were in a high-walled, desert canyon that ran roughly south, and in the distance, toward the canyon's mouth, I could see the gleam of a wide river. I assumed it was the Grand, the river now called the Colorado—and I realized with amazement that Lazarus, Perdy, and I had come up with the fleeing Vasquez before he could manage to reach his permanent camp at the confluence of it and the Dolores.

Her sides still heaving, Perdy stepped slowly forward, and I found myself in a sort of daze from which I could not escape. Oh, I was aware of everything around me—Lazarus's panting, Perdy's steps and deep intaking of breath, the raucous cry of a crow somewhere in the distance, the nickering and head-tossing of several of the Ute ponies, the stumbling shuffle of the big sorrel as it rose to its feet and wandered from the trail, and most of all Vasquez's consuming anger as he watched me riding slowly toward him.

But the daze I felt was caused by the sight of Steenie Bergman, and more and more she was the only thing I could really see. Oh, she was some dirty, all right, but I expect that I looked the same. Her lovely dark hair with the fiery glow of sunsets in it was disheveled and unkempt. Her dress was torn, and her petticoats showed through in several places. One of her shoes was missing altogether. And as I got closer, I could see burns on her wrists where she had been bound.

Put all those things aside, however, and it will be easily understood what I was seeing about Steenie Bergman, and why I was in a daze over it. Her head was high, her proud chin was thrust out with determination, the mysterious blue-gray of her eyes flashed with unconquerable spirit and the same look of eagles I had seen in Perdy's eyes and the eyes of Lazarus—and her lips, showing red and warm even through the dust and grime of six days' hard riding, formed clearly the words, "I love you."

Dazed with the sight of her, dazed with the knowledge that nothing had changed, dazed with the understanding that a creature so perfect and so lovely could love me—I measured my thoughts!

What did it matter that I faced the most vicious killer I had ever known? What did it matter that half the Ute nation was staring me down, armed to the teeth and ready on the instant for the warpath? What did it matter that I was alone with only a gaunt coyote-dog and a stove-up little southwestern mustang to side me? Or what did it matter, finally, that I was so exhausted I could hardly sit upright in the saddle?

Very little did it matter, and I knew it. What mattered was the girl standing proud and straight before me. What mattered was the dog and horse facing forward with me, not stumbling — but strong and ready to go again if need be.

And what mattered most was that I knew, just as I knew everything else about that moment, that the Lord had brought me there. He had heard my father's blessing. He had heard Eph's promise. And he had heard my cries and pleadings. And, just as surely, the Lord God of Israel had been kind enough to answer. He had given me Gideon Monson, Ephraim Hanks, and Lot Smith. He had given me Lazarus, and he had given me Perdy. And I could see then that he was willing and happy that Steenie and I should give ourselves eternally to each other.

Only there was still the little matter of my somehow getting her away from Vasquez.

"Jons," Steenie cried, "I knew that you would come! I told everybody . . . ouch!"

Vasquez grinned again as he squeezed her arm — but the grin was wiped off his face as Steenie lashed out with her one remaining boot, kicking the filthy slave-trader in the shin.

"There," she shouted as he dropped her arm and grimaced in pain. "You touch me again, you filthy beast, and I'll—"

"Steenie," I shouted frantically when I saw her stepping toward the man instead of away from him, "don't fight — *run!*"

"What?" she asked, looking at me, surprised.

"Run! It's your best chance—"

But by then it was already too late — for the Indian standing behind her suddenly reached out, grabbed her hair, and yanked her close, putting his arm around her neck.

She struggled against him, kicking and swinging her arms, but the touch of a knife under her chin quieted her, and her eyes opened wide at me.

"Jons, please . . ."

And then Vasquez angrily reached out and jerked Steenie

away from the Indian. Then he, too, threw his arm around her neck, choking her into further submission.

"There, you little minx! Now you're gonna watch the kid die."

"Father," I prayed silently, "thou knowest that I come into this camp of the Philistines as unarmed as poor old Samson was. Give me therefore, I pray, the jawbone of an ass —"

"That's far enough!"

Vasquez's gravelly voice stopped me at about fifteen feet, and so I sat on my horse, looking at him. He was big, all right, and evil to the core. I could see clearly the cruelty in his eyes, and suddenly I understood how this man had been capable of murdering Ben Crost and the Indian called Knife. There was a darkness within him, a darkness beyond skin and hair and whiskers that Ephraim Hanks had spoken of at one time, that came from being devoid of God's Spirit. And this man *was* devoid of that Spirit, I could tell that.

"So, it's you who's been followin' us?"

"Partly."

Vasquez grinned. "For her? She isn't worth it, kid, and now you've come a long way just to die."

"He won't . . . die," Steenie gasped, never taking her flashing eyes from mine. "The . . . Lord will fight our . . . battle, and . . . and I'll be going home with him."

Well, I flushed with pride, but Vasquez only laughed derisively.

"Take you *home?* This kid? That'll be some trick, outnumbered the way he is."

"He will," Steenie declared, suddenly struggling again. "I . . . I know he . . . will!"

Vasquez laughed again as he clamped his arm more tightly against Steenie's throat — and again I felt chills at the vileness of the man. He was truly one who deserved to die. Yet Brother Brigham had counseled us to avoid bloodshed at all costs in our war with the army. Was this no less a war? And was I no less a Saint than the brethren on the plains of Wyoming?

In my mind I could hear Al Bagley questioning me about

what I would do if it came to the question of killing or being killed, and again I was brought up short by the answer. I didn't know what I would do. I truly didn't.

But then I realized, abruptly and with sinking heart, that it hadn't come to that choice anyway. I was completely unarmed, and there was no way I could fight and defeat this wicked man who stood so arrogantly before me with Steenie held so cruelly against him. Nor could I possibly fight the Utes who backed him.

"Dear Lord," I pleaded in my mind, "show me the jaw-bone—"

"Get down off that horse and draw your gun!"

"I . . . I'm unarmed," I admitted quietly and to my mortal shame.

"Jons, noooo . . . !"

Vasquez laughed with glee. "Then get down off that horse and die, you young fool. I've got a wedding to arrange here, between the girl and old Chief Tavagoop, and I don't have time to waste on you!"

"Unngh," the Ute next to Steenie grunted, the one who had held her with the knife to her throat. Then he reached and pinched her again.

"*Tsharr nan-zitch*, white girl, she not *tick-i own-shump*, she not eat enough to be good squaw." The chief laughed, and the other Utes laughed with him. "But *towats* Tavagoop fix that soon enough."

Vasquez and several of the Indians laughed again, but I didn't, and neither did my Steenie.

"Jons," she whispered, her eyes momentarily filled with fear, "*please do something.*"

Well, I wanted to do something. With all my heart I wanted to. Trouble was, my mind was an absolute blank. All my prayers had come to nothing, and I had no single clear idea—

"Get down!"

Numbly I pulled my foot from the stirrup, lifted my leg, swung it over Perdy's back, and slowly swung to the ground.

"Dear Father," my mind cried out as I did so, "please show me the way."

"Move away from the horse!"

I did, or rather I took a step to do so. But maybe I had been in the saddle for too long. Or maybe it was still the effects of the poisoned water.

But maybe . . . maybe it was because of something, or Someone else! Whatever the reason, my legs had gone numb—and with my first step, my pins literally collapsed, and I found myself seated ungloriously on my rear in the dust and scrabble of the high-walled canyon floor.

And as I sat there, dazed, I found, too, a stone beneath my hand—rounded and smooth, about the size of a fire-hardened, clay marble.

Vasquez laughed uproariously, and Steenie closed her eyes so that she would not see my humiliation. Even the Ute warriors grinned and chuckled at my foolish ineptness, saying *"Pe-up,"* over and over, and snickering about it.

But me, my mind was racing. In my fall, I had found the stone beneath my hand in the dirt of the canyon floor, and in that instant I felt, too, the awkward pressure of the forgotten object in my rear pocket.

"Lord God above," I muttered, glancing upward, "hast thou shown me the jawbone?"

A shot rang out, and dust plumed upward an inch from my closing left hand. I started, moving my gaze instantly to the grinning José Vasquez.

"Get up," he said with a snicker as he shoved the one single-shot pistol into his belt and pulled out another. "There ain't no time left for praying, but I can't see no sense in making even a fool die on his rump. Now on your feet! *Pronto!*"

Well, I stood, and then with a fixed look and my right hand reaching toward my hind pocket, I started toward him. "Friend Vasquez," I said, suddenly smiling a little and feeling better about things, "let go of the girl and give it up. This day you have been delivered into my hands."

The man was startled, so much so that his jaw flopped

open — and even the Indians took a hurried step or two backward and lifted their weapons a little higher.

"Hold it . . . " Vasquez gurgled as he once again tightened down on Steenie's throat.

"No," I said, still walking, "nor will you continue to abuse my Steenie. Release her, you infernal fiend, and prepare for your Master to impress some new thoughts upon your mind."

As Vasquez's jaws refused to come back together, and as the dusky audience waited spellbound for my own execution, I smiled even wider and drew to a halt some five feet before the vaunted slave trader and my wide-eyed sweetheart.

"Are you ready, you miserable excuse for a human being?" I asked, grinning thinly. "You're a coward through and through, and that's the weakness old Gideon told me you'd have. If folks aren't afraid of you, then you're finished. Well, Steenie's not afraid of you, *Mister* Vasquez, and neither am I! Because you're a *coward*, and I'm calling you."

It was Vasquez's move then, and he made it like the man he thought he was.

It was a pretty good move, too.

But it just wasn't good enough.

He had hardly started to lift his second pistol when Lazarus launched himself from my side, taking dead aim on Vasquez's leg just above the kneecap.

At the same time, my right hand came forward from my rear pocket with the old elm-crotch slingshot that had sealed my betrothal to Christena Bergman. My other hand flicked fast as a snake's head to fit into the sling's worn leather the smooth round stone I had been given moments before, the stone that was the general size and heft of a fire-hardened marble or a cast-iron horse chestnut, the stone that was fittingly native to the high-walled desert canyon.

Thus was I armed.

Vasquez yelled bloody murder as Lazarus clamped down on his leg, and Steenie threw her elbow angrily into his paunchy gut. But as it turned out, I never really needed Steenie's nor the dog's diversionary tactics, not at all. The Lord was with me, and the deed was done almost before it had begun.

Long before Lazarus had clamped teeth on the leg of the startled slave trader, long before Steenie's dainty elbow had driven shoulder-deep into Vasquez's soft solar plexus, my hand had loaded the sling leather, hauled it to full, ear-lobe stretch — and released it with a wicked, whirring "wwhhhrrraaannng!"

The heavenly selected stone took Vasquez squarely between the eyes. His dog-bit yell blended with the thunderous report of his single-shot pistol as his trigger finger jerked to send his shot crashing harmlessly into the earth in front of me. While the blast of the black-powder load was still bounding back and forth between the high cliffs, Steenie jerked free. Vasquez then straightened up, quivered, and slumped at the knees. Then he fell like a rotten tree — trembling and slow, and with a terrible crash that sent the dust puffing even further than my own fall had done only moments before. And when he struck, the slave trader lay cold as the stone with which the good Lord had so deeply impressed his mind.

With some embarrassment, I lifted my gaze from the fallen slave trader to the love-filled but nevertheless dumbfounded stare of Christena Bergman. Nor did I fail to note the almost reverential awe with which the twenty or so Ute warriors were presently regarding me.

"If you'll look," I said carefully, "you'll find that the miserable heathen there on the ground is merely unconscious and likely won't suffer from permanent impairment."

Everyone continued to stare, and so self-consciously I lifted the old slingshot so they could see it better.

There was a universal cry of fear from the Utes, and they would have fled the spot instantly if I had not held up my other hand with the command for them to stop. With abrupt suddenness they did, their eyes wide, and I spoke again.

"Uh . . . actually it has been some time since I fired such a shot from this," I declared, wanting them all to understand. "But it was fairly simple, likely not even of semifinals quality. Certainly it was not such a shot as would have won for me the

'Chief Keokuck' shoot-off, back in Mount Pleasant, Iowa, where Ed and Billie Kitch were judges. Not, at least, two years ago when I actually won it."

Well, the Utes saw that I had said my piece, so still staring, they backed off another step or two, their eyes glued to my slingshot. The chief and the other brave who had flanked the downed Vasquez carefully mounted their ponies, and then as a man the entire group turned horses and spurred frantically back up the canyon.

That left Steenie and I suddenly alone, and neither of us could do much more than stare at the other.

"I . . . I knew you'd come," she whispered, stepping toward me.

"It was a long ride, and . . . well, I took too long."

"Pretty near. When you said you weren't armed, I wanted to break free and thump you one. But my goodness, who'd have ever have thought you were planning on using your . . . er *my* slingshot."

I dropped my eyes. "I . . . I wasn't. It only came to me when I fell on it. I think that was the Spirit, telling me what to do. I . . . Goodness, Miss Steenie, if you ain't a sight for sore eyes."

Now Steenie turned bright red, and her hand went self-consciously to brush a strand of lovely hair from her forehead. "I . . . I surely must be a mess. Jons, I—"

"You look mighty good to me."

"I . . . I do?"

"Better'n anybody I ever saw in my life."

"Just goes to show a person that love is blind. For that matter," she said with a sigh, smiling into my eyes, "you are about the most handsome man I ever laid eyes on."

Steenie came into my arms then, her eyes suddenly alive and dancing . . . and then she batted her long, dark lashes, setting my heart to beating like Perdy's hoofs on a hard-packed trail. Against those eyes I didn't have the chance of a horned toad in heaven—but consarn it, I didn't care, either. I was willing to get lost forever in her love—

Suddenly I felt the gentle nudge of Perdy's velvety muzzle

pushing against my back, forcing me forward against the woman of my dreams. I drew her more closely to me, and in an instant we were holding each other fiercely, our tears flowing freely and our murmured "I love yous" blending over and over together. And while Perdy nuzzled against the two of us, I felt upon my feet the happy thumping of plumed coyote-dog tail — and I knew that Lazarus was pleased, as well.

Truly, I thought, as my arms held the willing and wondrous softness of Steenie Bergman, was I ever a blessed man. The world was a wide and wonderful place, the Lord God of Israel was ruling firmly from His heavenly throne, and the four of us would stand as a witness of that to the end of our days.

And forever after, I knew as I held Steenie close. Forever and ever after, as well.

Epilogue

"Did you have to fight the Indians, Pa? Did you, huh?"

Fondly I ruffled the hair of the small boy and girl who sat spellbound upon my knees—and then I winked at their older sister, who sat on the floor before me.

"Fight them," Steenie answered for me as she turned from the pan where she was cutting apples for a pie to give our needy neighbor. "We very nearly did, Little James, getting away from them. Those poor Indians practically worshiped your father after he wiped out José Vasquez, calling him Heap Chief *Punker-ro*—"

"Tell us what that means, Ma."

"I don't know," she said, giggling, while I frowned at her. "Something like 'The Scrawny Little Man with the Forked Stick and the Go-Fastest Hands in All the World,' or some such nonsense. The way those people pampered your father was an eternal shame, and I was thankful when Gideon finally came and got us out of there."

"Uncle Gideon finally caught up with you?"

"He certainly did," I told them, "just a day later. I thought he'd never get there, I was so tired of being toasted and feasted by the Utes, eating dog and other such delicacies."

"It's a good thing they didn't eat Lazarus," Little James said, looking at the aged tawny brown coyote-dog who was sleeping soundly on the hearth before us. "We wouldn't have anybody to watch over us when we play."

"That's right," I agreed softly, gazing fondly on the elderly canine, who was practically immobilized now from the old gunshot wound that had turned to arthritis after a long and hard-run race. "Besides that, he'd have been way too tough to eat."

"And what about that mean Vasquez?" our daughter Mary Caroline asked. "Did you have to kill him when he awakened?"

"Of course he didn't, Mary Caroline," Steenie answered. "Your father vanquished the powers of evil that day with the one weapon a man such as Vasquez has no defense against—ridicule. The story spread from the Indians outward, the slave trader became a laughingstock wherever he went, and your father's triumph was as complete as Wellington's at Waterloo."

"And do the Indians still love you, Pa?"

I grinned, looking up at Steenie. "I reckon they do, Little Elinor—but they don't love me as much as they love your ma. Never did. Why, old Chief Tavagoop still has a hankering for her, and every time he comes here—"

"If that old fool pinches my arm one more time," Steenie flared, shaking a rolling pin in one hand and putting the other firmly on shapely hip, "then I'm going to take this rolling pin and knock him all the way to kingdom come!"

Wide-eyed, the children stared at their mother. But me? I only grinned as I looked at the beauty of her anger. "Steenie, of a truth it is Tavagoop's only good way of telling you that he approves of what you're eating."

"He's telling me I'm getting fat!"

"Not fat," I grinned. "Just . . . uh, more pleasingly plump."

The rolling pin swooshed closely above my head, the children squealed, and I chuckled. At that instant the door opened, and Old Gideon Monson, the friend of my youth, creaked through.

He was moving steady enough, like always, but slow, very slow, and my heart swelled with worry over him. He did not seem aware of the laboring in his thin old chest that even I could see, or of the aches that surely must be in his stringy old muscles. Or, if he was aware, he never let on. He just allowed his old feet in his worn boots to shuffle forward, and in a miraculous sort of way he followed after them.

"Morning," he groused, teetering toward a chair and plopping himself into it, his walking stick still held before him.

"Morning, good and faithful friend," I smiled. "Have you eaten yet this glorious day?"

Gideon nodded affirmatively but nonetheless kept his eyes fixed firmly on the instantly discovered, rapidly developing apple pie.

"Talk Bible to us, Pa," little James pleaded. "Do it, please?"

Again I ruffled his hair. "Verily I say unto thee, my children," I growled fiercely, "if thou ceaseth not to pester thy father with such frivolity, behold the heavens shall open and an angel shall come down to box thine ears."

"Your own ears, more than likely," Steenie said as she laid the dough over the apples and began pinching the pie edges into shape.

"Amen," Gideon growled. "Amen, brethren and sisters, and amen. Who's the pie for, Miss Steenie?"

Gideon still called her that, in spite of the fact that she was so obviously a Mrs. And Steenie loved him for it, she truly did.

"A needy neighbor . . . " she replied coyly.

"Hummph," Gideon grunted as he pulled himself to his feet. "Fine thing, fixing apple pie and giving the whole blamed thing away. Reckon I'd do better dropping in on the Widow Maria Crost."

"A needy neighbor," Steenie finished, smiling sweetly, "name of Captain Gideon Monson. Unless that same captain's in such a terrible hurry this morning to go visit the lovely Widow Crost that he can't wait for his pie to bake up proper."

Gideon stood still, but a wide grin spread slowly across his wrinkled old face. "I'll be waiting right here, Miss Steenie. You can count on me."

"I always have, dear Gideon," she said, patting his hand. "I always have."

The old man blushed and shuffled his feet, and then abruptly he looked over at me, remembering. "Friend Jons," he croaked, "this Sanpete air must be powerful good for mustangs. Perdy's foal has foaled, herself, this morning. Yes sir, Perdy's a grandma again. The new one's a scrubby little gray colt with stubby neck, hammered head, and the look of eagles in his eye. I thought maybe you might want to get rid of him, he's so dad-blamed ugly."

"Hallelujah," I said as I stood with my excited children in my arms. "I reckon we'd better keep him, if he's that ugly. Shall we go, children, and see this newest wonder that the Lord has sent to bless our family?"

Excitedly they agreed, and Steenie placed the pie in the oven. Then she turned with a secret smile and batted the biggest, darkest-lashed blue eyes in all of Utah Territory at me, setting my heart pounding and reminding me that she too was going to be bringing forth a wondrous addition to our family, a child to replace our little Peter, whom we had laid away to rest the February past.

With a sly wink I set little James down and took my wife's hand. I squeezed it tenderly, and then all of us filed out of our home together.

"Hallelujah," I breathed again as I looked off through the glorious Sanpete morning toward the corral.

"Amen," muttered Steenie Bergman Soderberg as she held tightly to my hand and arm.

And left with the last word, crippled old Lazarus, the scraggly coyote-dog and sometime canine philosopher who was limping silently beside us, shook his head in resignation at the mental condition of the poor fool humans he was bound to live with and protect.

"Aaarrowww," he howled, probably in self-pity—and then he limped off ahead of us to say congratulations to the hard-hoofed grandmother, the beautifully scrubby little old gray mustang mare we still called Perdy.

Historical Note

The Utah War, during which our story takes place, is one of the least understood but most fascinating episodes in Mormon, and American, history. It pitted against each other two forces that, from start to finish, should have been united. One of the fundamental beliefs of members of The Church of Jesus Christ of Latter-day Saints is that the nation known as the United States of America was raised up by the hand of God. Mormons believe that those who founded this nation were inspired and that the Constitution they framed is an inspired document. The Mormons, who had been driven from Illinois in 1846 to settle in the valley of the Great Salt Lake a year later, strongly believed this. In the West they were no longer part of any state in the Union, but they had no desire to break off from the United States. The majority of them were American citizens, and they wanted to remain such.

Therefore, less than two years after they first moved into the Great Basin, the Mormons organized a provisional state government and applied for statehood as the State of Deseret. However, for a host of political reasons, Congress rejected their application, ignored their protests, and organized the Territory of Utah instead.

With a territorial government, the Mormons did not have the right to elect their own officials. Instead, these offices were to be filled by appointments made by the president of the United States.

President Millard Fillmore, acting upon the advice of Colonel Thomas L. Kane, an influential non-Mormon friend of the Latter-day Saints, appointed Brigham Young as governor of the territory. However, the president filled a number of important but lesser offices with politicians from the eastern states. Some of these men had a true desire to serve the people, but many more had their own selfish political ambitions in mind, and they made no attempt to understand the Saints.

Soon after arriving in Utah, three of these men, Chief Justice Lemuel H. Brandenbury, Associate Justice Perry E. Brocchus, and Territorial Secretary Broughton D. Harris, left the territory, angry that the people had not willingly accepted them, and returned to the East, where they spread false reports about the Mormons in Utah. Called by the Mormons and the Eastern press the Runaway Officials, these men claimed, among other things, that they had been compelled to leave Utah because of the lawless and seditious acts of Brigham Young.

Daniel Webster, U.S. secretary of state, investigated, determined that the allegations were false or immaterial, and ordered the three to return West. They refused and resigned, and the issue was dropped.

Meanwhile, the biggest political issue of the 1850s was the question of how much control the federal government should have in determining the domestic affairs of the territories. The issue almost split the Union in the decade before the Civil War. According to the Missouri Compromise of 1820, Congress had the authority to decide whether or not slavery could exist in a territory. After a bitter debate in Congress in 1854, this law was replaced by the Kansas-Nebraska Act. According to this new law, pushed by Stephen A. Douglas and the Democrats, Congress had no right to decide whether slavery could exist in a territory; only the people living in that territory could decide the issue by popular vote. This was called "popular sovereignty," and, though opposed by many, it became law.

Many of the law's opponents linked it with the Mormons and their practice of plural marriage. They hurled this argument at the Democrats: "If the people of Kansas can decide by popular vote if slavery is legal, then surely the Mormons can decide the same question about polygamy by popular vote." Of course, few in the East believed that the Mormons should practice polygamy, so the argument was very powerful.

The Republican Party, organized in 1854, opposed the extension of slavery into the territories and felt that Congress should have power to make slavery illegal. In 1856, when they ran John C. Fremont for the presidency, this was a major plank in their platform. James Buchanan and the Democrats, on the other hand, supported popular sovereignty.

To further their cause and to make slavery appear even worse, crafty Republicans determined to link slavery with polygamy in the minds of the people. Most Americans already considered polygamy a terrible sin, and if it could be linked, in the public eye, with slavery, then both would be made to appear more evil. Consequently, in almost every Republican rally that year, there were banners that read, "The abolishment of slavery and polygamy; the twin relics of barbarism!"

In spite of these contiguous contamination tactics, the Democrats won the election, and James Buchanan was elected president of the United States. However, many times he was accused by others of aiding and encouraging the immoral (as they viewed it) practice of polygamy. This no doubt rankled James Buchanan.

Meanwhile, those appointed to replace the Runaway Officials proved to be better men than their predecessors. As a result, there was little conflict between the Mormons and the federal officials between 1852 and 1855. This situation changed, however, when two new judges were appointed in 1855. One of these was Judge William W. Drummond, and the other was Judge George P. Stiles, an apostate Mormon.

When Drummond, a heavy drinker, an avowed agnostic, and a user of vile and profane language, arrived in Utah, he introduced the woman with him as his wife. Often she even sat with him on the bench. Soon, however, it became known that his *real* wife and family were in Illinois, abandoned, and that the woman with him was a harlot. Since he was adjudicating so strenuously against the "immoral" practice of polygamy, the Mormons were outraged, and they let it be known.

Finally driven to resignation, Drummond returned to the East in a huff in the spring of 1857, soon after James Buchanan took office. Upon his arrival, Drummond made a number of serious allegations against the Mormons. Among other things, he accused them of wholesale murder, immorality, and rebellion against the United States.

At the same time, Judge Stiles forwarded to Washington an affidavit affirming many of Drummond's charges. Thomas S. Twiss, U.S. Indian agent on the Great Plains, felt that the Mormons were gaining too much influence among the Great Plains Indians, so he also wrote and complained. And finally W. M. F. Magraw, a government mail contractor who had been underbid by the Mormons and was angry at them for getting the mail contract from him, wrote Buchanan and made other false charges.

Newspaper editors, knowing that anything abut polygamy or the Mormons was "hot copy," eagerly seized upon these false reports and published them as the true state of affairs in Utah. Some of their stories were outright fabrications, and others were greatly exaggerated. (For example, see the various issues of the New York *Daily Times* of May 1857.) In this manner, fuel was heaped upon the fires of public opinion, which were already burning against the Saints. As a result, the American public was aroused against the "wicked," "immoral," and "rebellious" Mormons, and there was a popular clamor in the North for the government to do something about the "Mormon problem."

In the eyes of many aroused Americans, President Buchanan was neither acting fast enough nor decisively enough in dealing with the Mormons. This view was exemplified by a letter that "Amicus Curia" wrote in 1857 to the editor of the *Daily Times*. Published on the front page on May 27, 1857, the writer says: "Had Fremont been elected, with his anti-polygamy plank in his Presidential platform, you would have seen General Harney out as far as Fort Kearny, a distance of full three hundred miles, with the proper antidote for Mormonism, and a prompt and efficient man en route for Utah to ease GOV. YOUNG of his Gubernatorial honors; but for fear of displeasing the Mormons . . . the whole summer will be spent in talk and . . . feeble, undecided action. . . . Have not the American people the right, and is it not their duty, to demand speedy and decided action on this vital subject?"

Another writer, in the Santa Fe *Weekly Gazette*, stated: "Religious fanaticism, when excited and aroused, is the blindest species of madness, and is regardless of consequences. . . . While we may regret the loss of life that is likely to follow this madness, of these deluded people, yet we cannot but regard their action as a blessing to the cause of truth, for it must result in their extinction as a people in the United States. . . . The day of doom of Mormonism, we trust, is fast approaching."

Of course, the Mormon editors lashed back as best they could. George Q. Cannon, editor of the *Western Standard* in California, wrote: "The editor of the Herald deceives himself and those who believe what he writes, when he says that 'the days of Mormonism at Salt Lake are numbered.' The cannon are not cast, the powder and ball not manufactured, nor the men to use them either born or conceived, that will destroy 'Mormonism.' Mark our words gentlemen, it will live, though all earth and hell array themselves against it."

Goaded by these and other statements and pressures, President Buchanan acted. He did not investigate the charges made by Drummond, Stiles, Magraw, and Twiss at all. He accepted all charges at face value, mobilized 2,500 troops of the United States Army, and appointed a non-Mormon, Alfred Cumming of Georgia, as governor of Utah.

In July, the first troops left Fort Leavenworth on their way to Utah, acting officially as a *posse comitatus* to see that Cumming was properly installed as governor, to preserve the peace, and to see that all federal laws were obeyed by the "rebellious" Mormons.

However, Buchanan did not inform Brigham Young that he had been replaced as governor, nor did he inform the Mormons that he was sending an army west. In fact, he canceled the mail contract to Utah in a deliberate attempt to prevent the Saints from knowing that an army was coming, or why.

With no news but rumors being brought to Utah by returning missionaries and incoming emigrants, the Mormons were left to ferret out the facts of the government expedition for themselves. They quickly learned *about* it, but it was much more difficult for them to ascertain *why* the army was coming.

Because of previous experience with murdering, ravaging, raping, and pillaging mobs in Ohio, Missouri, and Illinois, the Mormons naturally expected the worst. They had been driven from state to state before, even by official armed state militias, and so this threat from the national government was looked upon as the final, ultimate mob. Consequently, the Saints determined to prevent the army from entering the Valley, at whatever the cost.

Historian Leonard J. Arrington writes: "The territorial militia, which was called the Nauvoo Legion, was mustered into full-time service under the leadership of General Daniel H. Wells. This force, consisting of about 3,000 men, was the kind of citizen army that younger officers were inclined to belittle, but which the old professionals never took lightly. As a later observer wrote, it was an 'uncouth, undisciplined, and ragged set of men,' with 'every variety of weapon known to civilized nations,' but it was a group, which in its own habitat, fighting for homes and families, could be ferocious and deadly."

Engaging in guerrilla tactics, the Mormons barricaded Echo Canyon and annoyed and hindered the army in every way possible. Under explicit orders to engage in no pitched battles, groups of Saints destroyed bridges, burned army wagons and supply trains, stampeded and took to the Valley herds of government animals, and burned the grass on the prairies. Without killing or wounding a soldier, they prevented them from entering the colonized part of the territory, forcing the army to spend the winter on Black's Fork, near Fort Bridger.

Men such as Orrin Porter Rockwell, Colonel Robert T. Burton, Major Lot Smith, and Major Ephraim Hanks led these raids, and the accounts in our story are taken from their personal and official records.

It was a frustrating time for the army. Colonel Alexander (known as "the Old Woman"), who was never officially in command, was nevertheless all alone at the front. Concerned by reports of Mormon preparations for war; beleaguered by the guerrilla fighters who were constantly harrassing his troops, destroying his supplies, and stealing his animals; and pushed by anxious [in]subordinates, Alexander finally decided that the safest and surest way into the valley was to avoid Echo Canyon altogether.

Accordingly, under Jim Bridger's direction, he pushed up Ham's Fork, intending to come around and down by the Bear River. But the command, not moving fast enough, finally bogged down as the weather turned foul and then worsened. Numerous accounts of dying animals and struggling soldiers bear evidence to the trial Colonel Alexander and his men endured just getting back to where they had started. And they had lost an entire month going absolutely nowhere. At this point, Albert Sydney Johnston finally arrived to take command, and the only thing left for this angry commander to do was to order his frustrated and exhausted men into winter quarters.

The Mormons, with the help of their God and his weather, had obviously won the first round.

The only soldier allowed to enter the Valley in 1857 was Captain Stewart Van Vliet, who came to arrange for supplies for the advancing army. Courteously received by Brigham Young, he could give no suitable answer as to why the army was coming. Hence the Saints were even more convinced than ever of the "mob" intentions of the army.

But though Van Vliet's mission failed there, it was a huge success in another way. The captain, after spending several days carefully observing conditions in Utah, came away convinced that the Mormons were a good but misunderstood people, not guilty of the crimes charged against them. He was also convinced that the army could not beat the Mormons at war in their own mountain strongholds. Heading east, he expressed these views freely, and word of them began to spread.

President Buchanan had been riding high on the tide of public opinion when he called out the troops to go west, but he soon learned that public opinion is capricious and unpredictable. When by winter the army hadn't accomplished anything but the spending of huge amounts of money and being embarrassed by a ragtag militia, the American taxpayers began to squirm uncomfortably. Shortly, after further "reflection," influential Americans began to publicly criticize the government for sending an army west in the first place.

By January of 1858, congressional leaders and newspaper editors had taken up the cause and were pressuring the leaders of the government to end the "war" and the resultant waste of money and manpower. President Buchanan, acutely aware of the shift in public opinion, began looking for an easy but respectable way out of the mess he and others had created.

At this point Colonel Thomas L. Kane, still the Mormon's friend, was asked by a messenger from Brigham Young to go to Washington to speak to Buchanan in the Saints' behalf. Finding the administration anxious to get the whole affair settled amicably, Colonel Kane left Washington and came to Utah via the isthmus of Panama and California. There he explained to the Mormons that the army was not to be a mob but was sent as an assurance that Alfred Cumming would be accepted as governor.

Meanwhile, Governor Cumming and the other federal appointees had spent the winter with the army at their temporary settlement called Camp Scott, near the remains of Fort Bridger. It was not a comfortable camp, and it was described by Charles A. Scott: "Rather tough times now, not enough to eat and blest with a ravenous appetite: Intensely cold weather, Sentinels have to be relieved every hour to keep from being frost bitten, as it is, when they come off post, they look like venerable patriarchs, their breath being frozen in their beards, eyebrows and even eyelashes. When we are not on guard, six or eight of us have to take a wagon and go out daily to the Cedars about four miles from Camp and haul in a load of wood by hand (because the animals are gone to Henry's Fork for forage)."

After meeting with the Mormons in Utah, Colonel Kane sped east to meet with Governor Cumming; and at the Colonel's request, Cumming came back to Utah with him.

Alfred Cumming was surprised at what he found. Not only were the vast majority of the Saints a sincere, devout, and orderly people who wanted only to be left alone in peace, but they were willing to abandon their homes, burn everything, and move south rather than turn their belongings over to the army.

In fact, even while he watched, all Mormons living from Salt Lake City north were actually leaving. More than thirty-five thousand men, women, and children ultimately packed their things into wagons and headed south, some to Provo and other Utah County areas, and others even farther south. Their abandoned homes, with straw piled high against them, awaited the torch should Albert Sydney Johnston's army force its way into the Valley, and Governor Cumming was astounded to see this.

Finally, he was also astounded to discover that the Mormons were perfectly willing to accept him as their governor and would give him every iota of respect that he actually earned and deserved.

While these things were happening in Utah, opposition to the "war" continued to grow in the East. More and more it was becoming obvious that the war was politically and economically motivated and had very little to do with the Mormons. The main schemer in this was Secretary of War John B. Floyd, an avowed secessionist who used the facade of a Mormon rebellion to scatter U. S. forces and arms preparatory to the impending Confederate Rebellion. Further, in later Congressional investigation, it was shown that he, in cahoots with William H. Russell of the firm Russell, Majors and Waddell, had defrauded the government and others of over $7 million in connection with the freighting of military goods to the West. Truly was it called a "contractor's war." Under an increasing barrage of criticism from all sides, and before he had received Governor Cumming's report, President Buchanan appointed a peace commission to go to Utah carrying a proclamation of pardon. This proclamation stated that though the Mormons were guilty of treason and sedition, all would be pardoned who would submit themselves to the authority of the federal government.

The Mormons, always sustaining the Constitution and the government, laughed this document to scorn. Yet Brigham Young and the other leaders, anxious to end the conflict, saw the value of it. Knowing that it was the administration's attempt to save face, and knowing too who his own people really were, Brigham Young signed it. In doing so, he said: "As to the gentlemen Commissioners, they have no power to investigate the past, but (are) to inquire if we will submit to the constitution and laws of the United States. We always have, and always expect to. I have no (reputation to uphold)—no pride to gratify—no vanity to please. If a man comes from the moon and says he will pardon me for kicking him in the moon yesterday, I don't care about it, I'll accept of his pardon." (*Comprehensive History of the Church* 4:433.)

Meanwhile, the move south continued, ultimately lasting from March until about the middle of May. Governor Cumming, on one trip south with Brigham Young, passed about 800 wagons in one day. "Is there not some way to stop the moving?" he asked the Prophet, to which Brigham Young replied that if the troops were withdrawn from the territory, the people would stop moving.

John R. Young, who was returning to Utah from a mission to Hawaii, described the move south as follows:

> At Parowan, two hundred miles south of Salt Lake City, we encountered a scene that I shall never forget. I remember distinctly the "Exodus," as it was called, from Nauvoo, when sixteen thousand souls left their homes and commenced that marvelous journey of fourteen hundred miles to the unknown valley of the Salt Lake. But that exodus was like a small rivulet by the side of a mighty river when compared with the thirty-five thousand men, women and children that we now met in one continuous line of travel.
>
> Horses, oxen, and cows were harnessed or yoked to wag-

ons and carts; and one family by the name of Syphuis, was moving their effects on a handcart drawn by a pair of yearling steers. Mothers and children walked along as merrily as if going to a corn husking; each family moving its little bunch of cows and flock of sheep, and all starting on the journey to Sonora, in Mexico, or some other place.

At times we were compelled to drive our wagon for miles outside the beaten road, everywhere hearing and seeing evidences that increased my gentile companion's wonderment of the marvelous power held by Brigham Young over this people.

A pioneer teenager penned the following description:

> We packed all we had into father's one wagon and waited for the command to leave. At night we lay down to sleep, not knowing when word would come of the army which we thought was coming to destroy us. . . . There were seven of us children in the family.
>
> We put away all our playthings, for the days found us so frightened that all we did was follow father and mother from place to place, looking into their faces for a word of comfort and a look of cheer. One morning father told us that we should leave with a large company in the evening. He said little more. There were packing and the making of bread.
>
> Along in the middle of the day father scattered leaves and straw in all the rooms and I heard him say: "Never mind, little daughter, this house has sheltered us, it shall never shelter them . . . " I did not understand him then, but as we went out of the yard and joined all the other people on the main road I learned for the first time that the city would be burned should the approaching army attack the people.
>
> That night we camped on Willow Creek in the south end of the valley, and at ten o'clock every soul with bowed head knelt in prayer to God. As I dropped to sleep I heard my mother whispering that the Lord had heard our prayers and that our homes should not be burned. I cried and cried, but at last I dropped to sleep.

There is no doubt that it was a trying and uncertain time for the Saints. Many truly struggled, but others were full of faith and gave the army very little attention. John Pulsipher recorded in his diary:

> The U.S. army East of us have wintered very well, & are threatening to come upon us & make a final end of all that will not join them. Truly this is a trying time — Destruction stares us in the face which every way we turn — They that have not the Holy Ghost the Comforter in them, are beginning to tremble. The prophet Brigham is as calm as if there was no danger — says *move South and see the Salvation of God.* And almost the entire people say Amen to it & are as happy as were the children of Israel led by Moses, anciently when they passed thro the red Sea.

So the Saints went south, difficulties were finally ironed out, and, as a final agreement between the peace commissioners and the Mormons, the army was allowed to come into the Valley. According to the agreement, they were to pass through the city unmolested, providing that they not stop and that they camp at least forty miles away. The commission forwarded a letter to that effect to General Johnston, who, upon receiving the news, "took off his hat with the insignia of a general on it, threw it on the ground, stamped on it, and said: 'Damn such a government. Here we starved and froze all winter, and now that we have these (Mormons) right where we want them, they are going to get off without shedding one drop of blood. Damn such a government.'"

Nevertheless, on June 26, 1858, the army finally, and very, very peaceably, entered Salt Lake City. A correspondent for the *Atlantic Monthly,* traveling with the army, described the scene as follows: "It was one of the most extraordinary scenes that have occurred in American history. All day long, from dawn until after sunset, the troops and trains poured through the city, the utter silence of the streets being broken only by the music of the military bands, the monotonous tramp of the regiments, and the rattle of the baggage wagons. . . . The stillness was so profound that during the intervals between the passage of the columns, the monotonous gurgle of the city creek struck every ear."

And gentile editors back East, watching the unfolding drama with amazement, made such comments as:

> Whatever our opinions may be of Mormon morals and Mormon manners, there can be no question that this voluntary abandonment of forty thousand people, of homes created by wonderful industry in the midst of trackless wastes, after years of hardships and persecution, is something from which no one who has a particle of sympathy with pluck, fortitude and constancy can withhold his admiration. Right or wrong, sincerity thus attested is not to be sneered at. True or false, a faith to which so many men and women prove their loyalty by such sacrifice, is a force in the world. . . . When people abandon their homes to plunge with women and children into a wilderness to . . . they know not where, they give a higher proof of courage than if they fought for them.

Thus concluded the Utah War. As historians Richard D. Poll and Ralph W. Hansen put it, at an estimated cost of between 20 million and 40 million dollars, the United States Army received field experience and lessons in geography. The freighting firm of Russell, Majors and Waddell made enough profit to become objects of later Congressional investigation. With "Buchanan's Blunder," the Democratic administration complicated its already difficult political situation, and Buchanan ended up serving only the one term. And while Alfred Cumming became governor of Utah Territory, Brigham Young remained leader of the people.

Though *In Search of Steenie Bergman*, set in the midst of this conflict, is fictional, we used accurate historical information in the book's setting. Ephraim Hanks's exploits, spiritual and otherwise, are documented in his biography, listed below. Lot Smith's adventures were also recorded by himself and published years later.

An interesting verification of Lot Smith's account is given by William F. Cody, who later became famous as Buffalo Bill. In 1857, at twelve years of age, he was a qualified teamster but had had to secure his mother's permission to travel west with Lew Simpson. His account in *The Great Salt Lake Trail* of Smith's capture of the government train is fascinating and adds the detail that Smith had earlier traveled with the train for a few days, posing as a teamster. Cody also recorded that he admired the Mormons for their pluck.

Orrin Porter Rockwell led the first raid on the troops at Pacific Springs, which failed only when the bell mule got caught in the brush. And, with the exception of the Mountain Meadows Massacre, which is not part of this story, the shooting in Echo Canyon took one of the only two lives lost by bloodshed during the war. The other life, that of the trader Yates, was apparently taken by Bill Hickman somewhere near the head of Echo Canyon. Dan Jones verified this murder, and his statement is published in *Forty Years Among the Indians*, also listed below.

In the Valley, weapons and munitions factories flourished as described, and martial law kept people from traveling freely in the mountains. Emigrants, who literally traveled westward side-by-side with the government trains and troops, pushed ahead and arrived in the Valley early, and the songs recorded in our story are two of the many that were sung by the two factions.

Slave trading between the Indians and the Mexicans was a terrible problem for Brigham Young and the Mormons during the early years of Utah, and President Young finally pushed a law through the territorial legislature, making it illegal for Mexican traders to even enter the territory. It is unknown whether or not any Mormon women or children were ever sold into slavery, but not a few vanished at the hands of Indians, and their whereabouts was never again discovered. It is very possible that these became slaves.

Finally, it was quite surprising for the authors to discover that the Saints, in their journals and other writings, called the government by the sobriquets "uncle" and "uncle Sam." We had assumed this to be a more recent appellation and so have no idea where it actually originated.

Our research led us to many sources, and for the convenience of the reader who may wish to pursue further study of the Utah War, they are listed below.

Alber, Sarah Pulsipher. "History." *Pioneer Journals*. Dugway, Utah: Pioneer Press.

Alter, J. Cecil. *James Bridger: Trapper, Frontiersman, Scout and Guide*. Columbus, Ohio: Long's College Cook Co., 1951.

Arrington, Leonard J. "Mormon Finance and the Utah War." *Utah Historical Quarterly*, 20 (1952): 219–37.

————. "The Utah War." Typescript in authors' possession.

Bailey, L. R. *Indian Slave Trade in the Southwest*. Los Angeles: Westernlore Press, 1973.

Baily, Paul D. *Holy Smoke: A Dissertation on the Utah War*. Los Angeles: Westernlore Books, 1978.

Bancroft, Hubert Howe. *History of Utah*. San Francisco: The History Co., 1899.

Berrett, William E. *The Restored Church*. 15th ed. Salt Lake City: Deseret Book Co., 1955.

Brooks, Juanita. *On The Mormon Frontier: The Diary of Hosea Stout*. 2 vols. Salt Lake City: University of Utah Press, 1964.

Carter, Kate B. *Heart Throbs of the West*. 12 vols. Salt Lake City: Daughters of the Utah Pioneers, 1939–1951.

Carter, Kate B. *Our Pioneer Heritage*. 12 vols. Salt Lake City: Daughters of the Utah Pioneers, 1958–1969.

Carter, Kate B. *Treasures Of Pioneer History*. 12 vols. Salt Lake City: Daughters of the Utah Pioneers, 1952–1963.

Cheney, Thomas E., ed. *Mormon Songs from the Rocky Mountains*. Austin: University of Texas Press, 1968.

Cody, William F. *The Adventures of Buffalo Bill*. New York and London: Harper & Brothers, 1904.

Cooley, Everet L. "The Utah War." Unpublished master's thesis, University of Utah. Salt Lake City, 1947.

Flake, Dennis D. "A Study Of Mormon Resistance During the Utah War, 1857–1858." Unpublished master's thesis, Brigham Young University. Provo, Utah, 1975.

Furniss, Norman F. *The Mormon Conflict, 1850–1859*. New Haven, Conn.: Yale University Press, 1966.

Gottfredson, Peter. *Indian Depredations in Utah*. Salt Lake City: Merlin G. Christensen, 1969.

Gove, Jesse A. *The Utah Expedition, 1857–1858*. Concord: New Hampshire Historical Society, 1928.

Hafen, LeRoy R., and Ann W. Hafen, eds. "Diary of Captain Phelps."

The Far West and The Rockies Historical Series, vol. 8. Glendale, Calif.: Arthur H. Clark Co., 1958.

————. "Documentary Account of the Utah Expedition." *The Far West and the Rockies Historical Series*, vol. 8. Glendale, Calif.: Arthur H. Clark Co., 1958.

Hanks, Sydney A. and Ephraim K. Hanks. *Scouting for the Mormons on the Great Frontier*. Salt Lake City: Deseret News Press, 1948.

Inman, Henry, and Cody, William F. *The Great Salt Lake Trail*. Williamstown, Mass.: Corner House Publishers, 1978.

"Journal History of the Church of Jesus Christ of Latter-day Saints." 1857–1858. Salt Lake City: L.D.S. Church Historian's Office.: Salt Lake City, Utah.

Jenson, Andrew, comp. *Church Chronology: A Record of Important Events*. 2nd ed. Salt Lake City: Deseret News Press, 1899.

Jones, Daniel W. *Forty Years Among the Indians*. Salt Lake City: Juvenile Instructor, 1890.

Langley, Harold D., ed. *To Utah with the Dragoons and Glimpses of Life in Arizona and California 1858–1859*. Salt Lake City: University of Utah Press, 1974.

Lamar, Howard R., ed. *The Reader's Encyclopedia of the American West*. New York: Thomas Y. Crowell Co., 1977.

Larson, Gustive O. *Outline History of Territorial Utah*. 3rd ed. Provo, Utah: Brigham Young University Press, 1972.

McAllister, John D.T. "Diary." Typescript at Brigham Young University, Provo, Utah.

Poll, Richard D. and Ralph W. Hansen. "Buchanan's Blunder: the Utah War, 1857–1858." *Military Affairs*, 25 (1961): 121–31.

Pulsipher, John. "Diary." Typescript at Brigham Young University, Provo, Utah.

Roberts, B. H. *A Comprehensive History of The Church of Jesus Christ of Latter-day Saints*. 6 vols. Provo, Utah: Brigham Young University Press, 1965.

Schindler, Harold. *Orrin Porter Rockwell, Man of God, Son of Thunder*. Salt Lake City: University of Utah Press, 1966.

Smith, Lot. "The Echo Canyon War: Lot Smith's Narrative." *The Contributor*, 4 (1882–1883): 27–29, 47–50, 167–69, 224–26.

Tracy, Albert. "Journal of Captain Albert Tracy." *Utah Historical Quarterly*, vol. 13 (1945).

Tyler, Daniel. *History of the Mormon Battalion*. Salt Lake City: Juvenile Instructor Press, 1885.

Vetterli, Richard *Mormonism, Americanism and Politics*. Salt Lake City: Ensign Publishing Co., 1961.

Whitney, Orson F. *History of Utah*. 4 vols. Salt Lake City: George Q. Cannon and Sons Co., 1904.

Wells, Junius F. (Vaux). "The Echo Canyon War." *The Contributor*, 3 (1882): 50–54, 84–86, 102–5, 146–49, 177–79, 215–17, 270–74, 296–99, 339–43, 380–83.